A
CAPITOL
CRIME

A CAPITOL CRIME

Lawrence Meyer

THE VIKING PRESS   NEW YORK

First published in 1977 by The Viking Press
625 Madison Avenue, New York, N.Y. 10022
Published simultaneously in Canada by
The Macmillan Company of Canada Limited

Library of Congress Cataloging in Publication Data

Meyer, Lawrence, 1941—
   A Capitol crime.

   I. Title.
PZ4.M6126Cap   [PS3563.E875]   813'.5'4   76-53795
ISBN 0-670-20336-X

Printed in the United States of America

for Aviva

A CAPITOL CRIME

1

Crime is not my beat. I know some people would disagree and call me more than a shade naive, but I take a philosophical view of these things. I cover the United States Senate.

I work for *The Washington Journal*, the largest newspaper in what official Washington refers to as "our nation's Capital." I went to college, but I managed to get over it. I survived two years in the military, worked for a couple of smaller papers, and then broke into the big time with the *Journal*. My work brings me into contact with most senators, various congressmen, assorted lobbyists, Cabinet members, and an occasional President. From time to time it's exciting. Most of the time, it's a living.

I've never been able to get my juices going day in and day out the way some reporters do about the job. Les Painter was that way about his work. He really believed that what he was doing was the most important thing in the world. He certainly was the most promi-

nent journalist in Washington. By the standards of the profession—
such as they are—he was very good at what he did. So good, in
fact, that plenty of people were glad when he was killed, or rather,
I should say, murdered. And that's how I got into the whole thing.

Painter's column, "The Inside Track," was carried by three
hundred and fifty daily papers in the United States and abroad. He
had a radio show and a weekly television program. If he called, you
called back. If he said you were being investigated, whether you had
known it before or not, that was reason enough to hire a lawyer. If
he printed a charge, a congressional committee had hearings to find
out about it. Careers were made and broken by his column. Sometimes he made a mistake, but not often. It was not so much that
he had a passion for accuracy as that he had a sense of when he was
wading into murky water and had to be more careful than usual.

I used to see him once or twice a week. We weren't close, but
I guess I was as friendly as any reporter ever got with him. He had
a wife and four kids. But they came second to his job. He managed
to squeeze them into his schedule, a compromise that he made with
his career, but if he had had to choose, he would have left his wife
without a husband and his kids without a father. And that's the
way it turned out in the end.

Some people thought he was a son of a bitch—a mean, unscrupulous, self-righteous egomaniac. That position had some merit to it.
On more than one occasion I heard about stunts he had pulled that
would have kept me awake past my normal bedtime worrying. He
didn't worry. He slept fine. I'm still here and he's not—but I'm not
sure what that proves, either.

His body was found on March sixth, four months before the
convention was supposed to start in Chicago. He was pulled out of a
utility manhole in a sub-basement corridor of the Capitol. He had
one neat little bullet wound next to his heart. Death, according to
the coroner's report, was instantaneous. Les was not a big man, so
whoever had killed him didn't need to be Hercules or Wonder
Woman to drag him to the manhole, take the cover off, and drop
him where he wouldn't be in the way.

After that, it was just a matter of time until the body was found.
He had been dead about three days when he was pulled out. A
janitor, cleaning the corridor, had noticed a disagreeable odor; he
found the body and called the Capitol police.

The Capitol police, who are about as effective as scarecrows,

2

called the Metropolitan police, since the murder occurred in the District of Columbia. I got a call about two in the morning from my desk at *Journal* telling me to go on up to the Hill. I won't say I wasn't upset to find out that Les was dead, but I wasn't exactly incapacitated either.

When I got there the police photographer was taking a lot of pictures, and the other officers were going over the immediate area with their equipment, looking for clues. A couple of FBI agents were hanging around in case it looked as if a federal crime were involved.

The police didn't find much. The coroner established later that Les had been killed without a struggle. He had been shot only once, at close range. Powder burns on his coat and skin showed that the gun had been next to his body when it was fired. His wallet had been taken, along with his watch and a ring he wore. Painter usually had more than a hundred dollars in cash in his pocket. He had seventeen cents when the police got to him. The murder weapon, they later established, had been a .38 caliber pistol. It was not recovered.

Even though I cover the Senate, the story was really not mine to report. It was Sid Jacobson's, our police reporter. He was there, too, wearing his black raincoat and beat-up hat pushed back on his gray head. He had a toothpick in his mouth, as usual. The police let him get up close. I had to stay back about twenty feet. Most of what I learned about what the police found I got from Sid. The police sometimes forget that Sid is a reporter. Sid does, too, and that's not entirely to his credit. But in general it helps in a pinch to have someone like him around who's on good terms with the law.

I hung around for about an hour and then left. When you work for a morning paper, there isn't much you can do in the way of a story in the middle of the night. We had caught a couple of thousand copies of the final press run with a brief story setting out the bare details of Les's murder, how the body had been found, etc. The desk told me they didn't have an obituary on him and asked me to write one. I said I would in the morning. The one thing someone in the business ought to get when he dies is a decent obituary.

I wanted to go back home and get some sleep. But first I had to go see Mary Painter. I wasn't that close to her and I didn't know her terribly well. But what I knew about her I liked. I thought it was important to see her. I'm not exactly a Tory when it comes to tradition, but when a man is murdered, his widow and children, especially the children, ought to know that someone besides them appreciated him. Painter was the best in the business, something they knew without hearing it from me, but I wanted to show my respect. Maybe I hoped that someday someone would feel the same way about me.

I stopped my car for a minute when I got to the foot of Constitution Avenue below the Capitol. Sometimes I think the entire structure, all eighty zillion tons of it, will sink by its own sheer weight and inertia. Judgment Day will come to Washington, and the swamp the city was built on will swallow up the political Sodom and Gomorrah.

But that night, so help me, even while they were pulling Les Painter out of a hole deep in the bowels of the Capitol, it gleamed with a ghostly, brilliant white light, as if the Capitol's marble were emitting the light and not merely reflecting it. A low-lying ground fog crept over the grounds, where crocuses and daffodils were beginning to peek out of the soil. Across the river, where the Grand Army of the Republic had kept Robert E. Lee and the Confederacy at bay, I could hear the hum of a propellor-driven plane. It was one of those unseasonably warm nights we get in Washington in the late winter, and it held out the seldom realized promise of a long and beautiful spring.

2

The lights were on in the Painter home when I drove up. They lived out in Maryland in one of the expensive, new, plastic suburbs. The house was a sprawling, one-story brick affair with no particular character or charm. The only thing you noticed was that the developer, in deference to the price he had gotten for it, had built only one other like it on the block. A couple of unmarked cars so plain they had cop written all over them were parked in the driveway.

I rang the doorbell. A man answered. He wasn't family and he wasn't a friend I had ever seen before. He was beefy, with a shiny gray suit, wash-and-wear white shirt, and a blue tie that he had been wearing since the early nineteen-fifties. He had a bulge under his left armpit.

"I'd like to see Mrs. Painter," I told him.

"You a relative, friend, or a reporter?" he asked.

"I'm a friend and a reporter," I told the cop.

"Sorry. We're talking to her now. Why don't you come back tomorrow, or give her a call."

"Well, it's nice of you to offer, but unless you've been hired as a domestic by the family, I'd be grateful if you'd step aside." He started to answer, but I cut him off. "You're out of your jurisdiction," I said, walking in.

He didn't like it much and me even less, but he stepped aside. Mary was sitting in the living room talking to two other men, and her oldest daughter, Alice, who is seventeen or eighteen, was sitting with her. I didn't see the other kids. Mary gave me a wan kind of a smile and held out her hand. I took it, half shaking it and half holding it.

"It was nice of you to come, Tony." Her eyes and nose were red, making a face that was normally only barely attractive homely. She had managed to put on some makeup and to comb her hair, but even on her best days she was not someone you would look at twice.

When I first came to Washington I expected that the women would be as glamorous as the men were supposed to be. I found out quickly that few of the men were glamorous and even fewer of the women. Just about everybody in Washington comes from somewhere else, usually a small town or city. They leave simple lives to come to Washington and they live simple lives when they get here. They do a lot of posturing in public, and the ones who are good at it get ahead and the ones who aren't don't. But at the end of every day, when the television lights go off and the microphone stands come down, after the last cocktail party and the last lobbyist dinner, they all trudge off to wherever it is they lay down their bones for the night. And the ones who keep their sanity and keep their lives on an even keel, no matter how "exciting" their days, usually come home to someone who looks more or less like Mary Painter.

"Sometimes he told me what he was doing in detail and sometimes he didn't," she was telling the men. "If it was really important, really big, he usually got very tight about it."

"And was he talking to you about his work or not?" The speaker now was a thin, pale-faced man who had introduced himself to me as Lieutenant Thomason. The man with him, a chunkier type, with a pleasant, florid face, was taking notes.

"You mean lately?" Mary asked.

"Yes, I'm sorry. I should have been clearer," Thomason said.

"Well, he was tightening up. All he said was that he was work-

6

ing on something big—very big. He took his work very seriously. All he said—and I never pressed him for details about what he was doing—was, 'This is a very good story.' That may not seem like much to you, but it was. The bigger a story got, the quieter he got. And I never saw him as quiet about a story as he was the last few weeks."

"Mrs. Painter, I imagine that your husband had files, uh, notes for the stories he was working on?"

"Yes, he did."

"I'd like to take a look at them," Thomason told her earnestly. "You understand. It might tell us what he was working on and help us find his, uh, killer."

"Well, yes, I do understand, Lieutenant." Mary paused and thought. "If you could give me a little while to make arrangements, then I'll see how I can help. I can't promise you everything. Mr. Jordan here can tell you," she said with a gesture toward me, "that my husband was a fanatic on the subject that a reporter's notes were his own and nobody else's. But I'll try to help you." She sounded distracted.

Thomason started to say something, but then he saw that Mary Painter was beginning to cry again and he held it. "I'll come back in the morning and we can talk about it then. I hope you can get some rest in the meantime," he said, casting a suggestive look at me.

I nodded gravely and got up. "I'll see you and your men to the door, Lieutenant."

"Your name is Gordon?" he asked me in the hall.

"No, no. Jordan. Tony Jordan. I was a friend of Les Painter's," I answered.

"What do you do?" he asked. "You a reporter?"

"Yes, for the *Journal*."

"I see," he said. "Well, Mr. Jordan, I'd like to speak with you in the next day or so if you don't mind. You may be able to help. I'd appreciate it if you would try to convince Mrs. Painter to let us look at his files. I understand her feelings. But I can always get a warrant for that stuff. Then she would be upset, and I would be, and it would just make things more difficult. And I can't wait too long, either."

The edge in his voice was not easy to ignore. He meant what he said. I understood Mary's feelings perfectly, and Les's, too. But I didn't see any point in giving a lecture to the Lieutenant there at the door about the comparative perspectives of cops and reporters. For one thing, Thomason and I both knew, without saying so, that the police had been dying to get their hands on Les's files for years. For all I knew, Les had a file on Thomason.

"What's it look like, Lieutenant?" I asked, trying to change the subject.

"It's too soon to tell," he said. "It might be a grudge or it might have been armed robbery that went amok or it might have been something else."

"A stickup?" I asked, skeptical. "In the Capitol?"

"I don't know how long you've been in Washington, Mr. Jordan, but there's nothing sacred to a lot of people here about the Capitol. We have robberies, rapes, and murders within shouting distance of the Supreme Court. And we'd have them on the White House lawn, too, if there weren't a fence and electronic equipment to keep people away. So mugging is a possibility."

"If you think it was a holdup, then why the interest in his files?" I asked.

"Because," Thomason said with a patronizing tone, "maybe it wasn't a holdup. So we'd be grateful for some cooperation, O.K.?"

"I'll talk to her about it, Lieutenant." I tried to sound reassuring. I fully intended to talk to Mary at great length, but that did not mean that I'd try to persuade her. It meant that I would talk to her.

He thanked me and left, taking the stocky man and the doorman with him. I went back into the living room. Mary Painter had composed herself. "Tony," she said to me, "I can't let them go pawing through his files. He didn't trust the police or the FBI and neither do I. I told them this story must have been big, but I don't think they understood. Tony, I never saw Les like that before. He was totally absorbed. Neither Larry nor Steve knew what it was, either. You know, usually he asks them to take a piece and help out when it's more than he can do quickly by himself. But last week Steve told me Les wanted to do this one alone, that it had to be done that way." She started to cry again. "Otherwise he might still be alive now."

"It may not be that way at all, Mary," I said. "Thomason just told me it might have been a holdup."

"In the Capitol?" she asked, incredulously.

"That's what I said, but he doesn't rule it out. It seems an unlikely place to *plan* to kill someone, which I guess would be the alternative. As for his files," I said, putting my arm around her, "I think you should do what you think he would have wanted you to do. But you're going to have to fight if you decide to hang on to them. So you'd better keep your lawyer informed."

"I will," she said, giving me that wan smile again and patting my hand. "I will."

"I'll call you in the morning," I told her.

"Thank you, Tony. Thank you for coming."

3

I got to work around eleven. Ordinarily, I go straight up to the Hill, but the Senate wasn't meeting and I had to write Painter's obituary. Several people stopped at my desk to find out whether I knew anything more than what had been reported in the paper. I really didn't, but we spent a lot of time talking about Les.

I was more or less confident that the police would work it out sooner or later, assuming Les's murder involved something simple like a plain ordinary mugging and assuming they put any kind of effort into it. Neither assumption was a proposition I would have bet my last dollar on. Except for some scraps of paper with names and numbers on them, Les had been stripped clean. That indicated robbery. The Capitol did not strike me as a place to choose to kill someone, which also indicated a robbery gone amok. But Painter did have a lot of enemies, and he could have been killed by any one of a number of them.

Police can't do much to stop a murder. They're even worse at solving a mystery. Washington has more than sixty unsolved murders on the books. Most of the ones that get solved involve either a robbery or two people who know each other fighting in front of witnesses, with one pulling a knife or gun on the other. The premeditated murders don't get solved so easily. If it wasn't some kind of mugging, then whoever did it had planned it carefully. I thought about it some, played with it, and dropped it.

If it *was* armed robbery, then Painter's death was senseless, but no more senseless than a lot of other things that happen in Washington—just closer to home.

Sometime around mid-afternoon, while I was still struggling to do justice to Les in the obit, I stopped to call the "Inside Track" office. Steve Brandon answered. Steve was one of Les's assistants, along with Larry Quirk. Among the three of them they had kept the "Inside Track" chugging along, if you'll forgive the pun. Brandon and Quirk were young but first-rate, considering what they had to produce and the time they had to do it. I couldn't have managed to slice the world up the way they did, and I kind of admired their straightforward view of life.

If they were going to keep the column alive, they were going to have to devote about twenty-six hours a day to it. Even then, it was going to be hard.

"How you making out?" I asked Brandon.

"Oh, I guess we'll both survive," Steve answered in a slow way, as though he had been giving it a great deal of thought.

"You seen the police yet?" I asked.

"They were in this morning, early. They wanted to see Les's files, but I told them that none of the good stuff was here. It's all at his house, in that office vault he built. He wanted it somewhere he knew was secure. This place over here is about as secure as the State Department."

"You got any thoughts about what happened?"

"Well, he was working on something very, very good. One reason no one missed him was because he said he would probably be going out of town this week and we should take care of things . . . you know, the column and the broadcasts. And he usually didn't call while he was away unless he needed something, which was rare. And he never called home. When he showed up in the office one morning, you knew he was back."

Brandon said Painter had been out of the country shortly before he was killed. They knew that because his secretary, Dinah Berman, had had to run over to get his passport renewed on a moment's notice, and he had brought her back a box of Swiss chocolates on his return. Brandon had asked Painter about the trip, and Painter had muttered something about "need-to-know basis" and cut him off.

"I asked Quirk if he had any better idea than I did about what Les was up to," Brandon went on. "We had a good laugh about what sorry investigative reporters we were—to work for a man and not know what the hell he was doing. So the answer is no, I really don't have any thoughts on what happened. In a way, I guess I'm hoping his death had something to do with his work. That would fit the conspiratorial view we have around here, and would at least give it all some meaning. If it was just a robbery or a random killing, it would make everything seem much more absurd than it already does."

Brandon said that as far as he could tell neither Dinah nor Moose Petowski, Painter's office boy, knew anything. According to Brandon, Moose and Painter had barely been speaking to each other.

"They had a couple of arguments over the last three weeks because Moose was slow in getting some stuff Les wanted," Brandon said. "Moose is very hung up on the notion that he's much smarter than people think he is and he resents the way people treat him. He thinks everyone sees him as a dumb jock type—and he's right. Because that's what he is."

We talked a little bit more and agreed to keep in touch. Then I called the Painter home. Alice answered and told me her mother was still out "making arrangements." She said the police were waiting and Lieutenant Thomason was wearing a hole in the carpet, being very official and anxious to talk to her mother.

Back to the obit. It was almost finished, and I was going to go downstairs for some coffee when my editor, Frank Elliott, asked me to come into his office.

Elliott was a figure of some controversy in the newsroom. Most of the troops, me included, thought he was one of the best journalists in Washington. He brought some perspective to his job. At some point or other in his life he had flirted with socialism. He had moved past that to some other persuasion I never quite pinned down, but it left him solidly nonpartisan as far as the political structure of Washington was concerned. It really made no difference to him who was in. From his perspective, they were all part of the same gang— to be watched closely and never, never to be trusted.

"I'm not happy with the coverage we've been giving the new

campaign bill," he told me. "The one Higgins and Americans Together are sponsoring."

"Well, the bill is a lot of bullshit," I said. "Assuming it would work, which it won't, it hasn't a chance of passing the Senate when the House sends it over. Phil Higgins left the Senate and put himself in charge of Americans Together so he could wash the politics off of himself, become a statesman, and then run for President. And now he's running for President. Fine."

"I've been reading the paper myself," Elliott snapped. "When you get around to telling me something new, I'll be glad to listen. In the meantime, you're working for me. So you might be interested in what I think. One, whether it's bullshit or not, that bill has a lot of people on the Hill in a sweat, including lobbyists. Two, your forecast on legislation has been wrong from time to time. Three, Higgins *is* running for President and that has to be conveyed. Just because it's no surprise and just because his bill doesn't stand much of a chance are not reasons to cover the story inadequately. You can tell people both of those facts, but you can't tell them if you don't write the stories. I'm tired of using this junk from the wires. I want something more substantial."

"Right."

I considered Frank Elliott a friend and he considered me the same way. We had some bitter arguments from time to time. He asked a lot of his staff, but he gave a lot, too—attention and interest to reporters and editors who cared as much about what they were doing as he did. In this case, he was right. He was bringing an informed opinion to bear on the problem. I was acting on prejudice.

It wasn't until five-thirty or so that I finally got downstairs for my coffee, and my phone was ringing when I got back, so I had to run the last fifty yards to my desk. It was Mary.

"Tony," she said, "I'm in a little trouble." She didn't sound too worried.

Still, I was concerned. "Is there something I can do? What's happened?"

"Well, I've been thinking and thinking about Les's files—and I decided I couldn't wait to see how things went. I could see Lieutenant Thomason was intent on getting into them and I just couldn't let that happen. So, uh, I, uh, burned them."

"Sure, nothing wrong with that. If you get a sympathetic judge, he might let you off with probation."

Mary's laugh sounded forced. "I expected a little sympathy from you," she exclaimed. "I thought you'd at least see it the way Les did. His files were *private*! And given a choice between letting his murderer get off and opening them to the police, I'm sure he would have said no to the police. He's not here, so I did it for him. And if you're any kind of a friend at all, find something nice to say, because Lieutenant Thomason has plenty of unpleasant comments."

"I'll come visit you every Thursday," I told her. Then I paused. "You must be crazy! I take the First Amendment seriously, too. But I'm not sure this is the time and place—"

"Well, I am. And I'm sure Les would be too. You don't know what was in his papers, but I got a peek at them more than once. They could have kept a blackmailer, political or otherwise, in business for the rest of his life. The police would have loved them. The FBI would have loved them. But it's too bad, because they're not going to get them."

"If it's done, it's done," I said. "You can't recapture the moment. What are they going to do with you?"

"They haven't quite decided. Maybe nothing. Lieutenant Thomason left here pretty mad." Mary paused, with a kind of gulp. "The funeral is the day after tomorrow, Tony. It'll be at our church out here."

"I'll be there," I said. I hung up the phone, dumbfounded with surprise and admiration. I had never figured Mary Painter to be that kind of woman. I had liked her well enough, but she seemed innocuous. She was turning out to be much gutsier than I had thought. She always seemed to hang on Les when they were together, so I had assumed she lacked a strong personality or separate identity. Maybe I was wrong. It wouldn't be a first.

4

The memorial service for Les Painter was held in the local church out in his Maryland suburb. Twenty years ago cows were still grazing on the land where the big frame building stood, and it was probably a nice place to bring a girl on a sunny spring day. You could get in your car, drive for about forty-five minutes or so and forget you were anywhere near a big city. If you were hungry, you could go to some little place where it was entirely possible that they baked their own bread and the pie you ordered for dessert.

Now the cow pasture was the site of a tacky little development called Ivanhoe Court, with about four hundred families. Next to Ivanhoe Court was a place called Camelot Hills. It went on that way for miles. After King Arthur had contributed what he could to the plunder of the country landscape, they had started in with Robin Hood and the whole Sherwood Forest motif. Except that some of these developments cost more than others, the families who lived in them all had a great deal in common—especially their desire to escape the overcrowded conditions of the city and to move out to the fresh air and open spaces of suburbia, where they lived twelve houses to an acre and choked on the exhaust from the cars that they all had to have to go anywhere.

I was standing outside the church taking in as much of this little corner of America as I could from my vantage point when Lieutenant Thomason got out of a cream-colored unmarked police car and walked over to me.

We exchanged morning greetings.

"I tried to call you last night to ask you some questions, but no one was home," Thomason told me. He couldn't help sounding accusatory.

"I ate dinner out, came home for a little bit, and then had to go see someone."

"Certainly. No need to explain. I just wanted to speak to you about Mrs. Painter. Have you talked to her recently?"

"The day after I saw you at her house."

"Did she tell you anything about her husband's files?"

"Such as?"

"That she had destroyed them."

"She told me that, yes."

"And what did you tell her?"

I was beginning to get annoyed. "Look, Lieutenant. I don't make it a practice to tape my calls because I consider what someone says to me over the phone to be a matter of interest to that person and to me only. If I think other people may be interested, I take notes. Then I translate my notes to a piece of paper which I give to an editor, and eventually what I write winds up in your newspaper. But my conversation with Mary Painter wasn't like that. It was personal, which means we talked about things that were private."

"Mr. Jordan," Thomason addressed me with a tired, formally polite air of resignation. "You have a job to do and I have a job to do. The more you cooperate with me, the easier my job is, the quicker I find Les Painter's killer, the quicker that person gets tried, and the quicker I leave you and everyone else alone. You understand that. So why make it difficult?"

I had heard it all before, and Thomason had said it all before. It was a well-rehearsed speech, the polite number he did for people he didn't think he could lean on harder. Police officers—the better ones

16

at any rate—all act as though they had been to charm school. The trouble is that they deal with recalcitrant people as though they were preadolescents having a tantrum rather than adults with real and substantial differences of opinion that prevent them from doing what the police ask. I was annoyed at being made to feel like a child. And I was remembering all the times over the years when I had asked—usually without satisfaction—for small pieces of information from a police officer. I wasn't enthusiastic. Irrational? You bet. I never held myself out to be Socrates.

More than that, I didn't see any point in trying to explain to him why Mary Painter had done what she'd done. He was part of her problem as far as that was concerned. Everyone wanted to look at those files—the FBI, the Internal Revenue Service, most of the committees on Capitol Hill, the Republican and Democratic national committees, and probably the KGB.

What kept them all from satisfying their desire—leaving aside the KGB—was the First Amendment. The police and the FBI had been trying since before I came to Washington to find out what Les had, but he was not—unlike some other reporters—in the business of sharing his information with the authorities. If he thought something was true and worth knowing, he printed it in his column. Then they found out about it when everyone else did. But if he didn't choose to print it, it was because it wasn't true or it wasn't worth worrying about or he still had more work to do on it. Whatever the reasons were, he regarded his files as inviolable. Mary understood that. She understood very well that sources are everything to a reporter. Without sources, we might as well stop publishing. We would have to rely on the government for all our news. They could tell us or not tell us, and in a lot of situations we would have no way of knowing what the facts were. A reporter without sources is a ship without water. Some people, Thomason probably included, might like it that way. They think that newspapers are nothing but a nuisance in the first place.

"Lieutenant, Mary Painter has been on her own since she turned twenty-one. She doesn't check out with me before she indulges her pyromaniacal impulses. She and I are not close friends. I know her because I was friendly with her husband, but I wasn't intimate with him, either. No one was. Les Painter was much too busy setting the world straight to have a lot of friends.

"So whether I agree or not with what she did is beside the point.

17

I wasn't responsible. I didn't know about it in advance and even if I had, I doubt if I could have done much to stop her."

We might have gone on for quite a while that way except that the President came up with his entourage and distracted everyone. When his car pulled up behind the police escort—the Montgomery County police were having a terrific time blowing their sirens—the Secret Service men jumped out and started scanning the small knot of reporters who were standing around talking and smoking before going inside. And then out came the President. He looked gray, tired, and a little low on energy. He didn't focus on the situation for a second or two, but then, recognizing some of the reporters, he went over to shake some hands and chat. The Secret Service men, who had moved ahead, slowed down and stopped. For a guy of sixty-three, the President was still in remarkably good shape, even if he wasn't exactly in prime condition. But since he was nearing the end of his second term, that wasn't hard to understand.

After a few moments he turned to go inside and the rest of us followed. He went to the front pew, where Mary Painter was sitting with her kids, shook her hand and theirs, said a few words to her and then went to his seat on the aisle in the second row.

Funerals by definition go on too long. Les Painter's could not be an exception. The minister read some passages from the Bible and then Philip Higgins gave the eulogy. I thought that was a little unusual, since reporters normally aren't that close to people they cover, and Higgins was a major politician. But Higgins and Painter were extraordinarily alike in a way, and their attraction for each other had been strong. They shared the same evangelical fervor—"vision of America" Higgins called it in his eulogy of Painter—and they were really on the same wavelength much of the time. Higgins was one of the heroes in Painter's columns, one of the few good guys taking on the bad special interests. I don't think that Higgins got a good press from Les because they were friendly. I think they were friendly because Les honestly admired Higgins.

Higgins, though, was low key in what he had to say about Les. He went through Les's life—how he had come to Washington from the West after the war, had started out as a copyboy in one of the smaller bureaus, had hustled his way into a reporting job, then had gotten a string of good stories and finally a Pulitzer Prize. Higgins included a lot of rhetoric about how Les believed in purifying the political process, working for the kind of nation and world we wanted our children to grow up in, and that sort of thing.

In a way, Higgins looked very much in his element standing there above the congregation. His black hair showed streaks of gray, especially around the temples. His blue pin-striped suit fit as if it were tailor-made, which it was. The white shirt and dark tie gave him the proper somber appearance. And he stood above us, lecturing us on how the country and the world ought to be, what our obligation was, and how important it was that we stood ready to respond. Toward the end it came perilously close to being a campaign speech. But Higgins managed to keep it within the bounds of good taste and to wrap it up before it got out of hand—which was why he was, after all, a pro and why he stood a reasonable chance of winning the big prize.

After the services, I paid my respects to Mary Painter, who seemed to be holding up well. I stood around talking to some people for a while before starting back to the office. I gave a ride to Dan Reilly, a former newsman who had gone to work in the bureaucracy as a press aide. He called himself a flack, although those of us who had known him from before had too much respect for him to follow his lead. Now he was working on the Hill for a California congressman, Ray Williams.

Reilly had a face flushed from too much drinking back in his old newspaper days. He had sworn off five years ago, switched to coffee and had begun living a quiet life. Except for chain-smoking Lucky Strikes, which left his fingers yellow with nicotine, Reilly now had no visible vices. He looked at the world through sad, watery eyes, seldom smiling. He was honest, alert and, most important for me, generally reliable in his information. I can't recall his ever knowingly spinning me on a story. When he had to earn his pay, he was open about it. He made no secrets about where his boss's interests lay, and he was loyal enough to keep his mouth shut when he thought they conflicted. Reilly was essentially a burnt-out case, a moral paralytic who could still distinguish between right and wrong but wasn't able to act on it. There are people like him all over. There is nothing particularly Washingtonian about Reilly. When you first come to Washington—when you're young and earnest—you expect that people in politics believe in what they're doing. Only later do you learn that for most of them those days are long since gone, and politics has become a way to make a living—like selling shoes, only more lucrative or like selling insurance, only superficially more glamorous. Washington is full of people, including elected officials, who once had all sorts of ideas about changing things. The longer they stay, the more like everyone else they become. Eventually they forget where they came from or why. The only important thing for them is staying.

In that respect, at least, Reilly was different. He didn't particularly want to stay. His problem was that he had nowhere else to go.

Since neither of us was in any hurry to get back to work, we stopped in Georgetown at a place on Wisconsin Avenue that specializes in crepes to have lunch before going back to work.

Reilly had a cup of coffee and I played with a glass of white wine until lunch came. "How long do you think it will take the cops to find Painter's killer?" Reilly asked me.

"Probably quite a while," I answered. "Mysteries aren't the sort of thing the police are very good at solving. How long do you think it'll take?"

"They'll either solve it in a month or they'll never solve it," he said without hesitating. "If it wasn't a mugging, I think they'll never solve it. They won't want to. And if it was a robbery," he said with the off-hand manner of a man who's got it all figured out, "they can put enough talking money out on the street to bring in some information fairly quickly. But maybe that's not what we're talking about. Maybe somebody wanted Painter dead. Whoever it is would be smart enough and big enough or rich enough—which is the same thing—to stay away from the cops.

"But I don't think the cops care all that much about this case. It'll be big for a while and then something else will come along and they'll put it on the back burner, and in about two or three years *Newsweek* or *Time* will assign one of their junior reporters to do a piece on how the police were never able to find Painter's killer. And then the case will be really dead."

He lit another cigarette. "When I was a reporter I used to think I had some sort of automatic insurance policy whenever I was going after somebody—especially in the mob. I figured they were too smart to kill me because they knew that no newsman would let me die without doing everything he could to find my killer. But that's a bunch of bullshit. There's nothing automatic about it at all. The most important thing on the minds of most reporters in this town is getting out of the office in time to catch the bus home to Reston and getting August off so they can go to Martha's Vineyard."

I cut in, "I'm not so sure that's fair, Dan."

"I'm not so sure that's fair, Dan," he repeated, mimicking. "I'll make it easy for you. Name me five reporters in this town who would have the balls and the inclination to dig into the possibility that the President of the United States might be a crook."

I thought about it for a while. "I can think of three, maybe four. Stonington, Goldman, Peterson, and maybe Engelberg—if the President were a conservative Republican."

"Right," Reilly said. "And the rest of these assholes would be lapping it up at the White House briefings day in and day out. The Prez could be fencing stolen goods out of the Oval Office and they'd be reporting that he was operating a discount house to aid the consumer.

"The point is that when you go after someone, you're out on a limb. The only protection you have is your own wits, luck, and the instinct to save your ass."

"I like to think there's more going for me than that," I said.

"You can think anything you want," he said. "I'm just telling you what is. The cops aren't going to find out who killed you, Painter, or any other reporter unless it's some black kid from Seventh and P. And if you think some other reporter is going to do it, you are going to be sorely disappointed."

The waitress brought our crepes and we started eating. I was starved, but Reilly only picked at his lunch. I had a salad, which was all right—Boston and iceberg lettuce with a garlic dressing—and an apple-and-sausage crepe. The sausage had a kind of spongy texture and was under-seasoned. If I had been writing a review, I would have given the place no more than half a star out of a possible four. I left the table sustained, but that was about all.

I dropped Reilly off at Sixteenth and K so he could catch a cab to the Hill, and then I parked my car and went up to the newsroom. With the Senate in recess, there wasn't a great deal to do if I didn't feel like doing much. And I didn't.

The newsroom was in its usual state of disorganization, with people standing around in groups of twos and threes talking about crabgrass, central air-conditioning, and nuclear disarmament.

I looked over the national-news budget—the list of stories the *Journal* staff was writing for the next day's paper, as well as the stories we were taking off the wires. The budget had its daily listing of disasters from all over—a tornado in Kentucky, a small earthquake out in California, unemployment was up, food prices were up. A scientist had announced the possibility that too much sexual

21

intercourse might contribute to cancer. Some hazards are better left unreported, if you ask me, but some newspapers think they have an obligation to tell it all.

Then I wandered back to our library to look at the clips of Painter's old columns, but not just for the hell of it. What Reilly had said at lunch bothered me, I guess because I thought his assessment might be right. The police weren't going to go out of their way to solve Painter's murder unless someone made a fuss about it. And it was unlikely that anyone except the *Journal* would, and the *Journal* itself wouldn't because that would look as if the *Journal* were throwing its weight around. And when the *Journal* threw its weight around, it did it quietly through the spoken, rather than the written, word so as not to compromise its image for disinterestedness, and so as not to leave a public record, in case at some later date the management decided to change tack.

I wanted to see what and whom Painter had been writing about for the past year or so. The clips from his column were arranged in monthly files—long, slender envelopes open at the top, each one labeled "Painter—The Inside Track." Painter's column appeared every day, rain or shine. His name was almost always on it alone, although he would share a byline with Larry Quirk or Steve Brandon if they had done all or almost all of the work on a particularly good story.

If I were looking for suspects, I might have found, conservatively speaking, about a hundred or so who could have killed Les Painter for a variety of reasons: revenge, to keep him from printing more of the same, to muzzle him for good, or whatever. I toyed with the idea that the CIA might be involved. They were a favorite target of his.

I found a couple of columns that intrigued me, though I'm not quite sure why. One was about Edward X. Dunphy, a lobbyist for several oil companies. Dunphy had a reputation as an easy touch for a buck. He had managed to avoid prosecution for violating federal campaign-spending and bribery statutes for years—one, by having good legal advice which kept him informed down to the last millimeter about where the line was drawn, and two, by being so well connected everywhere that it would have taken the grossest sort of violation to force Dunphy's friends to sit still for a prosecution. And Edward X. Dunphy, in public at least, was not a gross person.

Another bunch of columns concerned Henry Fisher, the chemical tycoon. Fisher's company, which he had started from scratch thirty years ago and which was still largely a family operation even though its stock was publicly owned, was under pressure from the Environmental Protection Agency to stop polluting the Wishbone River, where its biggest plant was located. Fisher had developed a keen interest in politics at all levels as a result of EPA's pressure on him. If EPA got what it wanted, Fisher's company could be wiped out. Fisher's whole house of cards, the tenuous empire he had built with mob money backing him, would come down, right on top of him. From what I knew about Fisher—the people he played with and the kind of game he played—he wouldn't let himself be restrained by the rules of polite society. And even if *he* would, the people behind him wouldn't.

Painter had done several columns and promised more about Fisher, detailing how he had funneled campaign funds to senators and congressmen even when some of them weren't running or had no opposition.

Another group of columns concerned Senator Layton Seld, whom Painter liked to refer to as Senator Sold. Seld came from the Midwest and presented himself as a liberal, which meant that he voted the way the AFL-CIO wanted him to on almost every issue. But Seld had discovered the confluence of interests beneath the surface antagonism between labor and management. That discovery had helped keep him in the Senate, where his attendance record was the worst.

He had made a brief run for the Presidency the last time out. Everyone thought he was crazy, since he would have had a hard time getting his family to vote for him, much less anyone else. But after the election he built himself a new house, so maybe he wasn't so crazy after all. I asked his press secretary a couple of times if I could see Seld's tax returns, and he always told me he was "working on it" but was "running into some problems." The main problem, I think, was that Seld didn't want anyone to see his tax returns. He probably would have preferred not to let the IRS see them, but he apparently did file them.

Painter's columns about Seld had to do mainly with his traveling habits, especially the free plane rides he took on corporate jets. Seld was forever showing up in Miami to speak at a manufacturers' convention or a labor conference, pulling off big fees for making stock speeches while missing key votes on the Senate floor. Painter apparently relished reporting Seld's activities in minute detail, including how he decorated his Watergate apartment, which he rented at a ridiculously low rate from some corporation.

Philip Higgins came up in a few columns, too, but he was always mentioned favorably. Painter especially liked Higgins's campaign reform bill, which Painter said would "do for American politics what the Water Control Act of 1966 will do for our nation's lakes and rivers—clean out the muck that's making them so filthy." Painter was about as subtle as a sledge hammer and he was no Hemingway when it came to style, but he got his point across and his point carried weight, which was all he cared about.

When I finished, just for the hell of it I made a list of persons I would consider suspects if I were investigating the Painter case. I put down Seld, Fisher, and Dunphy. Taken as individuals, they didn't seem like all that much. But powerful interests were behind them, and those interests had a great deal to lose. American industry had been built with muscle and other people's blood. Painter nosed around in places where the stakes dwarfed a mere man. One life more or less didn't make much difference in that atmosphere, even if Painter was more prominent than some faceless laborer. What really counted was profits.

So now I had a list. But then what? I've never been much good at that sort of thing—catching crooks with their fingers in the till, dredging through documents to get the goods on someone, tying a noose around someone's neck by examining public records. It takes patience, which I lack; persistence, not one of my strongest points; and time, which I did not have a lot of.

But Reilly was right about the police. Lieutenant Thomason seemed to care more about Painter's files than Painter's murderer. And if Reilly was right that Painter's murderer was someone big, I could wind up with my career a shambles or very dead. Neither of those prospects appealed to me, and since I like having myself around, I decided to kick it around some more before picking it up.

5

L es Painter's death didn't cause more than a momentary pause in the Capital. Nobody short of a President is indispensable here, and our experience in the past fifteen years or so indicates that we can change even them with less trouble than we had thought.

Washington is a city where news gets old very fast. The Presidential primaries, always a big draw for a town where the main occupation is politics, were already on us. At the same time, the Senate Rules Committee was about to hold hearings on Philip Higgins's campaign reform bill.

Under ordinary circumstances, Higgins's bill would not have been a major story. But Higgins was making the bill the cornerstone of his as-yet-undeclared race for President, and he had to be considered a strong contender—some thought the leading contender—for the nomination. And if he had the nomination, in what looked to be a Democratic year, then the chances were very good that he would be the next President of the United States.

I usually don't like to cover hearings. They take a lot of time, it's difficult to get enough space from the desk to write about the testimony intelligently, and they're downright dull. What I normally do is ask the desk to send someone else while I nose around and find out what's going on out of public view.

In the case of Higgins's testifying, though, I asked to cover him, an exercise of my prerogative since it was happening on my beat. I thought the story had a nice melodramatic side to it. Higgins had left the Senate to build grass-roots support for reforms he hadn't been able to legislate. Now he was coming back, with support inside and outside the Senate, to slug it out.

The problem was that Dan Felshin, our political reporter, felt *he* should be covering Higgins since Higgins was running for President, even if he hadn't formally announced.

The Solomon-like solution of the desk was to have both of us cover the story. I wrote the straight piece about the hearing, and Felshin wrote an interpretative piece describing the straitjacket Higgins was putting himself into by his proposal to limit political donations to one hundred dollars. Felshin considered Higgins a long shot, but Felshin had been wrong before.

With the knowledge that Higgins's testimony would be a media spectacular, the Senate Rules Committee had scheduled itself into the marble-walled grandeur of the Senate Caucus Room. Every time something historic happens in the Caucus Room, the *Journal's* national desk assigns a story about all the history that's taken place there. Since it's the biggest hearing room the Senate has, there's a lot to write about. The Teapot Dome hearings were there back in the 1920s. Joe McCarthy had a field day manufacturing Communists there in the early fifties, and it was there he met his match in the form of a strait-laced Boston lawyer from Iowa named Welch. John Kennedy used the Caucus Room to announce his Presidential candidacy in 1960 and his brother Robert used it again in 1968 for the same purpose. The Senate Watergate Committee held its hearings there in 1973. So a lot of the Republic's better and worse moments—which are which depends upon your point of view—occurred in the Caucus Room.

On television, the Caucus Room projects an air of elegance and dignity. The ceiling is about thirty feet high, a gold-leafed affair with enormous chandeliers. Roman columns and pilasters decorate the marble walls. Two oversized oak thrones are centered on the walls at either end of the room. And at the front is a table about half the length of a football field. The witness usually sits facing the senators at a smaller table which looks like a fold-up bridge table someone brought from home in the trunk of his car.

I arrived early enough to bring up a cup of coffee from the cafeteria in the Senate Office Building basement and to go through the *Journal* and *The New York Times* while the television camera crews were setting up for the hearing. The klieg lights that hang over the senators' table had been dropped so a couple of them could be turned around to face the table where Higgins would be sitting. He, after all, was the story, not the senators. As usual, the green baize on the senators' table did not quite fit, so that a third of the table was exposed, while the brown baize on the table where Higgins would sit was draped unevenly, so that it dragged on the floor on one side and hung only about three inches over on the other.

I turned around a couple of times to count noses in the crowd as the room started filling up. I was reminded as I turned, glancing over the room, that the paint was flaking. The paint job went along with the carpet, which was threadbare in a number of places—worn by the legions of senators, aides, reporters, and spectators who had trudged in and out of the room over the years. The first time I'd noticed the shabby condition of the Caucus Room, I had been surprised that the Senate hadn't fixed it up. But then I realized that the room looks elegant on television whatever the reality, and appearances are what count on the Hill.

Larry Samuels, Higgins's press assistant, came in about ten minutes before the hearing was supposed to begin and started complaining about everything—the lights, the microphones, the table, the room. That was mostly nervous energy and no one took it very seriously. The table was moved about six inches to the left and a couple of lights were adjusted. Samuels pronounced himself satisfied and he left to get Higgins, secure in the knowledge that he had earned his pay for the day.

Then a couple of minutes later a kid in his twenties came in lugging a briefcase and set it down on the witness table. I recognized him as Richie Vallone, Higgins's driver, errand boy, and general handyman. Someone had told me once that Richie had been in Vietnam, but I didn't know much more about him than that, except that he appeared devoted to Higgins. I had trouble understanding people like Richie who got involved with politicians. Politicians' work always seemed to me to be about deals—who got what, who got screwed, and who got paid, either over or under the table. I had no feel for the psychological role that politics played—giving people a way of making up for their own inadequacies by identifying with a cause or an individual. I was aware of that role, but I didn't understand it. It was so many different things to so many people—the spinster secretary who devotes her life to her boss; the suburban housewife who finds middle age approaching and nothing to show for her life; the young executive who is frustrated at work because he is not allowed to demonstrate his full potential. The bored, the turned off, the hopeful, the angry. Something along those lines might make a decent story, I told myself, if I could find a simple enough way to do it so that my editors could understand it.

I walked over to Richie. "How's it going?" I asked him.

"Hey, great, Mr. Jordan. Just great."

"When's he going to announce?"

"I'm just Mr. Higgins's driver, Mr. Jordan. He doesn't let me in on the heavy stuff."

"I thought you were one of his closest advisers," I said, kidding.

He smiled. "Well, he talks to me. He's good people. But I don't think I ought to go around saying what he tells me. It wouldn't be right. If you'll excuse me now, I've gotta get back outside."

Richie left and I wandered back to my seat to watch the show begin.

The opening of a hearing is a little like a pot of water starting to boil. You can see it beginning a long time before it actually does boil, and yet you're never quite sure of the moment when it actually starts to bubble. A few of the senators on the committee—but only Democrats—were around before the ten o'clock starting time. But Higgins wasn't there. Then Higgins came in, to be greeted by applause from the spectators. But Senator Donald Ludington, the chairman of the committee, wasn't there. Then Ludington came in, and since Higgins was huddled with a couple of his aides, Ludington had to look busy, too. No one should think that a United States senator was allowing the hearing to be delayed by a witness.

Finally it all came together. Higgins took his seat, Ludington banged his gavel, and the hearings were under way. Ludington kept his opening remarks very short as a gesture of courtesy to Higgins and asked him if he had an opening statement to make.

Higgins thanked Ludington and began reading his statement,

which had already been turned over to the committee, and to the reporters, television crews, and radio networks. Whatever the committee might think, Higgins was really giving his testimony for the six o'clock network news. The cameras were grinding away. The assembled senators were only props for Higgins as he removed the sixth veil from his candidacy.

"I see my testimony today as part of a larger effort to restore honesty, decency, and integrity to American politics," he read. "I believe it is feasible to wage a campaign for President demonstrating that it is not only possible but practical for a candidate to run successfully under the restrictions imposed by my draft legislation. I shall have more to say about this in a matter of days. I hope that this legislation will become law in this session of Congress. But if it does not," Higgins said with emphasis, "Congress should know that the next Administration may well make this bill its first order of business—to drive the money changers from the temple of our Republic."

At that point, the two hundred to three hundred spectators in the room, probably almost all from Americans Together, erupted into a prolonged ovation. He was not finally and officially a candidate, but he was the nearest thing to it. His staff had chosen this tortuous way of announcing his candidacy drip by drip so as to hog as much news time as possible—"maximizing media exposure" was the phrase they liked to use. He was going to have some rough spots to get through —raising enough money to campaign for the nomination, then getting it, and finally winning the election. But he had to be taken seriously. Americans Together had chapters in every state, and that provided the nucleus of the Higgins campaign organization. There were files of potential volunteers in each state, all the way down to the precinct level.

Higgins had served two terms—twelve years—in the Senate, so he knew politics and the players first-hand, knew where the bodies were buried, knew how the game was played, knew the weak spots of the other players as well as their strong points. He was photogenic, articulate, non-threatening to the working-class voters whose support any Democrat must have to get elected, and he brought that sense of mission that liberal Democrats always like their candidates to have. Americans don't choose a President every four years; they go around looking for a Moses. Usually they're disappointed, but Higgins was more than willing to play the part.

With his opening statement, Higgins didn't even bother addressing the committee. He spoke directly to the television cameras, peering into them with an intense gaze from those pale grey eyes of his. Higgins was one of those men who look neither young nor old. His hair was full and silvery in the way that men think gives them the distinguished appearance that suits their real selves. But his face, with its broad jaw and finely cut features, was unlined. Higgins was fifty-one, but he looked ten years younger. I don't think I need to explain why women, or at least many women, found him very attractive. He wasn't oblivious to that, but he wasn't preoccupied by it either. Higgins had a wife and three children, all of whom seemed to have come from central casting and fit the role of First Family perfectly. To all outward appearances, his family life was exemplary. But he also spent days and weeks away on political tours. Despite his sense of mission and his public image, he found time to relax and women to help him do it.

At this moment, though, he was trying to reform the political system and get himself elected President. He set out to parade before the American public battalions of villains with whom he proposed to do battle—Big Oil, both foreign and domestic; Big Business; Big Banks; private interests of all kinds.

"America is being carved up into a thousand feudal fiefdoms, and those who profit are the few in the aristocracy of special interests. The rest of us are becoming serfs, watching our lives and property being slowly taken over by them. I say it is time that we turn the country back to the people who made it great," Higgins read, as he got near the end of his statement.

When he finished, and the committee was preparing to ask questions, Higgins, by prearrangement, turned the witness chair over to Peter Stein, legal counsel to Americans Together. Then he slipped out, leaving Stein to clean up the debris like a janitor the morning after a New Year's Eve party.

During the first moments of Stein's testimony, the television camera crews, with their customary courtesy and respect for the dignity of the Senate, proceeded to break down their equipment as though the room were entirely empty. So Stein had to make himself heard over the clatter of valises being snapped shut. He bobbed back and forth in the witness chair, trying to maintain eye contact with the committee members while television crewmen kept stepping in the way to roll up their wires and disconnect their microphones.

Stein outlined the provisions of the bill, including the hundred dollar limit it would impose on the contributions that any person could make to any candidate in a single election. Corporations, companies, labor unions and associations would all be prohibited from giving money. The idea was to make every vote equal and to force politicians to pay attention to a broad spectrum of citizens.

Higgins had a potentially winning issue and had found a way to exploit it, but I was asking myself whether he really expected Congress to swallow the bill whole, and whether he really wanted it to.

When Ludington asked Stein if public financing weren't a good solution, Stein must have given at least five reasons why it wasn't, starting out with the matter of constitutionality and then moving on to the principle that a taxpayer's money should not go to support a candidate with whom he or she disagrees. Just about the point when my eyes were beginning to glaze over, I was saved—literally—by the bell, which signaled a vote on the Senate floor. Ludington announced a recess and the senators drifted toward the door. I decided to ride over to the Senate on the subway to see what was happening over in the Capitol.

6

The Senate subway is one of the technological concessions that the Senate has made to the Twentieth Century in the interest of saving time. Actually, there are two subways on the Senate side—one from each of the Senate office buildings to the Capitol. A third subway on the House side runs to the Rayburn House Office Building. You might ask yourself why the Senate, concerned as it is with conserving the senators' time, has built a subway but continues the practice of voice voting instead of doing it electronically. You might ask, but you won't get an answer that makes sense.

I rode over with Simon Walker, a Tennessee Republican who might have made a terrific President fifteen years ago if he had been from Illinois or Ohio and had been able to suppress his penchant for speaking his mind.

Walker was a great big shaggy bear of a man. He was one of the last remaining honest-to-goodness characters in the Senate. His breed was being replaced by the new, sleek plastic version that came with double-knit designer suits, patent-leather shoes, and glib statements which on close examination had all the substance of cotton candy.

"Ah am hanging on the edge of my chair waiting to hear if Philip Higgins has decided to run for President," Walker said with a whimsical smile as he squeezed into a seat next to me on the subway. "Ah thought all this time that he was merely trying to restore honesty and virtue to American politics, but Ah guess he decided that reforming the process was too slow and he might have to take the more direct route, bring in new personalities. And finding none up to his exacting standards, he may decide, reluctantly to be sure, that he will have to leave the peace and serenity of his reform efforts and join the crass business of politics again."

"How do you think he'll make out?" I asked Walker.

"Are we on or off the record?"

"Off, I guess." With Walker, there was no point in trying to pin him down for a quote, since he would slip on a mask and give me some kind of a rapid-fire incomprehensible statement.

"Some fellas around here don't agree with me," Walker said, "but I think Higgins is going to be hard to beat. And if he gets the nomination—which I think he will—he's going to be President. I could elaborate on that, but I trust my instincts. The people are tired of old farts like me. They think we're out of touch with what's happening in the country, and they don't trust all these young fellas who've come along. Higgins is something else, though. I don't agree with him, I don't especially trust him, but I can sense the kind of appeal he has, even in my state. And if he can sell what he's selling in Tennessee, then it's pretty strong stuff."

The ride from the Old Senate Office Building to the Capitol takes about thirty seconds, so we were pulling in as Walker finished his quick appraisal of Higgins's chances. I went up the short escalator with him and then we walked about twenty feet to the elevators— three on either side of the corridor. Assorted tourists were crowding around the elevators, but the chief operator moved them aside when he saw Walker coming and we got on the center elevator on the right, the one reserved for senators.

Walker got off on Two and went in to the cloakroom off the Senate floor to find out from his party whip what the vote was on and what the party wanted him to do. I went up to the Senate press gallery on Three, checked my desk there for mail, checked the gallery desk to see if anyone had called, and then called the *Journal* to check in. Everyone was in a meeting—one of about five that *Journal* editors hold every day—so I wound up talking to Melinda, the twenty-two-year-old brunette bombshell who answers the phone on the national desk. We had our usual suggestive conversation. Melinda and I gazed lustfully at each other across the generation gap but we never tried to bridge it, which was probably just as well. At thirty-eight, I still knew the moves, but making them was something else again. I told her to let Elliott know that Higgins's statement had gone as expected, that I'd probably need about a column, and that other than the Higgins story there was nothing doing.

"You still owe me that lunch, Tony," she reminded me.

"Listen, Mel, sometime between now and the day you bestow yourself for life on the grand prize winner, I'll keep my word to you. It may be only McDonald's, but I'll take you to lunch."

"O.K., cutie. I'll see you later."

I hung up and stood looking out the window over my desk. I had a view out across the Capitol grounds toward Northeast Washington. Over the top of Union Station, I could see the railroad yards, and in the far distance, hazily through the smog left by a million morning commuters, I could see the gold dome of the Shrine of the Immaculate Conception at Catholic University. There's nothing awe-inspiring about this view, but it beats looking at someone's dirty laundry.

The alcove where my little desk is located is one of the four large spaces that used to form an elegant corridor outside the balcony that rings the Senate chamber. The floors are Spanish tile. The ceilings have frescoes of historic scenes. In the alcove are about fifteen other small desks, each big enough for a typewriter and two small drawers. Reporters who regularly cover the Senate sit here. The main room has ten phone booths with government lines for reporters to make and receive calls. In the center, more or less, are four leather couches, back-to-back in pairs, and two large leather armchairs of the same dark brown color. A table set up over by a window is where press releases are left.

The general atmosphere is somewhere between a field hospital in a combat zone and a men's club. The ambiance is definitely masculine, even though about a third of the reporters at any given moment are women. Like it or not, the Senate is a male-dominated institution—on the floor, in committee, and in the press gallery.

Two frosted-glass swinging doors lead from this outer part of the gallery to the balcony over the Senate, where seats are arranged in four tiers on either side of the steep stairs. I've never counted, but I guess eighty to one hundred reporters could sit in the balcony. Usually there aren't more than five or ten, if that many, watching debate on the floor. The wire services have seats reserved in the first row, with phones under the writing counters so they can instantaneously relay news about the outcome of important votes.

I drifted down to one of the vinyl-covered barstool-type seats in the front row and watched the senators saunter in through the doors at either end and at the center of the chamber.

The Senate chamber is at one and the same time large and cozy. The four walls are marble, twelve feet high. Lush blue and gold carpet covers the floor. The old-fashioned desks are arranged in groups of two and three on broad tiers that make it easy for senators to come and go. Tiny microphones on each desk, when clipped to his lapel, allow a senator to address his colleagues in a whisper and be heard clearly.

A vote on the floor is about the nearest thing to mass confusion that I've ever seen in American government. The roll is read by a clerk, but most of the senators aren't there when their names are called. A lot of them just wander in, walk up to the desk in the front of the chamber, quietly tell the clerk how they're voting, and then stop to talk to colleagues. Naturally, when there are seventy or eighty senators on the floor, as there often are during a vote, those little clumps cause congestion, and the various conversations make it hard for the clerk to be heard and to hear. What usually happens is that some goody-goody senator asks the presiding officer to bring the Senate to order, if the presiding officer hasn't already taken the initiative himself. That's what was happening when I came in.

"The Senate will come to order," the chair was repeating over and over again, punctuating the statement with hard raps on the desk. "The Senate will come to order. Senators will please clear the aisles. Senators wishing to converse should move to the cloakroom. The Senate will come to order. Senators will please clear the aisles."

That's usually good for about ten seconds of order, and today was no different. I could see Walker down on the floor telling old mountain stories to Ludington and a group of other senators. In the back rows on the Democratic side, I could see Sprockett of Colorado, Martin of Illinois, Simpson of Nevada, and Delano of Maine rocking back and forth in their seats with laughter. Every time the laughter subsided, Delano would say something and it would start all over again. I was fascinated watching them, unable to decide whether their behavior was bad form, callous in the face of the serious matters they had to deal with, or a welcome relief from stodginess and pomposity, a refreshing puff of joie de vivre.

All of them were youngish men—in their forties and early fifties —well-known, moderately charismatic liberals. They looked good on television, polished in their public appearances, earnest enough to seem serious, yet detached enough to appear level-headed. They shared a weakness for female flesh and a capacity for strong drink. None of them would have been valedictorian of his class and maybe not even Phi Beta Kappa, but they worked at their jobs, for the most part.

Delano had enough skeletons in his closet to keep a pack of hounds in bones for a month. Simpson's father had made a lot of money as a movie star but had had the good sense to leave it at that —and the senator lacked his father's good sense. Sprockett had a reputation for hard work and paying close attention to detail. Martin liked to introduce bills—more than any other senator. He wasn't interested in *passing* bills, just introducing them, with an accompanying big splash back home.

So the four of them sat in the back row telling jokes, while some seventy-odd of their colleagues stood around on the floor and in the adjacent cloakroom talking, and the Senate voted on whether or not to cut off a million and a half persons from federal food stamps. The four of them were in their own little world, having themselves one hell of a time. It was the high jinks and rollicking fun of fraternity men rough-housing in the television room. If they had started throwing spitballs, it wouldn't have surprised me. In the midst of all that marble splendor, they seemed to have reverted to the carefree college days when a budget was nothing more than a spending limit imposed by the old man.

All that mingling on the Senate floor came as close as anything can to demonstrating the clubby atmosphere of this strange legislature, one of the most exclusive fraternities in the world. Despite Charlotte Daniels's presence, the Senate was a fraternity, and despite party differences, the Senate came to the aid of a colleague publicly embarrassed or legally threatened. When it moved against one of its own, always reluctantly, it thought in terms of minimum punishment rather than maximum. And when it punished, the offense more often than not was perceived to have been against the Senate rather than against the laws of the Republic, another citizen, or the country itself. The Senate will turn a blind eye and a deaf ear to drunkenness, adultery, theft, bribery, and other public and private indecencies of all sorts. But it will not tolerate an act that casts the Senate in a bad light. The American people might get the wrong idea.

After about ten minutes the senators started leaving the floor. I had had my recreation for the day and I started back to the hearing room. Stein was back on the stand, agreeing with Ludington that a hundred-dollar limit was severe, that the ban on organizational contributions was severe, and that the penalties—a fifty thousand dollar fine and five years' imprisonment—were severe.

"Severity is what we need, Mr. Chairman," Stein said earnestly, hovering over the microphone like a hawk. "We are not going to rid ourselves of the noxious influence of big money without taking some strong medicine."

"Do you see any constitutional problems with your bill as drafted?" Ludington asked Stein.

"We have prepared a brief dealing with a great many of the constitutional objections that have been raised, Mr. Chairman. I can summarize our arguments or submit the brief for the record."

"I think in the interest of saving time that you may submit the brief and the committee can study it, Mr. Stein," Ludington said. "With the indulgence of the committee and if Mr. Stein is agreeable, I would like to terminate your testimony at this point, with the understanding that you may be recalled to answer questions from other committee members at some later date."

Stein started gathering his papers, by now spread out all over the little table, to put them back into the two briefcases he had brought with him. He handed one of them over to the stenographer who was transcribing the hearings, and took a seat in the front row of the spectators.

The next witness was Mike O'Connell, labor's chief lobbyist. I could write a book about O'Connell and some day I may. O'Connell's physical presence is overwhelming. He stands a little over six feet and weighs close to three hundred pounds. During World War II he was a blimp. Now he is the legislative brains of the AFL-CIO and of almost every piece of social-welfare or civil-rights legislation that has been enacted into law by Congress in this generation.

The secret of O'Connell's success is that he knows, or at least tries

37

to know, everything about everybody. I never caught O'Connell ignorant of a fact pertaining to an important bill, unaware of a senator's position on a piece of legislation, or forgetful of a name. O'Connell is the nearest thing to a walking encyclopedia I have ever met. He often sounds as if he hadn't finished the third grade, though he put himself through college while working on the docks in Los Angeles. And his appearance can only be described as gross, from his size to his wrinkled shirts, food-stained ties, and rumpled suits covered with cigarette ashes and burn marks. But when I need a vote count before the vote, or when I'm having trouble with the machinations going on over amendments to a bill, I call O'Connell. He may not always tell me what I want to know, but he almost always has an answer.

More than that, O'Connell is a brilliant organizer. I have seen him, more than once, quarterback a filibuster to prevent the Senate from voting on a bill that seemed certain to pass, in order to give himself time to go to work. He gets on the phone to union leaders in a few states where he thinks a senator can be brought around, or he calls some big businessman he knows. He doesn't like to do it, but he will when it's important. It's all politics to O'Connell. A favor from a businessman now might mean a little easier time for him negotiating a new contract with a union the next time around. Or, it might mean a tougher time if the businessman doesn't help when O'Connell calls.

Now this bill that Higgins and Americans Together were pushing threatened to rob O'Connell of the essential ingredient that put him in a position to wield the power he had. During O'Connell's tenure, stretching back thirty years, the unions had grown to a point where they sat in on Presidential councils. They were consulted on matters of foreign policy. When a crisis threatened, union leaders were among the first outside the government to be called. O'Connell and the unions behind him had millions to spend on candidates. More than half the Congress enjoyed the benefits of union support. Union manpower registered voters, printed sample ballots, shepherded voters to the polls on election day—all the little jobs that get candidates elected.

O'Connell identified himself for the record and then launched into his testimony, a historical treatise on the role of organized labor in American elections. From there he branched out to the Constitution—the right of Americans to assemble and to petition their government. He mentioned the First Amendment's prohibition against laws restricting free speech.

"It is our position, Mr. Chairman, that the proposed bill would be such an unconstitutional infringement of the rights of our members and of all Americans to express their political preferences. Mr. Chairman, organized labor recognizes the desire on the part of many Americans to change the method by which we elect our public officials. We stand ready to support constructive changes within our constitutional framework, but we cannot support a bill that will muffle us and deprive us of our rightful voice. I will be happy to answer any questions."

Since O'Connell didn't like to testify and didn't like flexing his muscles in public this way, I had to conclude that he was taking the bill more seriously than I had. I made a note to myself to mention something like that in the story. O'Connell's testimony took about half an hour and then the hearing was over. I walked over to the witness table when Ludington recessed the hearing for the day.

"Making a rare public appearance, Mike?" I asked him.

"Hi, Tony," he said, looking up at me through a cloud of cigarette smoke. He coughed and then went on in that gravelly voice of his. "You know how much I love coming and sitting in front of these guys."

"So why bother?"

"This bill is tough."

"Come on," I said to him, with an air of disbelief.

"No, really. You ought to get out of Washington once in a while to see what's happening. We had a guy in Ohio, Delman, who was chairman of public works appropriations. Brought a lot of money into his district, kept the economy there moving and all the rest of it. We used to contribute ten or fifteen thousand dollars to his campaign at a minimum, whether he was opposed or not. We sent workers in to take care of things for him. He was one of ours.

"And everything that we did for him became an issue in the last campaign. Some kid barely old enough to qualify ran against him, and his chief issue was all the union help Delman was getting. At first we had a good laugh over it and so did Delman—until he realized that people in the district took it seriously. They didn't like it that we gave him all that help. They saw us as outsiders. They saw Delman's national prominence as a deficit, a distraction that kept him from paying attention to what they wanted. They thought he was too busy voting the labor line to pay attention to them. And that's happening all over America. You may not believe it, but it's true."

"What are you doing for lunch?" I asked.

"Well, I was supposed to go back to headquarters and eat with the chief, but he was called over to the White House, so he canceled. Where would you like to go?"

I suggested an over-priced restaurant around the corner from the Old Senate Office Building and we walked over there. We had to wait about two minutes for a table. It would have been twenty minutes except that O'Connell's is a recognized face. Being powerful in Washington means, among other things, not having to wait for a table.

We took our drinks to the table with us, ordered, and then got back to our conversation. "This is a strange time in this town," O'Connell said. "I've been in this town for thirty-five years. I came here when John L. Lewis was here. I've seen blood flow for organized labor. We had to fight to get into the White House, but we belonged there as much as the Chamber of Commerce, the AMA, the lawyers, the NAM, and all the rest. They had a right to say what was on their minds and so did we. And we still do. Guys like Higgins want to take the politics out of politics. They want to reduce everyone, regardless of who he is, what he does for a living, or what his interests are, down to equal size. That may sound like democracy to you, but it isn't. It's chaos. It will be a bunch of atoms floating around, looking for something to bring them all together. It's an invitation to the kind of mass movement that we've managed to avoid in this country for two hundred years, despite the efforts of Huey Long, Father Coughlin, and all the rest. The surest way to bring fascism to America is to destroy the power of organizations to speak for their members. What the hell did Higgins form Americans Together for—leaving aside the matter of his wanting to be President—except to bring pressure on the government?

"And you guys in the press are terrific. If a cop looks at one of you cross-eyed, you start screaming First Amendment. But let someone start talking about 'reforming the system' and you think he's a hero. You guys don't give a damn about anyone else's rights."

"I think you're overstating the case a little bit, don't you?" I protested.

"No, I don't think I'm overstating it at all. Our members don't always like the pressure we put on them to give us money so we can stay active politically in their interest. They don't think it brings them any benefit at all. They'd rather spend the hundred bucks on beer or a vacation than give it to the political fund so we can lobby a minimum-wage bill, or get safety standards raised, or get junior colleges set up so they can see their kids have a better education than they had. Then there are all the good-government types like the League of Women Voters who want to make it work the way they were taught it does in their high-school civics classes twenty years ago. The minute they see people organizing according to how they make their living, the good-government types start hollering about interest groups. Well, you tell me. If you spend a third of your day sleeping, a third eating, screwing, and getting to work, and a third of the day working, and the government pays more attention to the third of the day that you're working, don't you think you have a right in a democracy to try to influence what the government does to you during that third of the day?"

"Fine," I said, "but things are getting out of hand. Fortunes are made by people who do nothing but live off political campaigns."

"I can appreciate that. There's too much money in politics, O.K. Changes need to be made. But Higgins wants to come on with a goddamn meat cleaver and just chop things up. It's dangerous," O'Connell said, pausing to take a gulp of his drink, "but it's damn appealing to a lot of Americans. And that's what scares me."

If I had had half a wit, what O'Connell was saying might have told me something and saved me a lot of time later on. The point finally would come through, but later, almost too late.

7

I live in a nice old building off Connecticut Avenue just above where the city limits were back in the olden days. Years ago my apartment was part of a much larger flat that belonged to a Supreme Court justice. Back then reporters used to make about thirty-five dollars a week. Times have changed, but I don't get too smug about it. Some of my colleagues would be overpaid if they were making that now.

About once a week I have a lady come in to clean up the place. She keeps whatever diseases might be incubating in check and rediscovers a lot of my stuff that keeps disappearing. I am not what you would call a neat person. I was married once, but it didn't work out. From time to time I wind up at dinner parties sitting to the right of a widow, divorcee, or political wife whose husband is off anywhere except where he ought to be. When I'm not dining with the rich, the well-born, and the powerful, I usually eat out, although once in a while I make myself a meal.

When I got home that night it was about nine-thirty. I picked up a copy of *Time* to read the cover story on Bill Rosecroft, the senior senator from Pennsylvania, a Democrat and another leading prospect to be the next President of the United States. I was halfway through the piece when my phone rang. It was Charlotte Daniels.

Charlotte Daniels is a remarkable woman. She is only the third woman to serve in the United States Senate. She took over her husband's seat after his death seven years ago. He was a lot older than she, had done enough living to fill several lifetimes, and probably rendered the people of Nevada his greatest service when he checked out. He was not dedicated to the public interest.

Charlotte wasn't exactly a blazing reformer, but she had an independent streak. She was about thirty-one when Theodore Daniels died. I didn't know much about her formal education, but she had a fine, quick mind. She absorbed material quickly, she asked the right questions, she was able to read the politics of a situation, and she soon became a force to be reckoned with. The governor of her state had appointed her to avoid giving the vacant seat to anyone politically adept, on the theory that he could run for it himself in the next election. What the governor hadn't counted on was her political astuteness, her ambition and drive, and her ability to communicate with the voters in Nevada. She won easily in her own right, a year later, after getting the White House to accept a piece of legislation that her husband had been trying to get through for six years without success.

I had heard stories about how she got the President to change his mind, and I would have written it up if I could have nailed the story down, but it was likely that only two people knew the full story— Charlotte and the President. And neither of them was talking.

Charlotte Daniels was a beautiful woman, strikingly beautiful. She could be all business on the floor of the Senate or in a committee hearing and then be soft and sexy in the privacy of her Senate office. She held an animal magnetism for me. She knew it, and she knew how to turn her physical attractiveness to her advantage.

"Tony, this is Charlotte Daniels," she told me in a voice that wasn't entirely business.

"Hello, Senator, how you doing?"

"Fine, thanks. There's something I'd like to discuss with you if you're free."

"I can talk right now."

"I'd rather not.... You know I don't like to talk on the phone. If you could come over for about an hour or so, maybe we could have a relaxed conversation for a change."

"I'll be right over." I hung up the phone and, in deference to the dignity of the United States Senate, I shaved, showered, and put on fresh clothes.

Charlotte Daniels lived in the wooded area off Massachusetts Avenue, over near the British Embassy, on one of those streets that even most Washingtonians don't know about unless they get lost. In my case, I should have asked for explicit instructions about how to get there because it took me half an hour to make what was only a ten-minute trip.

I pulled up in front of a cozy little stone number with leaded-glass bay windows in the front, a garage, and a little yard with the grass carefully manicured and neatly laid flagstones. The house was bigger than it looked from the front, and in that neighborhood it was probably worth about $150,000, maybe $175,000.

I rang the bell, waited, and rang again. The porch light went on and I caught a glimpse of Charlotte's face looking out the window in the door before she opened it. "I was about to file a missing person's report," she told me as she pulled the heavy oak door open for me.

"I know. I was beginning to think I was one myself."

"Come on inside," she said, after hanging up my coat. She turned and led the way. She was wearing a black peignoir over a matching nightgown, which was scooped out low in front, revealing full, well-supported breasts. She wasn't wearing any shoes and she walked in front of me with the grace of a dancer. Her red hair, which was always striking against her white skin, was accentuated by the black of her peignoir. She had a vague odor of Arpege about her.

"You're wondering why I called you over," she said with a smile.

"You've found me irresistible for years and finally got up the courage to call and ask me for a date."

"Something like that. Why don't you get a drink and then come sit down over here and I'll tell you the whole thing." She dropped herself on the couch, tucking her legs under her and leaning forward to pick up her drink from the coffee table.

I didn't like the way things were going. I had come expecting to have everything on a professional basis—at least that's what I told myself—and she was carrying on like a siren.

But as soon as I sat down, everything changed. Suddenly she was

44

very businesslike. "You were friendly with Les Painter, weren't you." It wasn't so much a question as it was an opening statement.

"I was as friendly as anyone ever got with him. There were a lot of things about him not to like, friend or not," I told her. "If you were a friend, he made it a little easier, but I wouldn't say I was blind to his faults."

"Well, I understand that," she said. "I was the subject of one or two columns myself. Never anything terribly serious—there isn't anything like that to find out about me—but annoying. He had no compunctions about tearing you up one day and then calling you the next about something else, as though he had never written a word about you or had done you a favor by mentioning you."

"That's a special quality of insensitivity that we reporters like to have. Without that kind of chutzpah, he wouldn't have been so successful."

"Anyway," she said, "I've got a little problem here and I wanted to see what you thought I should do about it. We're just talking as one friend to another now." I said nothing, reserving my right to cut her off and change the ground rules if I got interested.

"Painter and I had dinner about ten days before he was killed. He called me up and asked to meet me somewhere. I wasn't terribly enthusiastic, you know. Eating dinner with him wasn't relaxing—he wanted to get straight to the point all the time. No small talk, no pleasantries, no good conversation—just listening and thinking about the next question he was going to ask."

"But you went?"

"Oh, I met him all right. I've been through worse ordeals. We went to Chez Michelle. I had a drink. He had a Coke. Can you imagine?" She stopped to wonder.

"He started asking me about Bill Rosecroft as though I were supposed to recite everything I knew. I told him I knew Bill had gone to Penn, had been a varsity rower or something there, that he'd been in the Marine Corps in Korea. After that it was law school and then politics. He never worked too hard at law—he inherited a lot of money somewhere—and he was in the Senate by the time he was thirty-five, what, ten years ago? And of course now he wants to be President.

"Painter said he knew all that. What he wanted to know was something else. He had a little trouble getting to the point, which surprised me. He said he wanted to know what I could tell him about Rosecroft's sex life."

"Painter liked to get it from the horse's mouth," I said, smiling.

"I told him that if I knew anything I certainly wouldn't tell him," she continued, ignoring my comment. "Then Painter got very charming and evangelical, all at once. You know how he could be."

I smiled for a moment at the memory of Painter at his best when he decided to appeal to your better nature—"for the good of America," he would say, somehow making you believe it.

"He told me that he was working on something very important, that it wouldn't be fair for him to go into a detailed account of what it was because if it weren't true then he would have damaged innocent persons, et cetera et cetera. He wanted me to trust him and to tell him what I knew, that it was important to the country to find it out sooner rather than later if it were true."

I smiled again.

"So I told him that I had gone out several times with Bill, for dinner, to a movie. I had had him over to dinner too, sometimes with others and sometimes alone. I like Bill. He's enjoyable to be with. He isn't heavy. He has a sense of humor. He manages to talk about things other than himself. And," she said, putting emphasis on this final point, "he is a *very* attractive man."

"What did Painter say about that?"

"He wanted to know if I had ever slept with him."

"And?"

"And I said no, I had not. For a while, I took it a little personally. I thought maybe I wasn't so attractive," she said, glancing down at her body. "I wouldn't want to be thought of simply as someone's recreation—I've been there once and I didn't like it. But I'm not ready to enter a convent yet, either. Anyway, Bill Rosecroft has never touched me. From time to time he gives me an affectionate peck, but that's about it.

"I'm telling you all of this for a reason," she added. "I guess what Painter was doing was important. He was unscrupulous sometimes, but not just because he was after a juicy story. So I'm telling myself that he was doing something important."

"Is there more?" I asked her.

"He asked me if I had ever heard of the Thursday Night Club. I hadn't. He said it was some group that Rosecroft belongs to. I started asking *him* questions and he gave me one of those looks. He was a very strange man. . . . He must have believed in himself a great deal."

' He never bothered to think about it too much, but you're right,"

I told her. "It was never a question with him. He took the importance of what he was doing and the righteousness of whatever it was as givens. You don't win a lot of friends that way, and if you're not as sure of yourself as he was, that kind of an attitude can be very intimidating. But he never had a doubt at all. He could outstare a snake. I don't think there was any situation that ever gave him the slightest pause. And people sensed that about him, that he was sure. His judgment was good. He knew when he had you, when he had enough information to do a number on you and make it stick. And finally," I added, suddenly gloomy, "he was just a victim of his own success."

"Is that what the police think?" she asked.

"I'm not sure what they think. I'm just assuming. And my assumptions aren't that good. I am merely mortal," I told her. "But you still haven't told me why you called."

"Well, it has to do with all this. I'm not sure whether I should go to the police and tell them all this, or just wait to see if they call me. I don't want to drag Bill into anything unnecessarily."

"I suppose if you really were terribly conscientious you ought to call them." She frowned when I said that. "But, if you're being conscientious about not wanting to hurt an innocent person, and if you answer their questions fully when and if they do call, then I suppose you will have done your duty as a citizen."

"That's the kind of answer I like to get," she told me with a smile, relieved to have me help her off the hook.

I changed the subject after that and we talked about Higgins's campaign bill, which Charlotte thought was a disaster. She always needed big contributions, she said, although the limitation would probably hurt her opponent more than it would hurt her. I told her my own estimate was that the bill had no chance.

"Well, it might pass," she said, leaning forward to pick up her drink and a cigarette. Every time she moved like that, she did it in a very slow, graceful, and deliberate way, pausing, knowing that I was looking, knowing that I knew she was aware of it. I was enjoying the whole game tremendously. When I struck the match she drew my hand close to her mouth and held it as she lit her cigarette. Then she let my hand go slowly—reluctantly, is what I was telling myself.

"Where do you buy your clothes?" she asked, rubbing the shoulder of my suit jacket.

"In a store," I answered cheerfully. "I'm already vain enough.

We don't need a detailed discussion of how much trouble I go through to make myself as attractive as I do in public. Look, I'm trying to impress my boss that I work long hours and go through indescribable tortures to report the news. I was planning to tell him tomorrow that I had put in a tedious night with a source, who would go unnamed, it goes without saying. You're ruining all my plans. Could we just keep this whole thing on politics?"

"I had no idea you were so dedicated," she said, grinning.

"I surprise myself sometimes. I think I better be moving along. I have a big day of news gathering ahead of me tomorrow, and you've got the cares of the Republic and the state of Nevada to worry about."

"There's no reason why you should feel you have to leave so soon," she said, folding her arms under her breasts and pushing them up ever so slightly.

"Well, it's nice of you to say so," I told her as I got up. "But I try not to get too close to my sources."

I left feeling so proud of myself for resisting temptation that I thought I would reward myself sometime later by giving in to it.

8

Time was slipping by and the cops didn't seem to be knocking themselves or anyone else out in a mad rush to find Painter's killer. I never thought the police could be accused of excessive sensitivity to the rights of criminals, but I was learning that there is a first time for everything.

Lieutenant Thomason called me a couple of times with questions, but I got the impression from the tone of his inquiry that he was writing a doctoral dissertation rather than investigating a murder. I couldn't very well criticize him, though, since I had been less than one hundred per cent cooperative in our earlier chats.

From the sort of questions Thomason asked me, I gathered that he was leaning toward the theory that Painter had been killed by a simple mugger who had robbed him. I didn't argue, but this made little sense to me. I was still brought up short by the location of the murder. The sub-basement corridor in the Senate is not your average spot for a stick-up. And then the body had been stuffed into that manhole. Bandits ordinarily aren't so concerned about hiding their victims.

I spent a lot of time thinking about it, rolling it over in my mind. If Thomason was wrong, I concluded, then Reilly had been right in saying that the murder would never be solved. Reilly's skepticism had colored my thinking ever since our conversation. Then there was the information that Charlotte had given me. I was becoming obsessed with the question.

I'm not sure exactly when I decided I would go ahead. I guess you could say I just slipped into it. I was fascinated to know about the lost days and hours of Les Painter's life shortly before it ended. Whom had he talked to and about what? It would be a hell of a story. In a way, for me, it *was* like doing a story, except the stakes were so much bigger. One person—maybe more—had a secret, and I wanted to know what it was so I could report it.

But it didn't stop there. A lot of people had not liked Les Painter. And I mean a *lot* of people. There were times that I wasn't crazy about him myself. Being a great reporter means, among other things, that you stop worrying about being liked. Great reporters have an internal gyroscope that keeps them on whatever course they've set for themselves. If they make friends along the way, so much the better. If not, tough.

Most of the time, though, I had liked Les Painter. I had liked him precisely because he didn't care whether I, or anyone else, liked him. I liked him because he was honest about what he did and about the way he did it. I liked him because he was one of the few persons in Washington who acted out of conviction, even if I had found him a little corny from time to time.

I was beginning to think that a lot of important people, without saying so, felt that Washington was better off without Painter. Painter had spent his professional life exposing political rot and now the rot would have its day with him. That, at least, was the way it was going. But I cared too much about Painter, about his work, and I guess ultimately about my work, to stand by and watch it happen without trying to do something.

But what was I going to do? I wasn't sure how to proceed once I had made the decision to play ersatz cop. I ran through a list of possible suspects, grappling for possible motives and framing questions for each of them. None of it made much sense, but I decided to focus on Seld first. Painter had said something in one of his last columns about having "more to say about Senator Seld's penchant for introducing special-interest legislation in the very near future." What had he meant? I called Larry Quirk and asked him, but he didn't know; Seld had been one of Painter's personal projects and he did most of the work on him by himself.

My next shot was to call a guy I knew in the United States Attorney's Office for the District of Columbia. We had known each other for about seven years, since the time when I covered the federal courts and the federal prosecutor's office. I had tried to keep in touch with him since I left that beat, so we had lunch occasionally or I would phone him and talk for a while. He liked to pick up gossip and I liked to keep an ear to the ground in case the D.A. got into anything I should know about.

I had a little trouble reaching him, but after the third try I finally got him. We made small talk for a couple of minutes before I came to the point.

"I don't know whether you can help me or not on this," I said.

"What's that?" he said.

"I was looking at one of Les Painter's columns the other day, one of his last ones. He mentioned Layton Seld and some special-interest investigation. I was just curious whether you had any kind of investigation going on down there involving Seld."

"Look," he said. "I've always tried to avoid talking about on-going investigations with you."

"So there is one."

"Let me finish. I'm not saying there is or there isn't."

"Except that you've always told me when the well was dry in the past."

"Maybe things have changed," he said.

"Is there any reason why they should have?" I asked.

"Not really," he said, chuckling.

"Then I'll proceed on the assumption that you would tell me if the well were dry," I said.

"All right."

"The problem is that that doesn't get me very far and I don't have a lot of time. Did Painter find out about the investigation or did you start looking into it after the column appeared?"

"Maybe you'd like to come down here and go through the files. I'm sure the judges won't mind. Grand jury minutes are secret, of course, but I can just explain that you needed them and I was trying to do my part for the First Amendment. Then you can come see me at the D.C. jail and help me find work after I'm disbarred."

"How long has the investigation been going on?" I asked.

"What investigation?" he answered.

"All right," I said. "Is there anything you can tell me?"

"In a word, no," he said. "I've already said more than I should have. You ought to do some more obvious things before you come around trying to pry information out of me. Why don't you check Seld's campaign expenditures and contributions?"

"Because he hasn't filed anything yet this year. The senatorial reports aren't due for months."

"I didn't say anything about his senatorial reports," he said.

"Oh. OH. *Right*," I said, "thanks."

"I didn't tell you anything."

"Right. I'll see you."

I went over to the Federal Elections Office that afternoon and checked out the filings for Seld's last Presidential campaign. Even though he had never been a serious candidate, the records took up hundreds of pages. I started going through the contributions, and noticed that the unions had really piled it on. Seld must have gotten fifty or sixty thousand dollars from unions alone for a race that lasted only six weeks. The expenditures took another several hundred pages. My problem was that I didn't have the slightest idea what I was looking for. All I knew was that something here was interesting enough for the U.S. Attorney to be looking at it, that Painter had probably known about it and Seld might have. So my efforts weren't a total loss. I knew there was some sort of an investigation. What stage the investigation was in I didn't know, and I didn't know whether Seld knew about it or not. More important, I didn't know if Painter had found out about it or had tripped it.

Anyway, I had enough to make a chat with Seld worthwhile. But getting to see him wasn't going to be easy. I'm not on his list of people to have over for dinner. On the occasions when he's figured prominently in any of my stories, he hasn't come off well. What can you say about a fifty-one-year-old senator who's a crook?

Given those parameters, as they say around Washington, I had to resort to witchcraft and smokescreens. The trick was to make him feel threatened without letting him know specifically what was on my mind. If he knew too much, he could either prepare himself or decide I was bluffing. If he didn't know enough, he wouldn't see any point to talking to me or he might think I was just trying to get his autograph. So I called Marion Wilson, Seld's press secretary, and told him that I wanted to speak to Seld. Something that might involve him had come up and if I were Seld, I would talk to me.

"What's that supposed to mean?" Wilson asked.

"I don't think it's all that opaque," I answered. "Let him figure it out. He'll know what I mean."

"I wish somebody would tell me what's going on," Wilson said.

"If Seld wants to tell you, he can tell you. That's his decision for the time being," I said.

Wilson closed the conversation at that point, which was just as well. I was beginning to run out of lines. He said he'd get back to me. I didn't want to press him because that would make me seem anxious. Since I still didn't know how to go about it, I really wasn't very anxious at all.

Then a few days later I ran into Wilson in the hall of the New Senate Office Building and we stopped to chat. "I'm not going to wait much longer," I told him. "I'm not going to let someone involved in a story dictate whether it runs or not by refusing to talk to me. If he doesn't want to see me, I'll just say that in the story."

"He's been really busy," Wilson said.

"Fine," I answered. "Just tell him I'm getting impatient."

The phone rang at home that night about nine-thirty, just as I was finishing a piece in *Esquire* by Alexander Cohen, another Washington reporter. "Eight o'clock tomorrow morning," the voice said.

"Couldn't we make it earlier?" I asked Wilson. "That way I wouldn't have to go to bed."

"You're the one who was in such a hurry. Take it or leave it. I had to bust my ass to get him to see you at all. He doesn't see what good it will do."

"Tell him that truth is its own reward," I said.

"I'll tell him when I see him and I'll see you at eight," Wilson said.

"I'll be there."

Actually I didn't mind at all. If I saw Seld at eight, I'd probably be the first person on his calendar, so I'd see him on time rather than having to wait the usual forty-five minutes to an hour for fifteen quick minutes.

I took a cab up to the Hill and had to listen to the driver moan to me the whole time about how much money he was losing when he could have been making two trips with a full car down Connecticut Avenue. I resolved to give him an extra nickel for his trouble and devoted myself to scanning the *Journal* during the twenty-minute ride.

I read in a magazine once that a successful executive's office is a reflection of his personality and approach to his affairs. Layton Seld's office was dull, cheerless, and in bad taste, all at the same time. The lime green walls were smeared with photographs of Layton Seld—Layton Seld shaking hands with the President, Layton Seld shaking hands with an astronaut, with a Cardinal, with Billy Graham, with a football player, a baseball star, et cetera, et cetera. You could see enough photographs and tributes to Layton Seld on the walls of his office to fill a small museum, if you could find a museum that was interested.

I was not kept waiting. He was on the phone when I came in and he ignored my presence while he spoke.

"I'm not going to commit myself. If they want to come to me and ask, then I'll consider it. My positions are well known. But I am not an active candidate." He listened for a minute. "That's right. . . . That's right. . . . That's right," he said. "And it's been a great pleasure talking to you, too." He hung up and turned to me. "Just a minute," he said, pressing a button on his phone. "Marion, would you please join us?"

"Well, it certainly is the season," he said, turning to me. "I'm getting all kinds of calls asking me if I'll consider running or am I available for a draft or am I available as a compromise choice if the convention is deadlocked."

"And what are you telling them?" I asked.

"Well, you heard me. I'm here, but I'm not going to seek it. I have my hands full just serving my constituency. If the convention decides it wants me, I'll be around."

Wilson came in and sat down in a chair over in the corner. We continued to make small talk for a few minutes and then I decided to get to the point. "I guess Marion told you I had something important to discuss with you."

"He mentioned you were anxious to see me," Seld said with a slight smile.

"It has to do with Les Painter," I told him.

"A terrible thing," he said. "Hard to believe that it could happen at all, much less right here in the Capitol. Do the police have any leads at all?"

"I'm not sure. They don't confide in me. Have the police talked to you?"

"No," Seld said, looking puzzled. "Why should they? I really didn't know Painter. I talked to him from time to time, when he wanted to check a fact or give me a chance to comment on a story where I was mentioned. But I didn't know him beyond that."

"I was looking through Painter's columns the other day, just trying to see whom he had written about in the last year or so. I found fifteen columns about you in the last four months. And this one, which was one of his last, said, 'We will have more to say about Senator Sold's penchant for introducing special-interest legislation in the very near future.' I suppose he must have talked to you about that," I said.

"No, I wondered about that when I read it myself," Seld said. "I have no idea what he was talking about. Did he ever speak to you about it, Marion?"

Wilson sounded as though he had been roused abruptly from slumber. "No," he said in a startled voice. "No, he never did."

"Well, what do you think it was about?" I asked Seld.

"I can't think of a thing. The only legislation I've introduced, aside from a few labor bills, are some things that some of my constituents requested to straighten out claims they have on file with the government. Those kinds of bills are introduced every day—that's the bulk of the legislation that moves through Congress."

"I have the impression that Painter was talking about more than that," I said.

"Well, now, what gives you that impression?" Seld asked. "Did he say something to you?"

"Les didn't discuss what he was doing with me. But it wasn't like him to drop broad hints unless he had something of substance. He liked to titillate his readers that way."

"Perhaps his notebooks or his private papers might help out."

"They probably would have been a great help," I said. "But I believe Mary Painter destroyed them."

"Well," Seld said, "I guess that disposes of that possibility. And I'm afraid I can't help you, either."

"I'm not sure you would want to help me," I said. "If I were in your position, I wouldn't."

"I'm not sure I understand," Seld said.

"If Painter had something that could damage you and if he

waited to print it until your senatorial campaign started, you could be in trouble. You have serious opposition in the primary and more serious opposition next fall, assuming you make it that far. If Painter had gone through your filings for the last campaign and then had looked at your legislative performance since then, checking the bills you introduced against some of the contributions made and doing some checking on the contributors, he might have found something."

"I guess we'll never know though, will we?" Seld said, "His secret died with him."

"I'm not so sure of that," I said. "His death isn't stopping the U.S. Attorney from looking at your campaign filings. For all I know, he was looking at them before Painter found out about it. Maybe he found out about the investigation from them."

"No!" Seld blurted out.

"What do you mean?"

"I don't mean anything," he shouted at me. "I want you to get the hell out of here. I don't like you coming around here and suggesting that I've broken the law and killed a man."

"Senator, I didn't say that."

"That's what you're thinking."

"Did you know about the U.S. Attorney's investigation before Painter talked to you about your returns?"

"I told you I didn't talk to Painter. And I don't know about any investigation now. I had the impression from Marion that you had something important you were about to write that involved me. If *that's* what it was, I'd like to get back to work. I'm a busy man."

"Do you want to give me a statement about the investigation?"

"When I'm informed that there is an investigation and I think it's important to say something about it, I will issue a statement."

"So when I write a story saying you're under investigation, what do you want to say?"

"No comment. I have nothing more to say to you—period."

All things considered, I was pretty happy with the way things had gone. Seld's little slip indicated that he *had* talked to Painter about his campaign reports but didn't know the U.S. Attorney was investigating them. Could he have thought that if he got rid of Painter, he could squelch the whole thing? Farfetched perhaps, but something to think about. I hadn't proved anything, and I didn't have enough to do a story. But I hadn't wasted my time. There was a good chance that Seld might be indicted on the campaign funding. And that was worth following up.

9

I went to the press gallery and read the paper for a while after leaving Seld's office. Dan Felshin had a story inside saying that Philip Higgins would formally announce his candidacy in a couple of days but would skip the New Hampshire primary. That brought the number of Democratic candidates to six, including Higgins, Rosecroft, and Warren Smith, the governor of Ohio, who was a favorite-son candidate. Thomas Powell, the senator from Wisconsin, was in the race but not going anywhere fast. Frank Henderson, the mayor of Los Angeles, was using the campaign as a platform for airing the problems of America's cities. That was one way to get an audience, but Henderson wasn't a serious candidate. Finally, there was Oren Fowler from South Carolina.

Fowler at one time had been a big segregationist, but that was before blacks in the South got their right to vote protected and the Klan put away its sheets. Now Fowler went around talking in code words about the "crime" problem and "preserving neighborhood schools" and "saving the little man." Fowler was not a serious candidate either, although he was aiming for enough votes to exercise some clout at the convention. He would probably want to be vice president, although it was inconceivable to me that he would get it. But stranger things had happened.

The Senate was working on an appropriation of about $2.5 billion for school lunches and related programs. I spent the rest of the day running around talking to senators and their aides trying to get a handle on the maneuvering over the bill. There were about eight separate votes on amendments before the bill itself came up for a final vote, and some of those were close, but the final one was one-sided, fifty-three to thirty-six in favor.

By the time I got through writing a story on it and hassling with the editors back at the paper over my interpretations of the votes, it was after seven-thirty. I won't bore you with the details.

Since I had no dinner plans but was tired of eating alone, I decided to give Charlotte Daniels a ring. I called her office on her private line. She answered. We talked about the votes for a minute or so, agreeing that things had gone pretty much as expected.

"You have dinner plans?" I asked her.

"Well, I have this damned reception to go to. The American Cattle Breeders. I'm supposed to be there now. I was just walking out when you called. By the time I get away from that, if I ever do, it may be after nine. Take a rain check?"

"Sure," I said.

I took a cab back downtown and went to a restaurant near my house, on the corner of Connecticut and R, where the food is passable but nothing to get worked up about. It was the kind of place where the tables are set for couples, but at most of them single men or women were eating solitary meals. A couple of these men and women had backed up three and four martini glasses or were killing off carafes of wine before wandering off.

I had work to do while I ate my dinner, so I couldn't enjoy the pleasure of numbing myself with cheap red wine. While I chewed on my steak, I read clips about Henry Fisher, the self-made chemical tycoon.

One clip, one of those profiles *The Times* does of people in the news, ran down his whole career—poor Jewish kid from the East Side of New York, worked his way through City College, went into the Army during World War II, served as a Ranger with umpteen

58

missions behind enemy lines, bought some surplus chemicals after the war and started his company, which was now worth more than a hundred million, married, broke boards with his hands for relaxation.

So Henry Fisher was the next person on my list of people to see. In a way, I was looking forward to that. At the least, it would give me an excuse to go up to New York. I might stay with a friend and make a weekend of it. I wasn't any clearer than I had been with Seld about what I was going to say, but I decided to wing it. I made some notes while I ate dinner, went home, read some more and went to sleep.

First thing next morning, about eight, I called Fisher's office in New York. I was calling from home, but I didn't have to tell him that. I told his secretary who I was and asked to speak to Fisher. After about three minutes, he came on the line.

"Yes, Mr. Jordan."

"How are you, Mr. Fisher. I was hoping to come up to see you over the weekend if it's convenient. I'm doing a story about the Environmental Protection Agency and I wanted to talk to you."

"Why can't we talk right now, on the phone?"

"I never feel comfortable talking to someone on a complicated subject over the phone," I told him. "I was thinking I could come up on Saturday to see you if it's convenient."

"I'm not so sure I want to talk to you. Every time I get involved with one of you guys, it always comes out screwed up, I look worse and I get myself in deeper. My lawyers keep telling me to shut up."

"I understand all that," I told him. I didn't like what I was going to have to do now, but I shut my eyes and went ahead. "One of the reasons why I want to do this story is that I want to show that EPA's enforcement of the law may give us clean air and water, but it will be achieved over the rubble of some pretty basic American industries."

"That's right. That's right," Fisher said.

"And I wanted to talk to you because I know that what EPA wants you to do could harm your company."

"Absolutely right."

"So I was hoping I could talk to you on Saturday."

"What's wrong with Friday?"

"Can't make it Friday."

"All right. Saturday. I'm not sure whether I'll be at home or in the city," he said. "You let my secretary know what time you'll be coming in—I assume you're taking the shuttle?"

I said I was.

"I'll have a car pick you up."

"I'd rather get there myself."

"Is it so important, Mr. Jordan? It's a convenience for me. This way I'll know you'll get here within a reasonable period of time, we can have the interview and get it over with. All right?"

"Fine."

"Just let my secretary know."

Saturday morning I got up about six to get out to the airport. It usually takes me about forty-five minutes to get myself together in the morning. It's not that the preparations are so elaborate. It's just that speed isn't one of my virtues at that time of day.

The weather was still kind of raw in Washington. Cherry-blossom time was coming, but it was only in the upper fifties with rain, clouds, and cheerless skies. If things went according to their usual form, spring in Washington would last about two days, to be followed by a vengeful summer.

When we landed at LaGuardia, it was raining and I was glad that I wasn't going to have to worry about getting a cab. Coming off the plane, I heard my name over the page and I went to the desk by the gate. An airline person at the desk directed me to a tough-looking character standing nearby.

"You Jordan?" the character said. "Mr. Fisher sent me to pick you up. You're supposed to come with me. Gimme your bag."

"Who're you?" I asked.

"I work for Mr. Fisher. C'mon."

This person was about five foot six at most and weighed about one hundred eighty-five or one hundred ninety pounds. He had on a grey gabardine topcoat over slacks, a blue double-knit jacket, a blue shirt, and a bright yellow tie. He was wearing a grey fedora.

"Does Mr. Fisher call you anything?" I asked him.

"Pete. He calls me Pete."

"What kind of work do you do for him?"

"A little of this. A little of that. I'm a jack-of-all-trades, ya know? I do what he asks me to do. He told me you're a reporter, so don't start getting personal. I don't need nothin' in the paper about me."

We walked outside where Pete had a black Lincoln Continental parked by the curb. "Get in," he told me. I obeyed meekly. He threw my bag into the front seat and slid in after it. Then he picked up a telephone next to the driver's seat and gave the operator a number.

"We're on our way," he said into the phone. "We should be there in forty-five minutes."

"Where are we going?" I asked him.

"Out to Mr. Fisher's house in Westchester. You ever been there?"

I said I hadn't.

"Nice place."

Fisher's place in Westchester had a gatehouse that I wouldn't have minded living in. The house itself was set about a quarter of a mile back from the road, up a wooded driveway. It was your basic $1.5 million house, with a central section, a wing on either side, a greenhouse out in back, a swimming pool, and a tennis court.

Pete pulled the car up in front of the house and took me in. The house had that put-together look that rich people have in their homes because they pay someone else to do everything for them. At the back end of the front hall Pete knocked on a door, and a voice told him to come in. Inside was a large room with huge windows looking out into the garden, and books and a fireplace on the opposite wall. Fisher was sitting behind a desk covered with Florentine leather talking to a redhead who had a blouse on about two sizes too small for her.

"Anything else, Mr. Fisher?" Pete asked him.

"I'll call if I need you," Fisher said.

"I decided we should talk here," Fisher said, extending his hand without bothering to get up. "This is my secretary, Lynne Von Kleeck. She'll take notes on the interview for me."

I had a tape recorder with me, so I didn't care one way or the other. I wouldn't have cared without the tape recorder. I find it interesting, though, that some people feel the need to protect themselves by having a secretary or some other witness present when they talk to reporters.

"Coffee?" Fisher asked.

I accepted the offer and Miss Von Kleeck lifted herself out of her chair to get it for me. I watched her pass my chair and then turned my gaze back to Fisher, who was smiling. "She's a very good secretary."

"I can see that," I said returning the smile.

Fisher was about fifty-five, a big, gray man with powerful, hairy arms. Even though he was clean-shaven, his dark beard left a shadow on his face. That, combined with thick, bushy eyebrows and brown eyes set deep in their sockets, gave Fisher a menacing presence. On his desk was a picture of him in a white karate gown, exchanging low bows with an Oriental man.

We sat making small talk for a couple of minutes. Miss Von Kleeck came back with my coffee, went back to her seat and picked up her stenographic pad. I pulled out my tape recorder. "Do you mind if I record this?" I asked Fisher. "I don't take shorthand and it sometimes helps if I want an extensive quote."

"Sure. Sure," Fisher said, waving his right hand at me. While I started in on the background that had led me to seek the interview—I was pursuing the line I had developed over the phone about EPA—Fisher lit a cigar—a Montecristo, from the color and smell of it. He noticed me watching him. "I pick these up in Europe whenever I'm there," he said. "I got these in Geneva a couple of weeks ago. You want one?"

I took one and put it in my pocket, thanking him and continuing with what I was saying. I asked him questions about his problems with EPA, how serious the threat to his business was, and what his alternatives were. We talked about that for half an hour or so, and then I tried to move the conversation around to Painter, doing it ever so slowly.

"I read somewhere that you've been trying to get the law changed and pressuring EPA to rewrite the regulations so you can get out from under."

"You read it in that goddamn Les Painter's column that I was buying senators and congressmen to try to save my neck," Fisher said abruptly.

"I don't think it was put quite that way."

"That's what he was trying to say."

"And your response?"

"I don't need a response any more. Les Painter is dead."

"Right. But the charge is still around. The ink's still on the paper."

"I have a right as an American to give money to political candidates. That's what the Constitution is all about. I have a lot of money, so I give a lot of money. I hope to get a sympathetic audience from a congressman or senator who gets money from me, but I don't ask for anything before I give or after."

"Just as a matter of curiosity," I said, "did Painter ever talk to you about your campaign contributions?"

"Certainly, a number of times. But the last couple of times he called me I refused to speak to him."

"Why?"

"Because it didn't do any good. I didn't expect him not to run the gossip—that would be expecting too much from a snake like Painter—but he never ever acknowledged when I *did* talk to him and offer an explanation. Then, when I stopped talking to him, then he said I refused to speak to him. I can't say that his death was a great loss for your profession."

"Is there any reason why you might have been worried about what Painter knew about you?" I asked him.

"Why don't you just ask me if I killed him?" Fisher said, with less irritation than I expected. "I want to put this off the record because I don't want my wife and kids reading about me in the context of a murder, even if I am denying it.

"I thought Les Painter was a creep, when I thought about him at all. He lived on rumors, gossip, and half-truths. I'm not sorry he is dead—I already said that—but I wouldn't have wasted my time killing him, which I could have done with my own hands," he said, holding them up like iron claws to emphasize the point. "Or I could have had him killed. Either way, the cops would have had to use damn near their full resources to pin it on me because I would have done it right. But before you go too far along that line, pal, let me assure you I had nothing to do with it. I'm just not sorry it happened.

"If you're interested," he said, changing the subject abruptly, "I'd be glad to show you around the place." I agreed, since it was clear that the interview was over. I got up and walked with Fisher into the hall.

"Why don't I show you the gym first and then we can work our way upstairs." Fisher opened a small, oak-paneled door and pulled a steel gate, standing aside to let me get on a tiny elevator, big enough for about 3.2 persons. We rode down and got off in a gym, a nice-size one, complete with weights, a regulation-size boxing ring, a rowing machine, one of those bicycles that you peddle but it doesn't go anywhere, and a steam room.

"I like to come down here and work out a couple of times a week," Fisher said. "I used to put on the gloves," he said, gesturing toward the ring, "but I'm getting too old and too slow to do that without the risk of getting hurt. I'm still pretty strong, though," he said, walking over to the weights and picking up a two hundred-pound barbell.

"You want to try it?" he asked me.

"No, thanks," I said. "I left my gym suit at home and coach doesn't like us to strain ourselves during the season."

"I heard you were cute," Fisher said. "I asked around about you before you came down. 'Cute but harmless' was what I heard."

"It's nice to know you're well thought of," I said.

"Let me show you the rest of the place before you go," Fisher said.

We got back on the elevator and he pushed a button for the second floor. "You have any favorites for President this year?" I asked him.

"I can live with almost all of them," he said. "I've given some money to Rosecroft because I figure he's got the best chance among the ones I can take. I think it's going to be a Democratic year this time around."

"How do you feel about Higgins?" I asked.

"He's one of the ones I can't take," Fisher said. "If he's elected, he'll be after me for sure. He's just like that goddamn Painter."

"You don't seem too concerned," I said.

"I think his medicine is stronger than what the country wants. If the Democrats can get organized, then I'm confident Rosecroft will get the nomination. And I'll take my chances with him."

"What about the Republicans?"

"I think it's going to be a Democratic year, but I'm not ignoring them."

We stepped off the elevator into a bedroom about forty feet long and twenty feet wide. I had trouble seeing my shoes in the carpet. Against one wall, which was covered with beige raw silk, was a canopied king-size bed with curtains drawn back and tied with silk sashes.

A frail woman in her late forties or early fifties, with pale skin and graying hair, was propped up against the pillows.

"This is my wife, Esther, Mr. Jordan. Dear," he said, turning to the woman, "this is Mr. Jordan. He's a reporter for the Washington *Journal*."

"Why is he here?" she asked, without acknowledging me.

"He's doing a story about my problems with the Environmental Protection Agency. I'm just showing him around the house."

"I wish somebody would get them to stop bothering us. The whole situation makes me terribly nervous—the constant pressure. We used to have such a nice life, Mr. Jordan, before the trouble started."

"I'm sure Mr. Jordan would like to see the rest of the house, dear," Fisher said, leaning over and giving his wife a kiss on her forehead. "I'll send the nurse up," he told her as we turned away.

Fisher guided me out of the room and whizzed me through the twenty or so remaining rooms in the house. We wound up at the front door, where Pete was waiting. Fisher held out his hand to me. "I'll be looking for your story, if you ever write it," he said, gripping my hand harder than I care to have it gripped. "Pete will take you wherever you want to go."

I got in the car and Pete pulled away. I asked him to take me into the city, to an address on the East Side where a friend lived. On the way in, I asked Pete how he had got to know Fisher.

"We were in the same company during the war," he said. "I was just a kid then, a replacement sent in just before the Battle of the Bulge. Mr. Fisher was my sergeant. We were on a patrol and the other four guys were killed by a mine He was wounded so bad he couldn't walk. I had to carry him. We had to hide from the Germans. At one point, one spotted us but I killed him before he could say anything."

"What'd you do, shoot him?" I asked him.

"Naw, that would have brought the others. I choked him to death. Nice and neat. Anyway, after the war, I looked Fisher up. I needed a job, and he said he was going to have a business and maybe there'd be something for me to do. I started out driving a truck, delivering chemicals for him. He kept his eyes open and when he saw other companies that weren't doing much business, he picked them up.

"He kept me around him even when the business got bigger. Sometimes when we go on trips and he can't sleep, we talk about the war. He still likes to talk about it."

"Does it bother you?"

"Me? Naw. It doesn't disturb me. You mean about killing that German? That wasn't the first guy I killed. It didn't bother me. Anyway," he said, closing off the conversation, "he's a good man to work for."

10

I had no way of knowing if I was proceeding properly or not. The meeting with Seld had left me wanting to know more, and the session with Fisher gave me the firm impression that he didn't think of life as a very expensive commodity. Still, I had a feeling that despite his menacing air Fisher probably had nothing to do with Painter's murder. I also had the feeling that my instincts here weren't based on anything remotely resembling experience.

But that didn't stop me. The next person to see was Rosecroft. He hadn't been on my list originally, but Charlotte Daniels had made me wonder. If Painter had shown an interest in him, why shouldn't I consider him?

William Francis Rosecroft was one of the most successful politicians in the United States Senate. By successful, I don't mean that his name was on volumes of landmark legislation or that he had won any battles fighting against the injustices of American society. He was successful in the only way that really counts with politicians—he had never lost an election.

The secret of his success is simple enough to describe, but it was a full-time job. Rosecroft made it a point not to be too far ahead or too far behind on any issue. He had developed to a fine art an instinct for judging the drift of public opinion, so that he could be there with the second wave—not the first, since that would have marked him as a crusader. Rosecroft's ability to be neither ahead nor behind on important issues indicated something else—a total lack of commitment to any principle beyond furthering his political career. In the league where he had been playing so far, his formula had worked. He had no serious enemies and a lot of friends. Labor liked him because he was predictable and respectable—which is to say non-threatening. Business interests weren't crazy for him but they weren't wildly against him either.

Rosecroft's strength was also his problem. Since his career had been associated with no cause except his own, he had no intense following to speak of, although his good looks and earnest manner made him popular with some young people—junior executives, insurance salesmen, housewives who wanted to "get involved," the kind of people who think that government should be a quiet, orderly, rational process where the public interest is easy to define, and usually coincides with what they want. He excited no passions, by design. Rosecroft knew that a lot of people don't want to be stirred up, don't want to be asked to sacrifice, don't want to be called to greatness or anything else. For such people, he was made to order.

Rosecroft's office had that same kind of efficient, nondescript quality that he had. I had made an appointment to see him at two-thirty. When I arrived I was greeted by the receptionist, an attractive young woman of twenty-five, pleasant, courteous, but not anyone you would fantasize about. She suggested that I have a seat while I waited. I thanked her but stood around looking at the pictures on the walls.

The pictures in the outer office were the usual mix. He had a picture of himself and the President standing in front of Independence Hall in Philadelphia during some ceremony or other. Then there was a color picture of the Senator somewhere in a Pennsylvania forest with autumn colors exploding around him. Another picture showed him throwing out a ball at the World Series in Pittsburgh. Pictures of Rosecroft accepting an award from B'nai B'rith, glad-handing black leaders in Philadelphia and American Legionnaires in Altoona—all of them wearing their American Legion campaign hats—snapshots of Rosecroft standing in Red Square, in Dublin, in the Colosseum, and outside the Knesset in Jerusalem. William Rosecroft was a man to leave no base untouched.

Surprisingly, I didn't have to wait long to see him. I would have thought that, with all of the business he had to go through when he came back to Washington from campaigning in the primaries, he would be over-scheduled. When I came into his office, Rosecroft was on the phone, talking a little, but mostly listening. Peter Goldsboro, his press secretary, was sitting on a couch by the window. He was wearing a dark vested gray suit with a white shirt and a paisley tie. Peter apparently thought he would be the next ambassador to the Court of St. James's if Rosecroft were elected. When I had first met Peter, he was working for the AP. He wore baggy pants, a corduroy jacket that I think was a family heirloom, and blue workshirts discarded by ditchdiggers. Peter had been in his man-of-the people stage then and had the appearance of the young Trotsky. I had liked him a lot. He had kept us on our toes at otherwise lackluster press conferences by asking good questions. Sometimes he was a little strident or belligerent, but his heart was in the right place. So we were all a little surprised when Peter had taken the job with Rosecroft. I never asked him why he had done it—gone over to the other side that way—because I wasn't that close to him. He had been with Rosecroft less than two years but had changed drastically. Besides dressing like a banker, he had begun talking and acting like one. When I called him with a question, he answered with the caution of a man whose words might decide the fate of nations. He had smelled the faint aroma of Power.

I nodded at Peter and took a seat in front of Rosecroft's desk and started doing a visual inventory of the room while he talked on the phone. On one wall were still more pictures, and I made a mental note to come back to those if I had time. Over the desk, or rather on the wall behind it, hung his oar from the heavy-weight crew at Penn. There was a picture there, too, of a twenty-year-old William Rosecroft standing with eight or nine other young men on the banks of a river holding their oars next to their shell. They were all smiling the carefree smiles of rich, well-born young men who have no greater worry than their next race. Then across the room there were some paintings of old, pre–Civil War Navy ships, along with a picture of a World War II destroyer. I wasn't clear what the destroyer was, since Rosecroft had served in the Marines during the Korean War. He had a blue and red Marine Corps emblem on display, too, along with a portrait of himself in his officer's dress whites twenty years ago, shaking hands with the Commandant of the Marine Corps. Next to that was a picture taken within the last year of Rosecroft shaking hands with the Commandant. I guess he liked the juxtaposition. On the mantel over the fireplace, Rosecroft displayed part of his collection of donkeys, carved, cast, and sculptured. He kept them around as conversation pieces, and their presence gave him yet another opportunity to talk with visitors about something other than matters of great moment.

His desk displayed the usual kind of clutter—papers, reports, letters to be signed, a ceremonial gavel he had gotten from somewhere, and a gold-framed color photograph of Rosecroft standing with his arm around a good-looking, almost pretty, young man of about nineteen or twenty. Rosecroft and the boy weren't looking at the camera so much as they were looking at each other. The picture appeared to have been taken within the last year or so. It had an intimate quality, as though the photographer had caught Rosecroft and the boy unaware, both standing bare-chested on a secluded beach. The photograph aroused my curiosity, especially considering what Charlotte had told me. I didn't have time to think about whether Rosecroft might be homosexual, because at that moment he finally stopped listening and spoke to the person at the other end of the phone.

"Margaret, I have to go. You talk to Mother and see if you can work out something and let me know. I leave it to you." He said goodbye and put down the receiver.

Rosecroft was particularly close to his sister, the more so since neither of them had married.

"I'll be with you in one more second," he said, acknowledging my presence for the first time. "Lenore," he said into a telephone, "bring me something to drink, will you please?" He turned to me. "How've you been?"

"That's a question I should ask you. You're the one who's running for President," I said.

"Well, I'm doing fine. We're going to go all the way. The polls look good, the money seems to be holding out, and we'll make a strong showing in the primaries. The convention will probably go past one ballot and I'll be able to carry it off."

He had talked about it so many times that his answers were mini-speeches. A question was really just a cue for him to launch into the next oration.

"You've looked at the bill that Higgins is pushing, I assume—the campaign finance bill?" I asked him.

"I, uh." He hesitated for a minute. "Of course that bill won't apply to this election or to the primaries. It hasn't passed yet and can't be retroactive if it does, which is questionable."

Rosecroft, among other things, was one of those people who spend an inordinate amount of time lecturing other people on the obvious. Some of his audiences find this stimulating, since they are too busy to discover these little pearls themselves. It was Rosecroft's way of trying to avoid saying anything, by suggesting that the questioner really didn't know enough to ask in the first place. It might work fine with the Rotary Club in Altoona, but I didn't feel like buying any.

"I realize that," I said. "I was wondering if you've had a chance to look at the bill and whether you have any thoughts about supporting it."

"Well, I've really been busy, you know," he said.

"Are you worried that your Presidential campaign is taking too much time away from your senatorial duties?" I asked, deliberately baiting him.

"I'm managing to run for President and perform my duties here," he said. "I've got a good staff, I keep in close touch with what's happening on the floor and with the legislation that I'm sponsoring. I've come back for the important votes."

"So what do you think of Higgins's bill?" I asked again.

"Tony, it really isn't something that I'd like to see become a campaign issue. It's a procedural question really, don't you think?"

"Senator," I told him, "I think it really doesn't matter what I think." I was exasperated. "The point is that Higgins is one of your principal opponents, he's running on a program of reforms, and that bill is one of the keys, if not *the* key, to his campaign. You may not feel like coming to grips with it, but it's there."

"Frankly, Tony," he said leaning across the desk and looking at me earnestly, "I . . ." At that moment he was interrupted by a black secretary who came in and set a Coke down in front of him. "Thank you, Lenore," he murmured. He lifted the glass and took a sip, set it down and turned to me again.

"Frankly, Tony, I want to be honest and candid with you."

"And I want you to be, Senator," I said, smiling sweetly. "I want you to feel that you can speak to me with the full knowledge that I won't share anything you say with anyone but my readers."

"That's the damn trouble. Look." Now he was transforming himself into a crisp battle commander. "We haven't worked out a position on this thing yet. We're still studying it, going through it carefully to study all the parameters of the thing. I'm getting input from a lot of sources and I don't want to tell you where I come out until we've heard from all stations."

"You don't like the bill," I said.

"I didn't say that. I said we're still looking at it."

"Is there any reason why you *should* like the bill?" I asked him. "I'm trying to find out what your position is."

"Can we talk off the record for a minute?"

"Why can't we talk on the record?"

"I don't want to be quoted. If you're interested in my position, I'll be glad to talk to you about it, but I would just as soon not be quoted on it right now—not until we've put something together."

"All right," I said.

"I think the bill is a bad bill. Higgins is right that it will transform politics, but I don't think that he or anyone else has a clear idea right now what that transformation will be. I've got staff working on it, studying it, and trying to put together a comprehensive position so that when Higgins starts showing up in the primaries, which I expect he will in the next couple of weeks, I can respond to the bill, criticize it, and put him on the defensive. You press fellows are all suckers for anything with a reform label on it, but a person has a right to spend his money to try to get a candidate favorable to his interests elected."

"Victory to the richest?" I said.

"No, not victory to the richest. The Democratic party doesn't traditionally represent the richest elements in this country. If you think too much money is being spent on campaigns, you can impose limits. But they shouldn't rob a person of his voice in public affairs. Part of the problem with Higgins's bill is that it denies what we've recognized as a basic right in this country—the right of citizens to organize to get what they want. If we take away that right, that will be the first step toward fascism."

It was a familiar refrain by now. The trouble was that it sounded infinitely more convincing coming from Mike O'Connell than it did coming from William Rosecroft. O'Connell really believed it, but for Rosecroft it was just a position. Rosecroft no more believed in what he was saying than a quarterback believes that a buttonhook pass is morally superior to an off-tackle slant. It was simply a question of which moved the ball better, which improved his chances of scoring and ultimately of winning.

"I think we have to be very careful about making indiscriminate changes." Rosecroft added, stopping again to drink some of his Coke. Peter was still sitting over on the couch, trying to look as if we were both getting it straight from the Delphic Oracle.

"Are you polling on this issue?" I asked.

"Well, we're polling on a lot of things, not to determine our positions but to find out how the message is coming across. I imagine we'll include a question or two on it to see what kind of impact Higgins is making."

"How much longer are you going to be in town?" I asked.

"I'm staying over tonight for a fund-raiser at the Hilton. We've got a vote tomorrow afternoon and then I have to fly out to Columbus for a rally tomorrow night. I'll go to Cleveland in the morning and then down to Dayton and Akron. From there I think I go to . . ." He paused for a minute, having forgotten where his campaign was taking him.

"Chicago," Peter said, wearily.

"Chicago," Rosecroft repeated. "Then we'll be back here the beginning of the week for a few days and turn right around and go back to Ohio. We're trying to maximize our time there in the next three weeks before the primary. I think we can get at least half of the delegates and do a lot better in Michigan and Illinois. It wouldn't hurt you to come out and see what the country looks like. You guys sit around Washington so much you forget that there are two hundred and eighteen million Americans out there who have to work for a living and who worry about more than whether they can give a hundred dollars or a million to a political candidate."

"I can talk to my desk about it, but we're already covered, I think, for the primaries. I'm not sure they'll want another body out there at this point."

"If I can help out, let me know," Rosecroft said. "I think you ought to see us in action. It would answer a lot of questions you seem to have about the way we approach things."

I wanted to bring up Les Painter, but I wasn't sure how to approach the subject. I decided to dive in and see where I came up.

"Did you hear Higgins's eulogy at Les Painter's funeral?" I asked Rosecroft.

72

"No," he said a little distantly, "I didn't go to Painter's funeral. I really didn't know him very well."

"Did you ever talk to him?"

"Oh, sure. I must have talked to him a dozen times or so, but never in any depth. I wasn't a source of his or anything like that. How is that investigation coming? What do you hear about it?"

"Not much. The police talked to me a couple of times but they didn't learn any more from me than I did from them. I hope that's not a reflection of relative knowledge."

"Do they seem to have any leads?"

"Not that I know of. What makes you so interested?"

"Who wouldn't be?" Rosecroft answered. "The most prominent columnist and investigative reporter in Washington is killed—murdered—in the Capitol by an unknown person. That's a pretty good story, isn't is?"

"Well, it was for a while, anyway. I think the police are operating on the premise that he was shot during a stickup."

"Any luck?"

"Well, as I said, I don't know what they've found out. But I think they're on the wrong track. I think his murder had something to do with his work."

"You have something specific in mind?"

"Not any one thing. He had a couple of things going. One involved a colleague of yours."

"Who?" Rosecroft asked, showing interest.

"I don't think it's nice to talk about people behind their backs, do you?" I said, giving him the closest thing to a coy smile that I could muster. "Then he was asking around about something called the Thursday Night Club, which I've never heard of."

"Well, it might have been just an armed robbery, you know," Rosecroft said abruptly.

"That doesn't strike me as very likely, Senator," I said. "The crime rate may be high in the Capitol, but the kind of crime that's committed here isn't violent."

"I suppose you're right," he murmured in a distracted sort of way. I got up to leave, pausing for a minute over his desk. "I was noticing this picture here of you and this young man."

"My nephew," Rosecroft said, a little too quickly and a little too loudly.

"I thougnt your sister was unmarried," I said.

"Well," he said expansively. "I call him my nephew. He's my

cousin's son. I don't really have any nieces or nephews and she's a widow, so I kind of fill in, help out wherever I can. He's in school now at the University of Michigan—junior year. Wants to go to law school after that, enter politics. I keep telling him he ought to make an honest living, but he's determined."

The joke fell a little flat. Goldsboro was on his feet, doing that stand-up paper-shuffle that aides do when they want to move you out of the room gracefully, in the hope that you won't notice you're leaving until you're gone.

"I appreciate your time, Senator," I said, holding out my hand. "Maybe I'll try to go out with you sometime in the next few weeks."

"Sure," Rosecroft said. "Peter can help you if you have any trouble with campaign staff." Goldsboro nodded gravely as though he'd just been given the message to Garcia. He came out into the reception room with me and stood while I picked up a pile of papers I had left on a table.

"You're starting to look like a character out of the ad for Chase Manhattan," I told Goldsboro.

"What? Oh. I know. I thought I ought to try to improve, in deference to him," he said, crooking his head in the direction of Rosecroft's office. "And he's got a point. He thinks nothing should distract people's attention from the candidate. If I look too scruffy, then people start looking at me when they ought to be looking at him.

"But that's not the only thing. I've been sitting in on policy meetings over at the campaign committee. We both agreed it would be a good idea for later on."

"You mean when you're in the campaign or in the White House?" I asked.

"Either way," he said with some embarrassment.

"Oh, Peter," I said with mock solemnity. "It is a very long road with lots of chuck holes and detours on which you are traveling."

"Meaning what?" he said, with a faint tone of belligerence in his voice.

"Meaning that I hope you have a road map, plenty of gas, and your corduroy jacket and blue jeans packed in a suitcase for the end of the trip when you rejoin us mere mortals."

"I've gotta go," he said, looking at his watch. "If you need anything else, call me. I'll get back to you." I watched him walk briskly down the hall and turn into his office.

74

11

I went to the paper after my talk with Rosecroft to collect my paycheck and to soak up a little of the atmosphere you find in a major metropolitan newsroom. It was about six-fifteen and roughly half of the reporters were pounding away on their typewriters, writing stories they had been sitting on since mid-afternoon. Many people assume that reporters like to write and that that's why they become reporters. Whatever reasons a reporter has for choosing the profession, an affection for writing isn't one of them. If newspapers had no deadlines, reporters would never produce anything. As it is, they spend their day talking on the phone to sources, talking to editors, talking to each other, doing anything to avoid staring at a blank piece of paper in a typewriter.

The reporters who weren't writing either didn't have stories that day or had already finished them. The ones who had already finished were a distinct minority.

I sat at my desk reading letters from various cranks, maniacs, and nit-pickers and the occasional admirers who write. Dan Felshin came over, pulled up a chair, and sat down.

"Higgins is announcing tomorrow at that headquarters they set up over on K Street. It's a bit of an anticlimax, considering it's been open and functioning for the last seven months," Felshin said.

"Well, you know how pols love drama," I said.

"Yeah, but this isn't even drama, it's burlesque. Anyway, he's finally going to do it. It will be a relief to have him in the race so we can stop hedging our descriptions of him. At any rate," he said, "I'm going to cover it. I just wanted to let you know in advance so that there wouldn't be any misunderstanding." Relations at the *Journal* among reporters whose beats overlap are like those between France and Germany in 1913—formally at peace but prepared to go to war at the drop of a hat.

"You didn't have to tell me," I told Felshin gallantly. "It's *your* story, after all."

"I realize that," he said a little waspishly, "but I thought it was the decent thing to do." I guess that remark was supposed to have struck a blow at me, but I ignored it.

"I appreciate your telling me," I said.

My phone rang. "Dinner tonight?" Charlotte Daniels asked.

"Gee, I'd love to, Senator, but tonight was going to be my night to continue my reading and memorization of this year's *Congressional Staff Directory*."

"Nobody loves a smart-ass," she said. "Take me to dinner and I'll take you to a high-powered cocktail party first where you'll get to rub shoulders with all sorts of famous people. Then I'll tell you about the inner workings of the Senate District Committee and then . . ."

"I'm already asleep," I interrupted. "I'll do it if you promise not to do anything to compromise my integrity as a reporter."

"Since when did you become so ethical?" she asked.

"I'm making a fresh start."

"It's a deal. Do you want me to pick you up?"

"Only if you're in a plain black chauffeur-driven Cadillac with White House markings. Otherwise I'll meet you at the cocktail party." She gave me directions and I told her I'd be there in half an hour.

That was before Frank Elliott came out of his office and asked me to come in "for a chat." "You know," he said in that ominous way he has of announcing that a lecture is coming, "it's a fortunate thing for some people around here that the practice of paying reporters according to what they produce went out after World War I."

"I think the Newspaper Guild and the Wages and Hours Act of 1938 had something to do with it, too," I said.

"Yeah," he said, brushing aside my little attempt to be helpful. "Because if we still did pay people based on what they wrote, guys like you would go hungry. If stories were air, you'd have suffocated weeks ago."

"You ought to quit while you're ahead," I said. "If bad metaphors were money, you'd be a millionaire. I've been working on a couple of things. There isn't a whole hell of a lot going on right now, and when I do try to get something into the paper that crack team of deskmen out there tells me how tight space is and to write it short."

"Everybody writes too long around here," Elliott said.

"Is this a colloquium on the problems of *The Washington Journal* or what?" I asked.

"What the hell is this business of your going to see Seld and accusing him of killing Les Painter?" Elliott blurted out.

"Now that," I said, pausing for emphasis, "is very interesting. Did Seld tell you that I had accused him of murder?"

"No, he didn't tell me. He told *him*," Elliott said, indicating by looking up that "him" was Franklin Walters, publisher of the *Journal* and guardian of the public trust. "Walters called down to let me know. Not, you should understand, that he wanted to interfere in any way, but just so that I could raise the matter with you to make sure you knew what you're doing. I wish to hell that Walters would get married again so he would have somebody else to worry about and leave us alone."

"He did get married—two months ago," I said.

"That was annulled," Elliott said.

"When did that happen?"

"A month ago."

"Jesus. You'd think after a while he would figure out that something about him is unattractive to women who live with him."

"Jordan," Elliott said with more than a trace of exasperation, "I don't want to talk about Franklin Walters. I want to talk about you."

"If more people took that kind of an interest in their fellow human beings," I said, "what a wonderful world this would be."

"What is this business with Seld?"

"The U.S. Attorney's office is investigating Seld to see if there were irregularities in the financing of his Presidential primary campaign the last time he ran."

"So do a story on it," Elliott said.

"What do I write for a second paragraph?" I asked him. "I've just told you everything I know."

"So get to work on it."

"You just told me you want to see more stories by me in the paper. How can I spend my time trying to dig up this story and at the same time be doing other stories on a daily basis to keep you happy?"

"You'll find a way, I'm sure," Elliott said. "I'm not so concerned about that as I am about your going around accusing people of murder."

"Seld is hallucinating," I said. "I did *not* accuse him of murder."

"What did you do?"

"I asked him if he had any idea what Painter meant in one of his last columns when he said he would have more to say about Seld very soon."

"What did he say?"

"First, no; then he blew up and threw me out of his office."

"Congratulations. Look. I don't give a shit what you do as long as you're careful. It's unseemly to go around affronting the dignity of United States senators by interrogating them as though they were Mafia hit men."

"I didn't . . ."

"I know. I know," Elliott said. "But you have to use tact."

"If I used as much tact as the police are using, I'd never get a story."

"It's reassuring to see that you appreciate the difference," Elliott said. "Your job is to report the news. The police's job is to solve crimes. If you ever read Aristotle . . ."

"I read him. I've also forgotten him."

"Apparently," Elliott said, beginning a lecture. "The world functions best when everyone does the job that he or she has to do as well as they can. That brings harmony, makes me happy, fills the paper with exciting news, keeps Franklin Walters off my back and me off yours. O.K.? Now. If you happen to stumble over Painter's killer and want to do a little piece about it, fine. Meanwhile, I would appreciate it if you would cover the United States Senate. Win a Pulitzer doing that and I'll give you a ten-dollar raise."

"Do you mean it?" I asked in my best eager-beaver voice.

"Well, now," Elliott said with mock gravity, "I'm not promising anything. But I'll see what I can do."

"Now that that's out of the way, let's talk about something else," I said.

"I have to go to the front page meeting," Elliott said, getting out of his seat.

"I want to go out to Ohio with Rosecroft soon," I said quickly.

"Who'll cover the Senate?"

"There's nothing important on the calendar for the next several weeks."

"Talk to me later." With that he was out the door.

As far as I was concerned, he had approved my trip to the Midwest. Elliott is one of the greatest procrastinators in the world when it comes to a decision involving money. The only way to deal with him is to present him with a fait accompli. If he doesn't like it, he gets mad. But there are worse things in the world than having him mad—like sitting around waiting for him to make a decision.

I went back to my desk to dig a razor out of my drawer so I could shave before meeting Charlotte.

The cocktail party was at one of the downtown hotels, in a room designed to mix sound so that no one could hear anyone else unless their heads were six inches apart and both parties were shouting.

At both ends of the room a cash bar had been set up. White-coated waiters mixed watery drinks in oversize thimbles for a dollar a copy—the proceeds to the Friends of Eddie Erlenborn for Congress. Eddie was from somewhere out west of the Mississippi, and I couldn't figure out what the hell all those people were doing drinking on his behalf. So far as I could tell, nobody at the party besides Mrs. Eddie Erlenborn had ever heard of him.

But the room was packed. The party was typical of Washington cocktail parties. It presented, like the geological structure of a mountain that's been defaced, layers of political history going back to the New Deal, the Fair Deal, the New Frontier, the Great Society, et cetera—all those Democrats who came to Washington and never got around to leaving, like pilgrims, except that they found Washington more lucrative than any Moslem ever found Mecca.

They were standing around drinking their watery drinks and shouting at each other, trying to carry on conversations. I caught Charlotte's eye while she was standing in a corner talking to a tall, heavy-set man who looked good for at least a ten-thousand-dollar contribution to her next campaign. We exchanged glances and then I went to a bar, shouldering my way through the crowd gathered around it, and got myself a bourbon on the rocks.

I looked around for someone to talk to. I saw Ernest Washburn, the Democratic senator from Indiana, talking to Valerie Simmons. So far as I know, Valerie Simmons's entire life consisted of going to parties and being mentioned in newspaper stories about people who were at parties. Since she was always at parties, I assumed she was important, but I never understood why. At any rate, Washburn *was* important. He was chairman of the Senate Finance Committee, and he was a serious person—or as serious as anyone else in Congress, at any rate. On the theory that I might salvage something out of the party, I struggled over to where Washburn was energetically making a point while Ms. Simmons listened with rapt attention.

I was hoping that Washburn would get a little oiled up and I could start asking him about some big money bills that were floating around his committee.

"After about two weeks, the first two weeks," he was saying when I came up, "your muscles start loosening up down here and the definition gets better. You find you can go farther and faster and your legs get surprisingly strong. Here," he said, taking her hand, "feel my thigh."

She knitted her brows as she extended a bejeweled, braceleted hand to feel his thigh through his gray glen-plaid pants leg. "Oh, yes," she said, gravely, "I see what you mean. Oh, yes."

Washburn looked up and saw me standing there. "We're talking about jogging," he said. "I jog. You should run to work, too, Tony. It would do you a lot of good."

"I know you do," I answered. "That's very nice. The thing I've always wondered about is how you get dressed. I mean who brings your clothes to the office and who takes care of getting them cleaned and all?"

"Somebody on my staff takes care of that," he said without interest. "The important thing is the extra energy that I have during the day as a result. I find it much easier to get through my day."

Not being able to bear another minute, I edged away, passing conversations on interior decorators, the price of steak, a new hotel in Puerto Vallarta, the likely political composition of the next Congress, who would win the New Hampshire primary, a new hairdresser in Georgetown, and Senator Frederick Quilling's bill.

The conversation about the Quilling bill featured Quilling himself. Quilling was from Missouri. He was relatively young, he was articulate, he was funny as hell in private conversation and a sure cure for insomnia as a public speaker.

Quilling's bill was a complicated piece of legislative drafting, but the effect was easy enough to explain. It limited the proportion of stock in any major corporation that could be owned by a foreign national or foreign corporation. The language of the bill was broad, but everyone knew that the real purpose was to limit the ability of Arab oil interests to buy into American corporations. Arab money was showing up everywhere, especially in an airplane manufacturing firm headquartered in Missouri. The employees of the firm didn't like the takeover attempt, the owners didn't like it, and the Defense Department didn't like it. The State Department had some problems with Quilling's bill, but the White House was staying out of it and it looked as though the bill was going to pass.

"I think we're in good shape if they filibuster," Quilling was telling a small group that surrounded him in a tight semicircle. "We'll let it run for a few days, then we'll present a cloture petition, vote, get the debate over with, and vote on the bill. We've got the votes to pass it in the Senate, and the House leadership says they have the votes over there. So I think we're in good shape."

"Have you heard from the White House at all?" someone asked him.

"Well, they sort of wish the issue would go away," Quilling said. "I think the President wishes the whole thing had never come up, but he's under a lot of pressure to sign it. He's under a lot of pressure not to sign it, too, but I think he will."

Someone asked Quilling what worried the President. "There's some concern—which I think is unfounded—that the Arabs are antagonized by the terms of the bill. They might read it not only as an economic affront—which it certainly is—but as a racial affront, which it's not meant to be. It has nothing to do with racial characteristics at all."

"The Arabs aren't doing anything that we haven't been doing in other countries, including Arab countries, for the last thirty or forty years," I interjected.

"That doesn't mean we have to like it or accept it," Quilling said. "In some of those instances, our investments were the only way those countries could develop. In other instances, we were attracted by favorable tariff policies. In any case, they couldn't or

81

wouldn't stop us. That's not the situation here. We're not power-less. We don't want to have our corporations dominated by foreign interests. And we're taking reasonable steps to block it. Some people think that's xenophobic. I think it's good sense."

I became aware of a slight pressure on my elbow. I turned slightly and found Charlotte Daniels, in a lime green tweed suit and a cream-colored blouse. "Take me away while my sanity's still intact," she said in a low voice.

"I didn't realize it was so desperate," I said, smiling. "Where would you like to go?"

"I'd like crabs. Do you have a car?"

"No. I left it at home."

"Mine's in the garage."

We picked up her coat and walked through the lobby to the garage next to the hotel. I paid the attendant and we waited with about six or seven other couples for our cars. Some of the women were overdressed, wearing full-length gowns and skirts, as though they had gone to a formal White House dinner rather than a tacky cocktail party for a minor politician. But I suppose when a woman spends her days imprisoned in a three-bedroom rambler out in Wheaton or Arlington, with only a shopping center to go to for excitement, then a night in town is a night on the town.

I stood watching a man near me who had a big cigar in his mouth and was counting a wad of bills. He didn't seem like a Washingtonian, but he wasn't acting like a tourist. He had on white patent-leather shoes, blue pants, and a light blue sport jacket. Char-lotte broke into my reveries. "What *are* you thinking about?" she asked.

"Where could that guy come from, dressed like that at the end of April?"

She glanced over and said quickly, "Kansas City."

"Missouri or Kansas?"

"Kansas."

His car, a powder blue Lincoln Continental, came roaring up the ramp and stopped on a dime next to him. He put away his wad of bills and fished out a pocketful of change, handing a coin to the garage attendant who held his door after doing a quick dust job on the windshield. The woman with him was having trouble getting into the car because she had had too much to drink and her full-length velvet skirt was making it hard to maneuver. But she finally managed and he pulled away after checking out his dashboard like the pilot of a 747 before starting a transatlantic flight.

Charlotte's car came up a few minutes later and I got behind the wheel and headed toward Rockville. "If you don't mind slumming a little bit, Senator, I can find you a first-rate crab dinner," I said.

She didn't answer. I looked over and found her with her head back and her eyes closed.

"This is one of the most exciting evenings I've had in years," I said. "First you force me into attending one of the most missable functions of the season, and then you pass out on me."

She opened one eye a crack. "Some men would give their right arm to have a beautiful senator captive for the evening. You want to conduct a Socratic dialogue."

"Would you like to talk about jogging? That's what Ernie Washburn was talking to Valerie Simmons about at the party."

"Did he tell her to feel his thigh?" Charlotte asked.

"You've had this discussion with him?"

"Are you kidding? Ernie's famous for that. You feel his thigh and then he starts showing you how your body can be 'firmed up' and then one thing leads to another and you wind up going to Ernie's apartment to see his jogging suit."

"You *are* kidding."

"I am *not*. Some women find him terribly attractive. I don't, but I can see where a woman might. For one thing, there's something very sexy about being able to hold someone so powerful a prisoner between your legs. Besides that, he's supposed to be very good in bed. And," she said by way of a crescendo, "he has very firm thighs."

"You know that for a fact?" I asked.

"No comment," she said, smiling.

The restaurant where we went for dinner is not in the standard tourist guide to the Washington area. For one thing, it's too far away and too hard for most tourists to get to. For another thing, it offers little more than crabs—huge, succulent hard-shell crabs, caught that morning in Chesapeake Bay, steamed and spiced, served on a table covered with newspaper. The only plate offered is a hard rubber board. No forks, but wooden mallets and knives.

We ordered spiced shrimp for appetizers, a pitcher of beer, and a dozen jumbo crabs to start.

We picked at the shrimp and sipped beer while we waited for the waitress to bring the crabs. I asked Charlotte about the Quilling bill. She said she thought it would pass and that the President would have no choice but to sign it.

"It's not going to put us in too solid with the Arabs," I said.

"That's an understatement," she said. "But he's got other things on his agenda, other battles he wants to win before he leaves office. If the President doesn't sign, then he's going to have organized labor jumping down his throat along with most of the Democrats and a lot of Republicans. It's one of those issues where he's going to wind up overlooking what he thinks is in the country's long-run best interest in order to accomplish some other things that he also thinks are in the country's long-run interest. That's what the game is all about, kid."

"Thanks for the lesson," I said. "Now, if I can return the favor, maybe I can show you how to take apart a crab." I picked up one of the crabs that the waitress had just dumped on the table.

"I hate to bruise your male ego," she said, smiling at me, "but I already consider myself something of an expert."

For the next hour, Charlotte and I grunted, pounded, and struggled with the crabs, getting relaxation from the effort and taking our minds off politics and government for at least a little respite. For the moment, anyway, nothing was more important than digging out all the crabmeat we could.

When we were finished and after we had washed all the grit off, I paid the check and we got back into her car to drive through suburban sprawl back into the city.

I was feeling contented from the crabs, the beer, and Charlotte's company. "Why don't you and I run off somewhere and live happily ever after on the seven million your husband left you?" I asked her.

"Because we'd both be miserable," she said matter-of-factly.

"We are anyway. At least we'd be away from this mess."

"We don't want to be away from it, really. You say you hate it and I say I hate it. We both complain about it. And we couldn't survive without it. We're addicts. Some people get their kicks making money. Others get it from sex, religion, or drugs. We get it from power—either from possessing it, or from being around it, or attacking it, which is the same thing as trying to get it. We're hooked. We're junkies on it. Why can't you ever take a vacation for more than a week?"

"Because I can't find anybody to water my plants?"

"Because you can't stand the thought you're going to miss something. This town is the capital of the world for you, for me, and for

84

all the other gnomes and giants in our happy little circle of how-ever-many-thousands it is. We're tacky, provincial, ignorant, uncultured, and unsophisticated, and we don't give a damn because we're all convinced that everything that matters—that really matters—happens here. All the rest of it—New York, Paris, Rome, Moscow—that's all icing on the cake. It's ridiculous. But it's the way we think."

"Nevada Senator Tells Las Vegas to Stuff It," I said, headline-style. "Washington Only Thing That Matters, Lady Solon Asserts."

We drove for a while without saying anything.

She finally broke the silence with a question. "What's happening with Painter's murder? Did you ever talk to Rosecroft?"

"I did."

"What did he have to say?"

"I never tell anyone what a source has told me unless it was on the record," I answered, robotlike. "I'll tell you this much. I asked him for a signed confession and he said he'd think it over and get back to me."

"What *did* he say?"

"He invited me to come out with him for a campaign swing."

"And you're going to go?"

"I think I will. Let me ask *you* something," I said, changing the subject abruptly. "Have you ever met or seen Rosecroft's nephew— a tall blond kid of about nineteen or twenty?"

"No," she said pensively. "I don't think I have. I've seen him with a lot of young kids—people on his staff. Mostly good-looking boys, but no one he's ever introduced as his nephew. Why?"

"Well, I saw a photograph on his desk of him and some young kid standing there with their arms around each other. When I asked him about it, he said the boy was his nephew. The picture made me uncomfortable, but I can't say it established anything.

"I've talked to some other people, too. It turns out that Layton Seld is under investigation for possible misappropriation of funds from that Presidential campaign of his four years ago. Painter knew about that. Or it could have been another guy I've talked to. Or it could have been someone else, or ten thousand other people. For all I know, you could have killed him."

"Thanks for the vote of confidence," she said.

I pulled up in front of my apartment and stopped the car. "Don't take it personally," I told her. "That's what you get when you make a professional inquiry of me while we're having a social evening."

"How would you like to kiss a senator goodnight?" she asked me.

She leaned over and I took her in my arms. I had intended to give her a light kiss and let it go at that. But she moved against me, pressing her full breasts into my chest and sliding her tongue into my mouth in a slow, provocative way as our lips met. It had been a while since I had been this close to a woman and now I was reluctant to let go. The smell of her was overwhelming me and I could feel the silky smoothness of her skin under her blouse while she caressed my neck with her lips.

We might have stayed like that for hours, passionately necking and petting in the front seat like two high-school kids, except that a car came up behind us and honked its horn. We parted and I pulled the car over, sat for a minute looking out the windshield, and then looked at her.

"We could go back to my place," she said softly.

"We could," I said, "but I can't. I have three bills to read before I get up to the Hill tomorrow morning and I have an eight-thirty appointment. Why don't we do a weekend sometime in the next couple of weeks? If you won't run away with me, you could at least spend a couple of days at the beach."

She nodded her head and leaned over to kiss me again. This time I kissed her quickly to make sure that I made good on my intention to get some work done before going to bed. I got out of the car and she rolled down the window. "Look at your calendar tomorrow and give me a call to let me know when we can get away," I said.

She said she would and then pulled away, her car moving quickly up the street. I stood there for a moment watching it before turning to walk through the courtyard and into my apartment building. It was about eleven-thirty, a time when smart people in Washington are off the streets.

Out of the corner of my eye, I noticed a man get out of a parked car that was sitting in front of my building with the lights out. I walked slowly into the dimly lit courtyard.

"Jordan." I heard a voice call behind me.

I turned. "Yes?" I said.

"Just wanna talk to you for a minute," the man said. He was about five feet away, coming up quickly. I looked at his face, but couldn't make out his features. Then I realized why. He had a nylon stocking pulled over his face, distorting it and making it unrecognizable.

"I don't think..." I started to say. But I never finished the sentence. A boulder apparently collided with my forehead. I staggered and fell, hitting the cold sidewalk, which felt oddly as though it was pitching and turning. Then I was turned over. Something hard hit me in the stomach, then in the groin. I heard myself groaning. Then I was picked up and felt something like a hammer slam into my jaw. After that, I don't remember much.

The man may have said "cover the Senate" or "stick to your business" or he may have said nothing and my paranoia may have been talking to me. I'm not sure.

When I came to, one of my neighbors was gingerly propping my head up. He was one of the people I nodded hello to in the morning but didn't know beyond that.

"What happened to you?" he asked.

My head was throbbing. One side of it was wet. My stomach and my groin ached. My jaw felt as though I had spent a week in a dentist's chair.

"Are you all right?" he asked again.

"I'm still taking inventory," I muttered. "Give me a minute."

"Sorry. What happened? Were you robbed?"

"I don't know. See if my wallet is in my coat pocket."

It was, and the twenty dollars I had in it was still there along with my credit cards, my press cards, and a lot of old laundry slips.

"It looks as though it hasn't been disturbed," he said. "You still have your watch. He probably was scared off before he could get your money."

"Maybe," I said. "Or maybe . . ."

"You think someone would just beat you up for the fun of it?"

I wasn't in a mood to discuss human motivation with this passing stranger.

"Look," I said, "if it wouldn't be too much trouble, I wonder if you could get me a cab or something so I could get to GW Hospital and get a Band Aid."

"Oh, sure," he said. "I'll be glad to take you in my car. Do you think you can make it over to the lot?"

He helped me get up, which I did slowly, in stages, and then we walked to his car. A bad cut on my forehead was bleeding heavily, but other than that I seemed to be all right.

He told me his name was Harold Waldman, he worked for the Federal Aviation Administration, he was a lawyer, he was engaged, he knew I was with the *Journal*. He told me more than I wanted to know. Someone was inside my head with a sledgehammer, pounding away.

When we got to the emergency room, it was after midnight. The staff wasn't especially busy, but it wouldn't have done for them to take care of me immediately. First they kept me waiting for about fifteen minutes, after putting some gauze on my head to stop the bleeding. Then I had to give a clerk my life's history and prove I had medical insurance. Harold stayed with me like an anxious grandmother throughout.

Finally, after about forty-five minutes, a nurse came and walked me back to a large room with several treatment tables in it. She motioned to one and I lay down. She took the gauze off the wound on my head and proceeded to clean it, using what felt like a combination of soap, steel wool, and sand paper. "Just lie quietly," she told me. "Doctor will be in to see you as soon as he's free."

I lay on the treatment table for another fifteen or twenty minutes, waiting for Doctor to come in. When he finally arrived he was a young resident who didn't waste any time on frills, and didn't bother to greet me in any way. He just grunted as he pulled the gauze quickly from the wound. I didn't want to seem ungrateful for the attention I was finally getting, and I said nothing. He went over to a cabinet by the wall, poured a brownish liquid into a cup, stood looking at it for a minute, and then drank it. I wouldn't have minded a little something myself for medicinal purposes, but he wasn't offering any. I looked him over. He was about twenty-eight or twenty-nine, medium height, unkempt brown hair, needing a shave, and weighing about a hundred and sixty pounds. When he finished his pick-me-up, he tossed the paper cup into a wastebasket and turned back to me.

First he took something that felt like sulfuric acid and poured it on the cut, cleaning it thoroughly. "Looks like brass knuckles," he said, acknowledging me for the first time.

"It felt like a rock," I said.

"Well, it's the kind of cut that knucks usually make," he said. "I'll have to take six or seven sutures to close it."

He threaded a needle with some white thread and proceeded to stitch me up. He hummed a nondistinct, off-key tune while he worked. I winced when the needle went through my skin but in my best John Wayne fashion said nothing. I've had more comfortable, enjoyable experiences in my life.

After a while I figured it was all right to venture a question. "Don't you usually give your patients something for their pain before you begin sewing them up?"

"Yeah," he said, putting the needle through again, "but you looked like you could take it." Had he been more charming at the outset, I might have taken that as a compliment, I was in such a dumb mood. As it was, I began to suspect that he was a novocaine junkie who was denying me my shot so that he could use it for a numbing high at the end of his tour of duty. "See your own doctor in about ten days to have the sutures removed," he continued, as he finished up his work. "You'll probably have a scar on your forehead and a black eye for a week or so."

I walked out to find Harold Waldman still faithfully waiting for me. There was a cop standing around and Harold asked me if I wanted to report the incident. I told him to forget it, I didn't feel like answering questions. Beyond that, I was tired of cops.

Harold drove me home, saw me to the apartment, and probably would have helped me undress if I hadn't assured him a hundred times that I was all right. It was about two-thirty when I finally got in. I admired myself in the mirror for about five minutes, staring blankly at my swollen, discolored face. Then I poured a Jack Daniels, drank it more quickly than good whiskey ought to be consumed, took my clothes off, and crawled into bed.

12

I had nightmares that night in which featureless men approached me as I was eating crabs and gazing across the table at Charlotte Daniels, who was arching her eyebrows and casting seductive glances at me. Just as I was about to put aside the crabs and move across the table to Charlotte, the featureless men started to pound me in the face with enormous wooden crab mallets. A passing policeman was writing parking tickets and warning me that if I didn't quiet down, I would be taken in for disorderly conduct. He called me "sir."

I woke up once around five, took another pill, and tried to go back to sleep. I was uncomfortable. My head still hurt, not to speak of my stomach and my ego. I kept playing through the scene over and over again, trying to figure out what it meant. If it was a robbery, how did the man know my name? If it wasn't a robbery, what was it? A warning? What was I being warned about? And if it was a warning, did he actually warn me? Why didn't he say something while I was conscious enough to hear it?

Maybe, I thought, it's too hard to beat someone up and talk to him at the same time. The Lone Ranger used to do it all the time on radio, but this wasn't radio. This was real. What did he say? "Stick to the Senate?" What the hell was that supposed to mean? The decent thing to do would have been to leave a card or a note. Clarity in communication, that's what I wanted. How was I supposed to alter my conduct if I didn't know what had been offensive?

The hell with it, I told myself bravely. For about forty dollars a week more than I made, I could hire a bodyguard and let him worry about it. Then all I would have to do was worry about how to pay the bodyguard.

Fortunately, at about six-thirty, I heard the paper plop down in front of my door and I was saved from my own idiocy. I began to climb out of bed, but the room started spinning and I fell back on my pillow. I lay there for a moment and then got up again, slowly this time.

The paper was full of the usual. They were shooting at each other in the Mideast; a robbery over in Northeast Washington ended with a ninety-miles-per-hour chase through mid-morning traffic; prices were up, employment down. A House committee was thinking about holding hearings to find out why Washington still didn't have a major-league baseball team. The Virginia suburbs were presenting record budgets. The Maryland legislature was rushing to close. It went on like that through eighty-eight exciting pages, and I haven't said anything about the financial news.

While I was sipping some coffee, the phone rang. It was Mary Painter. "I'm sorry to be calling so early, but I tried you last night and there was no answer. I wanted to get you before you left."

I told her it was all right, I had been up for some time. "What can I do for you?"

"The police have arrested someone for Les's murder."

"Who is it?"

"I don't know if you know him or not—he worked in Les's office. He was sort of a messenger and sometimes he did a little leg-work for Les."

"Moose Petowski?"

"You know him?"

"Not terribly well," I said, "I know him. I know who he is. I've

91

spoken with him. Why do they think Moose killed Les?"

"They asked me a lot of questions at the beginning. You know. But they didn't answer mine very well."

"What did they ask you about Moose?"

"If he owned a gun—I told them I didn't know. If he got along with Les—I told them that Les was not an easy person to get along with, and neither was Moose. They had quarreled. Les had fired Moose a couple of times and then taken him back. About a week before Les was killed, they had a big fight. Moose wanted to know when he could become a full-time legman. Les told him never, that he was too stupid, too slow. Les told him that he ought to think about some other kind of work, like being a truck driver or a hod carrier."

"Did Les tell you about this?" I asked.

"No, Moose did. He's been with Les for eight years, since he was in high school. He didn't have much of a family life. His father drank. His mother is dead. So I had him out to the house a lot. I thought he was a nice boy—confused, stubborn, and not very disciplined, but decent. He was very good with our kids when I had him babysit if we went out. Responsible and all." She stopped for a moment. I didn't say anything. "I don't think he killed Les," she went on, "Moose had a bad temper, but I just don't believe it. Tony, can you get him a lawyer? Somebody good? I'll pay for it."

This woman was a constant source of surprise to me. First, she burns her husband's notes, risking a contempt of court citation or an indictment for obstruction of justice. Then, when the police arrest a suspect for her husband's murder, she wants to lay out money to defend him.

"I've been up all night thinking about it," she said. "I was trying to figure out why Moose would have done it. I don't know what the case against him is, but I just can't picture Moose killing Les. It just doesn't fit. He and Les had had lots of fights and Les had fired him before. Why should Moose kill him now? I just can't accept it."

"Mary," I said, trying to ask the question as diplomatically as I could, "do you think Les would want you to be doing this?"

"I don't know what Les would have wanted," she said with a touch of anger in her voice. "Les is dead. I may have tried to do what he wanted while he was alive, but I have to start trying to puzzle things out for myself now. This is what I want to do."

She was very emphatic, so I tried to be businesslike. "When was Moose arrested?"

"He called me from police headquarters last night around eleven or so. He just kept saying over and over, 'I didn't do it. I didn't do it.'"

"Did he say when his arraignment was?"

"He didn't know or he didn't say. I'm not sure."

"O.K. Let me get off now and call someone. I'll call you back when I know something."

"Tony, there's one more thing," she said, pausing. "Moose or anyone else shouldn't know I'm paying for the lawyer."

"How about the lawyer?"

"Nobody. Just you and me."

"Terrific," I said. "I suppose you'll funnel the money to me and I'll write the checks. Then I can explain to my buddies how it is that I'm defending Les's accused killer with all this previously unknown dough. On top of that I can explain to the IRS where the extra income is coming from so I can pay taxes on it."

"We'll work out something with a bank."

"Suppose the lawyer doesn't like the arrangement?"

"Then you'll have to find someone else."

"You're not making this at all easy, Mary."

"I know. But I think of you as my friend, too, and I need your help."

"All right, Mary. I'll see what I can do."

I put the phone down. I didn't like it. Getting a lawyer for Moose was one thing. But shielding the source of the lawyer's fees was something else. In other circumstances I might have thought the deal was shady or suspicious. If I thought about it enough now, I might decide it was shady *and* suspicious. I sat there kicking it around for a while. First of all, should I go through with it? And second, if I did, who should I get? Who could I get? Who would take the case under the circumstances?

Those were reasons for not doing it. On the other side, I figured, were Mary's feelings. She knew Moose, knew what her husband's relationship with Moose had been. If Mary thought Moose was innocent, that should count for something. It was unconventional, but that was what was wrong with this whole thing in the first place. The police were proceeding in a conventional way and getting nowhere. Painter had not been a conventional person. He made up his own rules and stuck to them. Mary was doing that now. I had to decide if that was the kind of game I wanted to play in. When I started thinking about it I realized I had already made that decision.

I was in the game. I had a lot of misgivings about what I was doing, and about what Mary was asking me to do. I would just have to put them aside for the moment and proceed. I couldn't worry and act at the same time. That was a sure way to get nothing done.

So now I was back to the problem of finding a lawyer for Moose, the sort of problem I could work out only in the shower. Besides, it was getting late and I still wanted to make my morning appointment if I could. I took a quick look at myself in the mirror. My eye was swollen, blue, and very ugly. The bandage on my forehead was dramatic.

I got a plastic bag to cover my head to keep the stitches dry and stepped into a hot shower. Then I started leafing through the file cabinet in my mind, going over lawyers one by one. I must have thought of about fifteen or twenty different ones, rejecting some of them immediately, others after some thought, and putting a few in the category of possibles. Finally, my choice narrowed down to the one man I had thought of first, John Forman.

John Forman was one of the best lawyers I've ever seen. For one thing, he didn't play the game that some of his colleagues played. He actually defended his clients. He didn't urge them to plead guilty to some lesser offense as a means of saving himself time, unless he thought the case was absolutely hopeless. He wasn't afraid to defend unpopular causes—he had defended a lot of government workers who had gotten into trouble for their political activities during the early fifties, when McCarthy was cutting a wide swath through Washington. Forman was a fighter. When he walked into the courtroom, he was courteous but tough. He acted as though he was on his own territory, communicating to the jury a sense that he had absolute confidence in their intelligence and judgment and that when he was through presenting his case, they would agree that his client was innocent. In a quiet, dignified way, he was one of the most committed persons I knew. If I ever need a lawyer, John Forman would be my choice.

The only problem was, I couldn't be sure that Forman would remember me. He didn't cultivate the press the way a lot of other lawyers did. I hadn't had that much contact with him. And it had been several years since I last saw him. I was reluctant to refresh his memory by referring to the *Journal*, since this contact was a personal one and I wanted to keep the *Journal* out of it if I could.

It was eight-fifteen. I tried Forman at home. His wife answered.

94

I gave my name and asked to speak with him. He came on the line, polite but not overly warm, sounding as though he didn't know who I was.

"Have we met, Mr. Jordan?"

"Well, sir, we did meet several years ago when you were defending John Williams on a bank robbery charge. Do you remember the case? He had been tried first for conspiracy and when you won an acquittal, he was indicted on the robbery charge for the same hold-up. And you got an acquittal again."

The double jeopardy case with that rotten judge," Forman said. "I remember the case, all right, but I don't remember you."

"I talked to you quite a bit during the trial." I described myself to him, without mentioning the *Journal.*

"Are you a reporter, Mr. Jordan?"

Now I was in it. "Yes, I am. But this has nothing to do with my work. I'm calling as a private person."

"Fine. Why don't you call me at the office?"

"I'm afraid it can't wait. I'm calling you to see if you'll represent someone. He's going to be arraigned this morning downtown in Superior Court."

"What's the charge?" Forman asked.

"His name is Moose Petowski. He's charged with first degree murder." I was really backing into it, as though telling Forman everything at once would scare him off.

"Who is he charged with killing?"

"Les Painter."

Forman didn't say anything for several seconds. "I knew Les Painter, you know. I dealt with him from time to time. I respected him. I thought he went off the mark occasionally, but I thought he performed a service."

"I hadn't thought of that," I said apologetically. "I'm sorry to have put you on the spot."

"You're not putting me on the spot," Forman said. "This person has a right to be defended. All things considered, he probably needs all the legal help he can get. He'll need a good lawyer." Forman stopped for a minute. I didn't say anything. "I'm a good lawyer. Is there any reason why I shouldn't take the case?" he asked.

I wasn't sure if I was supposed to answer the question or not. I said nothing. "How is he going to pay the expenses? What about my fee?" Forman asked.

"That will be taken care of," I told him.

"By whom?"

"By someone interested in seeing that Petowski is well defended. You'll be paid through a bank."

"What kind of arrangement is that?" Forman asked. "It seems a little . . ."

"Shady?" I supplied, cutting him off.

"I suppose that's one word I might use. What about that, Mr. Jordan?"

"Mr. Forman, I called you because I respect you. I respect your work. I know the arrangement is unusual. Petowski may not want you for his lawyer for one thing. I'll have to talk to him, introduce you to him. I can give you this assurance. To the best of my knowledge, nothing in the arrangement I've described to you so far as I know is unethical or improper. If, at any time, I have reason to change that judgment, I'll tell you, and you can do whatever you think is proper."

He didn't say anything for quite a while. I could hear him breathing and his wife clattering around with dishes and running water in the background. "I'll come down for the arraignment, Mr. Jordan. We can talk after that about whether I'll take the case. I'd like you to meet me down at the courthouse in a half an hour, so we can talk to this person. You'll have to tell me what you know about him."

I got off after thanking him. I made a call to cancel my appointment on the Hill, which I wouldn't have been able to make on time anyway. I dressed quickly, considering my infirmity of the moment, caught a cab, and went down to the courthouse.

Forman was not much to look at. Short, middle-aged, drably dressed, and carrying a battered briefcase, he didn't look like a threat—or much of a hope—to anyone. But who was I to talk about looks? I introduced myself, apologized for my appearance, and we shook hands.

"We don't have much time," Forman said. "Petowski is supposed to be arraigned at nine-thirty. I want you to introduce me to him and let me talk to him, and then you stay here so I can talk to you after the arraignment." All of this was said quickly as we went down the stairs to the basement lock-up where prisoners are kept until they're brought to a courtroom.

Forman had a little trouble getting me past the U.S. marshal, but we finally got that settled and sat down at the plain blond-wood table provided for counsel and defendants in a barren, sterile room with institutional green walls. They brought Moose in in handcuffs, which the marshal did not remove.

Moose was appropriately named. He was about six feet tall, weighed two hundred pounds or so without any sign of flab. He had long blond hair which was uncombed, so that he had to push it out of his eyes periodically. He was wearing a light blue shirt and blue jeans. He nodded curtly at me when he sat down. He didn't smile, and he asked for a cigarette. Neither Forman nor I smoked.

"Moose," I said, "this is John Forman. He's agreed to defend you if you would like him to represent you."

"How am I supposed to pay for a lawyer?" Moose asked belligerently.

"That's taken care of," I told him. "You don't need to worry about it. Someone is paying his fees and expenses. I can't tell you who, because . . ."

"I don't like it," Moose said curtly.

"Look, pal," I said, restraining myself, "like it or not, you need a lawyer, a good lawyer. If you want to take your chances with a public defender who doesn't want the case and who'll advise you to plead guilty to something, or with a lawyer who'll take you only because he needs the money, then go ahead and turn Mr. Forman down. If you're convicted of first-degree murder, you can get life. If you plead to a lesser offense, you might get twenty years or so. If you want to act like a fathead, go on. You won't be hurting much. You'll go to jail. Painter's killer will stay free and we'll never know why he was killed. You'll have the satisfaction of proving to yourself that the world is out to get you."

"Save it," Moose said. "I *am* innocent. Not that I had any great love for Painter after what he said to me. But I didn't kill him."

"You agree to have Mr. Forman take the case?" I asked.

"Sure," Moose said. "What the hell. I need a lawyer."

I got up. "I'm going to let you two talk alone. Moose," I said, looking at him as sharply as I could, "you can trust Mr. Forman. For your sake, I hope you believe that."

I knocked on the door and the marshal opened it to let me out. I went back up the stairs. My head was pounding, but it was too soon to take another pill. I went to the courtroom and sat down, waiting for Forman to come back up. No one else in the room paid

97

much attention to me or my bandage. There was a young black woman waiting there with a child about two or three and also a middle-aged working-class black couple. They had seen plenty of people with black eyes and bandages. I wasn't anything special.

Soon Forman came back in. "With his attitude," Forman said, shaking his head, "the prosecution won't need much of a case to convict him. If he doesn't cooperate more than he did just now, I'm not going to be able to prepare an adequate defense. What makes you think he's innocent?"

"Well, I'm not sure . . ." I said. But then the magistrate came in, and our conversation was cut short. Petowski was the second person on the docket.

Any doubt that the case was important was dispelled when the U.S. Attorney himself, Harold W. Wyman, came in to argue the government's side. About seven reporters came in with him, including two from the *Journal*. I thought about crawling under a bench, but it was too late. Mitchell Strauss, the *Journal's* court reporter, sat down next to me.

"What the hell happened to you?" he whispered, looking at my face.

"Irate reader," I answered.

"Really," he insisted. "What happened?"

"Guy found out I worked for the *Journal* and complained to me that his paper is either late or not delivered at all. If you had ever worked in circulation you'd know how worked up people get about their paper. Don't ever tell people you work for the *Journal*."

"You going to give me a straight answer?" Strauss asked.

"You going to punch me in the eye if I don't?"

He smiled and dropped it. "What are you doing here, anyway?" he asked.

"Making you nervous," I said. "Stop asking so many questions."

Petowski's case came up and Forman went up to stand with him. Wyman stepped up and made a brief presentation. The government, Wyman said, had strong evidence making a clear link between Petowski and Les Painter's murder. The government had witnesses who had seen and heard a bitter fight between them less than a week before the murder. Petowski had been in the Capitol shortly before the crime occurred and he had made clear his animosity toward Painter. Wyman asked the magistrate to hold Petowski without bail until his case could be presented to the grand jury.

98

Then Forman argued against Wyman's request, asking the magistrate to set bail, which was pretty funny considering that Petowski had no money for bail. It didn't matter much because the magistrate denied Forman's request and ordered Moose held. The marshal took him away and the assembly that had gathered for Petowski's arraignment got up noisily and moved into the hall. Forman and Wyman were quickly besieged by reporters. Wyman waved them off, and they didn't get much more from Forman, who didn't know enough. to tell them anything anyway. When they had just about given up, Forman came over to me. "I'd like to talk to you again," he said quietly, so that the others couldn't hear.

"Well, not with them standing around," I said. "Suppose I call you at your office in about an hour or so?"

"I guess you're right," Forman said, glancing at the other reporters, who were standing five or six feet away, watching us talking. "Call me." He turned and walked away.

Strauss came up to me again. "What the hell was that?" he said, not bothering to disguise his annoyance.

"I was telling Forman that he should get elevator shoes so he doesn't look so short when he appears on television," I said.

"Goddamit," Strauss said. "I don't like it. In the first place, you have no business being down here. This is *my* beat. This is *my* story. In the second place, you talk to the lawyer for the defendant in a big case like this, and then you won't even tell me what the hell's happening. I'm going to call the desk and complain."

I didn't especially like the drift of Strauss's remarks. I had enough problems already without having to explain to Elliott and whoever else at the *Journal* might ask me what I was doing in the courthouse talking to Petowski's lawyer.

"Look, Mitchell, it's very simple," I said in a calm, reassuring way. "Les Painter was a friend of mine. Forman and I have known each other for a long time. I wanted to come down for the arraignment, that's all. As for Petowski, I'll tell you the little bit I know, but I really don't know very much."

"I'll share the byline with you," Strauss said, as though he were making an offer to divvy up a treasure chest.

"No, no." I said. "I'll tell you what I know and you confirm it somewhere else. Just keep me out of it. You don't have to say anything to the desk about my being here or talking to you."

"Yeah. Yeah," he said quickly.

I didn't trust him a bit, but I didn't have much choice. I told him what Mary Painter had told me—without telling him where I had heard it. He wanted to know who my source was, but I acted offended and he backed off. He had no business asking me that anyway.

When I finally got Strauss off my back, I went up to the Hill. The press gallery was half-empty since almost everyone had gone downtown to the National Press Club to cover Philip Higgins's press conference announcing that he was running for President. But I didn't get away entirely free. Rick Mason, who covers the Senate for the *Times*, was in the gallery, and he took one look at my face and started asking questions.

"What the hell happened to you?" he said, going over my face and body like a mobile camera.

"If I told you I walked into a door, would you believe it?" I asked.

"Nice try, but no cigar,"

"Tough game of touch football?" I said.

"Not bad, except that it's spring."

"Well, then, I was mugged."

"Welcome to Washington," he said. "Did he, they, or was it she, get any money?"

"No, the main damage was to my ego," I said. "You know I never carry more than five dollars in cash."

"Which reminds me," he said. "You owe me ten bucks."

"I'd pay you back..."

"But you never carry more than five dollars in cash," Mason said.

"I've gotta make a call," I said, cutting short the conversation. When I called Forman and asked him if he had made his mind up about the case, he went through a monologue not unlike the discussion I had had with myself earlier in the day. He listed the doubts he had about the case, including the unorthodox method of payment, Petowski's belligerence, and his uncooperative attitude. My heart started to sink. I had enough to do without leaving a trail around Washington finding Moose Petowski a lawyer.

"I've been practicing law for a long time," Forman was saying. "You develop a feeling about the clients."

"Do you have a feeling about Petowski?" I asked.

"Yes, I do," Forman answered. "I think he's probably innocent. It doesn't sound to me like the evidence against him is very strong. I've decided to take the case, assuming my fee arrangement is satisfactory. I'll need a retainer of five thousand dollars. I would like payment by check, not cash. How does that sound?"

I told him I thought it would be all right and I would see that he got the check as soon as possible. We agreed he would call me if he needed anything else. Then I told him what I could about Moose, including the details about the fight, and suggested that Steve Brandon, Larry Quirk, or Dinah Berman at the "Inside Track" office could tell him more. He thanked me and we both hung up.

Then I called my desk just to check in. Melinda answered the phone, all business. "Frank wants to speak with you," she said. "Hold on while I switch you."

"What the hell were you doing down at the courthouse?" Elliott demanded when he came on the line. "You were supposed to be on the Hill at eight-thirty this morning."

So much for Strauss, I thought to myself. "Les Painter was a friend of mine. I wanted to watch the arraignment."

"So then what were you talking to Petowski's lawyer about?" Elliott demanded.

"He wanted my recipe for meatballs stroganoff. He's been after me to give it to him for months and I keep forgetting to do it."

"I'll pass that and come back to it later," Elliott said. "Who messed up your face? Strauss said it looked like you had been mugged."

"O.K.," I said. "You want a straight answer, right? Promise you won't let this get around?"

"What is it?" Elliott said, not a little impatiently.

"I entered the middleweight class in the Golden Gloves. Last night was the qualifying round. I may have gotten roughed up a little, but you should see the other guy."

"Let's go back to the business with Forman," Elliott said, getting more annoyed.

"Let's drop it," I said. "If you want, I can file memos on what I do all day long—who I see, what I eat, who talks to me, what I read, who I sleep with. The only catch is that you pay me for my time, all twenty-four hours, on an overtime basis. You won't learn much, but then you can feel that you're in charge of my little life. Otherwise, my obligation to you begins at ten and ends at six-thirty."

"I don't think you have to go that far, Tony," Elliott said in a conciliatory tone. "Strauss was complaining that you were there, that you seemed to know things, and that you weren't telling him everything."

"Strauss is paranoid," I said quickly.

"Everyone around here is paranoid," Elliott said, chuckling. "That's a prerequisite for employment."

"What's going on today?" I asked.

"Nothing much. Higgins declared. Walters wants to have a chat with me today."

"For what?" I asked. "To talk about me again?"

"Now who's paranoid?" Elliott said. "I've got to go to the morning editors' meeting. Have you got any stories for the weekend?"

"Maybe something on the Quilling bill if I can get the reporting done today and write it tonight or tomorrow for Sunday."

"O.K. I'll put that down as a possible. I gotta go."

He hung up. I sat there for a minute thinking about my career. What I needed, I decided, was a long vacation or a suit of armor. I calculated my chance of getting either as somewhere between slim and none.

13

The next week or so was slow on the Hill, but busy for me. First, I had to run around getting Moose Petowski's defense fund set up. That was a little complicated because I didn't want to sign the checks and Mary wasn't going to either. We finally got an arrangement worked out with the bank.

Then Forman called me a couple of times to complain about Moose's attitude. I finally called Mary and told her that Moose was conspiring with the prosecution to get himself convicted. She agreed to try to do something to bring him around.

Elliott was on my back because I wasn't producing anything for the paper and couldn't be reached or found when he wanted me. Frank harbored old-fashioned ideas about employees' working full-time for the people who paid them.

I had some problems with what I was doing, too. I was afraid the news business might get away from me if I spent too much time on the investigation—even if nothing much seemed to be going on. That's usually the time that a lot's happening. But I didn't let my doubts stop me. I was committed to going ahead. If I got ulcers in the process, then I'd have to pay that price.

I dropped in at the office of "The Inside Track," one afternoon. The column was still publishing, although about twenty papers had dropped it after Painter was killed. The office itself, which was on K Street, wasn't terribly impressive. One entered a large room, where Dinah Berman, Painter's secretary sat. Two smaller rooms opened off a hallway behind her desk, as did a third room with a refrigerator, hot plate, the inevitable coffee pot, and a duplicating machine. Painter had used the larger of the two rooms, which had a terrific view of a brick wall on the adjoining building. Quirk and Brandon shared the other one.

As it turned out, neither Quirk nor Brandon was in. Since I had nothing better to do, I sat down and chatted with Dinah, who was opening the afternoon mail. We talked about Petowski while she opened the letters with a leather-covered letter opener that Painter had doubtless given her for Christmas or her birthday. He was not much on giving personal gifts or on splurging.

Dinah is a nice girl, as they say. Not terribly attractive, but not repulsive either, bright, but not overpowering. Pleasant, stable, and neat. The perfect sort of person to have in an office as chaotic as "The Inside Track."

We were talking about her love life, or lack of it, when she stopped for a minute to give a closer look to one particular bill. "Well, that solves that mystery, anyway," she said.

"What's that?"

"Where Les went on that trip he took before he was killed. Here's a bill from the Hôtel Suisse in Geneva for five nights. And here's another one for his airplane ticket." Both bills were on his American Express card.

I asked her if I could see the bills for a minute. She handed them across the desk to me. "Actually," she said, while I looked at the vouchers, "that makes sense. He brought me back those Swiss chocolates."

I wrote down the dates of his stay in Geneva and stuck around until she finished opening the mail to see if anything else turned up. Nothing did, and I made my way out as gracefully as I could without appearing too interested in what she had showed me. I went back to the *Journal* so I could check something out.

The *Journal* has bureaus in eleven foreign cities—London, Paris, Tokyo, Hong Kong, Moscow, Buenos Aires, Nairobi, Rome, Bangkok, Bonn, and Belgrade—staffed by *Journal* reporters. On top of that regular staff, the *Journal* has arrangements with correspondents in thirty or forty other cities where we pay them a monthly retainer or a fee for each of their stories we use. These are the "stringers," so named, I suppose, because they're kept on a string.

I walked over to the foreign desk, where Jim Hoskins was going through a pile of yellow, white, and green wire copy, mechanically putting some of it on a spike to be discarded, marking other pieces with a slug and slipping them into paper folders to be distributed to the foreign desk people when they came to work at three.

Exactly what Hoskins's title is at the *Journal*, I can't say. He is not an editor, because his job doesn't involve decisions about who should do a story or about the content of stories. I would say that his job was clerical, except that the foreign desk couldn't function without him, and to say that he's a clerk understates the matter. He knows where our correspondents are, who our stringers are, how to get messages to them, how to arrange airplane tickets and transmission of cash, what the exchange rates are, and all kinds of absolutely mundane and boring matters without which no foreign news would get to us from our people.

"Do we have anybody any good in Geneva?" I asked him.

He looked at me for a minute, sucked on his pipe professorially, and then answered. "Gerard Fournier."

"Is he any good?" I asked.

"He's reliable, fast, and accurate," Hoskins said. "He isn't able to leap tall buildings in a single bound, if that's what you have in mind."

"No," I said, "I just want somebody dependable."

"Well, he's dependable. What could you possibly want him for?"

"A favor," I said. "A favor that doesn't need to be broadcast around the newsroom. I'd be happy if you and I were the only ones who knew about it for the time being."

"That can be arranged," Hoskins said.

"I'd like him to check on something for me. Do we have to pay for that?"

"Not if it doesn't take too much time or cost him money out of pocket. He's on retainer," Hoskins said.

"I have to find out—if I can—what Les Painter was doing in Geneva in February. How should I do it?"

"Draft a message and give it to me. I'll have it sent with a notation that the reply should come to you."

"Who else will see it?" I asked.

"Outside of the guy in the wire room, just you and me. The wire room guy doesn't read the stuff except to see where it goes. I'll give the whole thing to you, all four copies. I take care of the billing, too, so you don't have to worry about it. What's this all about?"

"I'm not sure," I said, meaning it.

"O.K.," he said. "Ask a buddy to do a favor but don't let him in on the secret."

"I really don't know any secrets, Jim. I'm hoping Fournier can provide something."

"Well, draft the message and let me have it," Hoskins said, still not believing me.

It took me a while to write what I thought was a reasonably good query. Then I took it to Hoskins. My message said: "Please look into movements Les Painter while in Geneva February 9 to 14. Am especially interested to know whom he talked to and subjects of conversation. Stayed at Hôtel Suisse. Also determine if possible whether he left Geneva and went anywhere outside the city. RSVP Tony Jordan."

Hoskins looked at it for a minute and laughed.

"Something wrong?" I asked.

"Well, it's clear you haven't had much experience cabling. If all our wires were written like this, we'd be bankrupt. I'd like to edit it."

"Sure," I said.

He picked up a pencil and worked it over. It came out reading,

"PLS CHK GNV MUVMNTS LES PAINTER FEB 9–14. STAYED HÔTEL SUISSE. INTERESTED WHO MET AND SUBJECTS DISCUSSED. ALSO IF LEFT GNV FOR ANY NEARBY DEST. RSVP ASAP JORDAN JOURNAL."

"That's the way professional correspondents do it," Hoskins said tartly.

"Don't get smart," I said. "How fast can it be sent?"

"How about two minutes?" Hoskins asked. He got up and took it into the wire room, sat down at a teletype, punched it out, took the tape he produced, and put it on a machine. In about three minutes, he was done.

"Now what?" I asked.

"Now I get back to work, you leave me alone, and we wait for an answer. I'll let you know when I hear something."

I pestered Hoskins by phone for the next couple of days, but he stayed pretty good-natured, assuring me he had heard nothing from Fournier and would let me know as soon as he did. So when I found a message from him in the Senate press gallery about a week after my cable, I wasted no time. "What's up?" I asked him on the phone.

"Fournier has wired back," he said.

"What's he say?"

"You want it now?" Hoskins asked.

"What do you want me to do, go to a secure telephone? Give it to me in Navaho. They'll never know what you're saying."

"O.K.," Hoskins said. "Fournier says that Painter did two things in Geneva. He spent a lot of time talking to representatives of the Arab Consortium. And he went around trying to find out if Layton Seld had a numbered bank account in any of the banks in Geneva. Painter also checked in Zurich to see if Seld had an account there, Fournier says."

"Does he say whether Painter found out?"

"He hasn't been able to determine that. He wants to know whether you want him to do more or if that takes care of it." Hoskins said.

"Well, I want him to pursue it, both of those things."

"I don't know, Tony. This is going to start costing us."

"It's legitimate. If I can find out that Seld has a Swiss bank account, it ties in with something else that I'm working on. Don't worry about it. I'll take the heat. Just wire Fournier back to pursue the Seld thing and also the business about the Arab Consortium."

"Why the Arab Consortium?" Hoskins asked.

"Because it's there," I said. "How the hell should I know? All knowledge is relevant. Let me worry about why."

"O.K." Hoskins said. "I'll send it off."

I thought about what I ought to do—go talk to Seld again? Start making the rounds of Arab embassies? I didn't know what I should do. Finally, I applied an old rule that has always stood me in good stead—when in doubt, do nothing. It made sense. I really didn't know much more about Seld than I did before, except that Painter had had reason to think he might have a Swiss bank account. Whether Painter's suspicions were true, I didn't have the foggiest. Considering the warmth of Seld's feelings for me already, there was no point in going back for another round, assuming—a doubtful proposition—that I could get in to see him in any case.

As for the Arabs, that was less than nothing. Painter fancied himself, *inter alia*, something of an expert on foreign relations. For all I knew, he was simply carrying on extended discussions with Arabs about oil, not an unreasonable topic of conversation for a journalist. The Arab Consortium, representing Arab oil interests, would be a logical group to touch base with. Their Geneva office handled a lot of different business—public relations, negotiations, foreign investment, and occasional assassinations when one sheik fell out with another. Any one of those subjects, or all of them, might have been the focus of Painter's interest.

With Fournier checking into it, there was no sense in my broadcasting my ignorance by stumbling around asking questions. Let him give me something to get my foot in the door with and then I could pursue it.

As it turned out, even if I had decided to start knocking on doors, the telephone call I got that afternoon would have put me off. It was the publisher's secretary, Maria (pronounced Ma-rýe-a) Scott, daughter of a Georgia dirt farmer but she came on sounding like Vassar, Class of '60. She was summoning me to "luncheon with Mr. Walters in his dining room tomorrow at one."

I use the word summon advisedly. One was not invited to eat with Franklin Walters. He was not Louis the Fourteenth but he wasn't one of the boys either. The problem was that his merest whisper was amplified into a shout through the megaphone of sycophants surrounding him. Either consciously or fortuitously by instinct, Walters had managed to surround himself with aides who projected an image of him to outsiders as a mixture of Dalai Lama, Pope, and Philosopher King all rolled into one.

Not that I minded having lunch with Walters. He wasn't especially scary. No one had ever disappeared while dining with him. The food was usually pretty good and, it was free. Elliott had also been invited, as it turned out, and that was it—just the three of us for a *très intime* luncheon, surrounded by Walters's modern art.

Walters reminded me of a greyhound—elegant, sleek, and bred with a purpose in mind. He had been born to wealth and had been the whole route—St. Paul's, Princeton, staff officer in the Navy during World War II. If there was an establishment in Washington—

in America—he was part of it. The problem was that his intellect didn't match his station. Too much in-breeding had weakened the stock, which could have been strengthened with an infusion of a little common blood.

Walters was blind to his own shortcomings and to the failings and limitations of his class. He had confidence in his own ability and those like him to manage events, but that confidence was misplaced. Walters didn't know it, but time had passed him and them by. The world no longer was in their control. But his paper still paid the rent, still gave him leverage to wangle an occasional dinner invitation to the White House, still gave him the ability to pick up the phone and call almost anyone of importance in the world and get through without a wait. One of the reasons why he had such ready access to the powerful and famous was that they had access to him. Walters was not promiscuous in his granting of favors, but he did dispense them from time to time.

A favor usually meant that something was done—or not done—in the pages of the *Journal*. Getting something done was usually not so bad, because a willing editor could always find a drone to carry out a command. But not doing something was tougher. The *Journal* had a lot of good people working for it. When they got their teeth into something, they didn't like to let go. It was contrary to nature and to their professional instincts. People had quit the *Journal* over Walters's interventions in the past and others would probably quit in the future. They had their integrity and self-respect and he had his newspaper. It was as simple as that.

Maria Scott told us to wait when Elliott and I arrived. Elliott was a little fidgety, not because he was scared of Walters, although he may have been, but because he had a lot to do. And because he was just a fidgety person. It made me nervous being around him for any length of time. He jiggled his foot, scratched his back, flipped through a magazine, jiggled his foot, etc.

Finally Maria picked up her phone, dialed, and hung up after a brief conversation. "Mr. Walters says you may come in now."

We entered a long, narrow office with the desk placed at the far end of the room so we had to hike over to it. Behind it, on the wall, was the standard Washington collection of photographs. Walters was another one who needed to be reminded of his importance.

He got up and came around the desk. "Frank. Tony," he said, holding out a tanned manicured hand. "Nice to see you. Glad you could make it." I smiled, not because I was glad to see him, but at the unintended irony of his greeting. We shook hands, and I remarked to myself on his nice grip.

"Why don't we have a drink?" he suggested. We stepped over to a bar near his desk where liquor, various set-ups, and ice had been placed. "Tony, how about you?" I took a bourbon. Elliott had a martini. Walters had Dubonnet.

We stood around, or rather sat, making small talk—politics, the weather, where Walters had been on his most recent trip, the stock market. But after a quarter of an hour Walters got up and suggested we go to his dining room, next door. We followed him in and sat down at the dining table. A maid appeared through a side door and began the ritual of switching the service plates and replacing them with identical china that had been warmed. Then another maid brought out the entrée—roast chicken, rice, green beans, and hot rolls. Coffee was served, water was poured, and we were left by ourselves.

Walters finally got around to the reason for the gathering. "Tony, I understand you're inquiring into the possibility that Senator Seld is being investigated."

"I've been told that's the case," I said.

"I suppose Frank told you that Layton called me to complain that you had accused him of being involved with Les Painter's murder," Walters said.

"I think he overstated, rather, uh, misrepresented, the conversation," I said.

"Not that it matters," Walters went on, "since the police have charged someone with Painter's murder and presumably that takes care of that."

"Petowski still gets a trial," I said.

"Of course," Walters said. "Of course. Certainly he does. But that isn't a matter you have to concern yourself with any further, I should think." I looked over at Elliott, but he wasn't saying anything. Nor me.

"My concern is that the *Journal* should behave responsibly. I know that Seld overstated what you said to him, but the implication and import of the questions you were asking are clear."

"I suppose that's true," I said. "I tried to be diplomatic, but I still have to do my job. That's what it's all about."

"Certainly," Walters said. "I just want us to behave responsibly when dealing with people who hold public office. They have a right to be presumed innocent, too. We should be on firm ground when we approach a public official with anything even remotely resembling an accusation. I would never stop a responsible story from appearing in the *Journal*. I think you know that," he said, turning on a paternal smile that was meant to communicate wisdom and understanding. "I simply don't want to do or print anything irresponsible. You agree with that, don't you?"

"Whose dictionary will we use?" I answered.

"I'm sure it won't come down to semantics," he said, with a nervous little laugh. "You fellows downstairs are all so dedicated and worried about your professional reputations. You have to remember, I have my reputation to be concerned about, too."

There was the heart of it. I had never come up against Walters before, so I was seeing and hearing this act for the first time. A pall of depression started falling over me.

Walters changed the subject and we finished off the meal with trivia. Elliott, who apparently had been suffering from temporary deafness and loss of speech while Walters was working me over, rejoined the conversation. We finished, and Walters let us go without offering his ring to be kissed. We merely shook hands, and he told me, "We really should get together more often."

Waiting for the elevator, I turned to Elliott. "You were a big help in there. I want to thank you for your support."

"Don't worry about it," Elliott said. "You're not going to have any trouble with him."

"Why the hell didn't you say something?" I was getting a little hot.

"For what?" Elliott said, getting angry himself. "You think arguing with him makes a difference? You think you get anywhere with confrontations over issues that haven't materialized yet? You think I deal with him and his obstructions by throwing my glove down every time I disagree with him? I can handle him. I have handled him, but I do it my way. You just get the stories. I'll get them in the paper if they're worth getting in and when they're ready to print. And let me worry about how I get to sleep at night. You guys think you're up against the whole goddamn world, that there's a conspiracy against reporters to suppress the truth. Give me a little credit, O.K.? And give a little thought to the possibility that your way isn't the only way. I'll be there when it counts, buddy boy, don't worry about that."

I was not convinced. I suppose if I had bought what Elliott had said entirely, I would have told him what I had found out about Painter and Seld. But I had learned a long time ago that there is no point in telling an editor something you know until the situation is ripe. Talking too soon is a sure way of losing control. Our meeting with Walters reinforced my reluctance to confide in Elliott. Since I didn't know what I was going to do, I had no intention of letting him direct me, or try to.

In the meantime, I had a date with William Rosecroft. I wasn't dying to go campaigning in the Midwest, but he was right about getting out of Washington. And I wanted to watch him if I could. I wanted to know everything about him that I could learn—for a lot of reasons.

14

Rosecroft had hired a medium-size jet for his next-to-last venture into Ohio. The scene at National Airport was about what you would expect when thirty or so adult men and women get together at six o'clock in the morning to board an airplane that they'd rather not be on. Some of the reporters looked as though they hadn't slept at all while others looked as if they still were sleeping. There were the usual crack-of-dawn jokes and speculation about whether the plane would (a) take off safely, (b) fly safely, and (c) land safely. Then there were questions about what time they would start serving liquor on board. That discussion went on for about ten minutes, an indication of the subject's importance.

Since I was making this trip by special invitation of the candidate, I was supposed to get preferred treatment. Goldsboro had told me I would be "taken care of." That turned out to mean that I got to sit with Goldsboro. Rosecroft sat by himself on the flight reading memos, making some notes, and signing letters.

Goldsboro and I made a stab at small talk for the first few minutes, then dropped the effort. I looked out the window at clouds and Peter spent a lot of time trying to memorize the back of his hand.

When we landed in Columbus, we were met by an efficient young guy who was probably about twenty-nine, a lawyer dying to come to Washington to help make it safe for democracy. All he had to do was get Rosecroft elected. He introduced himself to Rosecroft as Ted Winters.

"Ted, good to see you," Rosecroft said, giving his hand a firm squeeze. Rosecroft introduced Goldsboro, John Thompson, a member of the campaign staff in Washington, and then gestured over toward the reporters, without bothering even to try introducing us. Rosecroft and Thompson got into a car with Winters and a Secret Service agent. "The media," as they like to refer to us on political campaigns, were shunted off to a bus for the two-mile ride to the shopping center that was our first stop.

The shopping center took about two hours or so. Rosecroft gave a little speech about how important it was for the future of the Republic that he be the next President and then he went around shaking hands, patting matronly cheeks, and kissing middle-aged women. You've seen it all before.

From there we moved on to a luncheon meeting of an Ohio teachers' convention where Rosecroft was scheduled to talk about why education is a good thing and why more money should be spent on it. The speech was supposed to be non-political. Sure.

Goldsboro handed out the text of the speech on the bus. I thumbed through it. It started with a story about Socrates and went on from there. Nothing like letting your audience identify with the greats.

When we reached the hotel, the delegates were milling around outside the banquet hall like a bunch of hungry cattle waiting for the cowhands to bring the hay. We went right in. I found a seat at a table with some teachers, male and female, from Akron, Dayton, and Columbus. A couple of the women weren't bad, if you go in for that sort of thing. I was strictly business on this trip.

Rosecroft was up at the head table, fiddling around with his speech and picking at the over-cooked roast beef. When the time came, the master of ceremonies made a lame effort to joke about the non-political invitation to Rosecroft. He registered about a one point five on the laugh meter but persisted with a few more jokes and finally turned it over to Rosecroft.

Rosecroft quickly demonstrated why he was successful in politics. He got off to a snappy start, telling three jokes that got good laughs. Then he acknowledged the presence of some important officials at the head table and some "good friends" out in the audience. He moved skillfully on, tracking his text but not following it so slavishly that it sounded as if he were reading it.

"When I went to college after World War II, I had among my friends and classmates any number of men who were being educated by the United States of America through the G.I. Bill. That legislation was an investment not only in those young men, but in America," Rosecroft was saying. "We have a chance to make a similar kind of investment today, not just in our veterans, who should be getting higher benefits—and they will if legislation I am sponsoring passes—but we should also be investing in every child in America. When we begin to look on educators as a resource, on an educated populace as a resource, when we begin to see the money we spend on education as an investment in the future rather than in terms of tax dollars spent for buildings and salaries, then we will have made a giant stride toward mastering our problems." Here Rosecroft was of course interrupted by an ovation. It was like coming before a convention of dairymen to convince them that everyone should drink more milk.

The speech went on that way for about twenty minutes. I wasn't going to rush to a telephone to file a story on it—as a matter of fact I wasn't sure I would file anything at all while I was with Rosecroft. I might wait and do a Sunday wrap-up on him or on the Midwestern campaign. I hadn't decided, and the desk hadn't given me any clear instructions, either.

After lunch, Rosecroft was mobbed by teachers, most of them in their twenties and thirties, who wanted to shake his hand, tell him that they supported him, get his autograph, and have their picture taken with him. A lot of them had little Instamatics so that they could record all the fun-filled action of the twenty-third annual Mid-Ohio Education Association annual spring convention in Columbus. A few of the bolder women actually got to kiss Rosecroft, who kissed back, so they wouldn't think he was a wooden Indian.

Thompson was standing about five feet behind Rosecroft checking his watch as though he were clocking a thoroughbred. He was responsible for keeping Rosecroft on schedule. The Secret Service agents kept looking around at the hands and faces in the crowd around Rosecroft. For all the expression they showed, they might as well have been robots. They didn't smile, frown, flinch, cough, sneeze, or do anything else that would have given them away as mortal. They just stood there looking, occasionally putting out a gentle hand that would quickly become firm if resisted, to guide someone away from Rosecroft if it got too crowded.

After about fifteen minutes of this, Thompson went into his number, moving forward to spirit Rosecroft away. Rosecroft left the teachers wanting more, one of the first rules of show business.

From Columbus we were to fly to Detroit and go to an automobile plant in time for Rosecroft to shake hands with the workers coming off the assembly line. Labor was pushing Rosecroft hard in Michigan, Ohio, and everywhere else. Higgins was showing up well in the polls, despite his late start. He and Rosecroft were about even in those two states, Rosecroft was doing slightly better elsewhere and Higgins was showing up very strong in California, Oregon, and New York. It looked as though Higgins might just pull it off, despite what the experts said, or at least come damn close.

The handshaking at the Ford plant turned out to be a mistake. Not that anyone assaulted Rosecroft. It was worse than that. Most of the men coming off the line—and the women—ignored him. Campaign staffs don't seem to understand that when people get finished with a job they hate, the last thing they want is to be held up at the end of the day.

An official from the United Automobile Workers was there with a megaphone periodically announcing that "Senator Bill Rosecroft is here to shake your hand." Rosecroft stuck to it, acting as though the response here was as enthusiastic as it had been at lunch. He had his coat off, the sleeves of his light blue shirt rolled up, his tie pulled down and his top button open. That was his way of showing he understood the problems of the working man.

We did that for an hour or so. Then we were supposed to drive to Ann Arbor, where Rosecroft was giving a speech to the Students for Rosecroft after dinner with some of them. Rosecroft invited me to ride with him. At first we chatted sporadically, while I looked out the window at the flat countryside where the trees were opening new leaves and farmers were plowing to plant corn and soybeans. It gave me a comfortable feeling to see the land renewing itself that way, so it was all I could do to force myself away from the lulling tranquility to discuss politics. For once, though—maybe because he felt the same kind of mellowness—Rosecroft let down his guard. He gave me an honest appraisal of what was happening. He lapsed into a monologue and I tried to say as little as possible.

"I think it's going well," he began when I asked him again how his campaign was doing. "Higgins is showing up a lot stronger than I ever thought he would though. I misjudged his appeal, maybe because I don't understand it."

"Reaction against Washington?" I asked.

"That's part of it, I guess. A feeling in the country that Washington is manipulating the people, that the public's interest isn't being served because we're too busy with special interests.

For me there just doesn't seem to be a way to talk about the 'public interest' in meaningful terms. It's all right in speeches—people like to hear it—but they sure as hell don't care about the public interest when it conflicts with their own special concerns. That's why I can't understand the draw Higgins has. I don't think people understand the full effect of the things he stands for. That campaign reform bill you're so interested in. The net effect of that bill would be to make it harder for people to come together to express their common concerns.

"Higgins isn't a liberal and he isn't a populist. I'm not sure that there's a precedent for what he represents in American politics. He's a true believer. Something took hold of Phil while he was in the Senate. I don't know what it was. When he quit to form Americans Together, I figured it was just a ploy to win the nomination. That was fairly effective. But I'll be damned! I mean, he actually seems to believe what he tells people."

"Maybe that's what sells," I said softly.

"Maybe," Rosecroft agreed. "Maybe it is. But the medicine is stronger than people realize. The trouble is, the rhetoric of politics being what it is—fear-mongering and all—that when you really want to warn people about something, they've been given so many false alarms, they don't respond. You see what I mean?" He really wanted me to answer.

"I'm not sure that I agree, Senator. No offense intended, but I gave up caring a long time ago who gets elected President. Maybe

117

I'm jaded and maybe if Higgins shakes things up a little, either by getting the nomination or by delivering a message to whoever does, that might be useful."

"I think you're wrong, Tony," Rosecroft said. "I think you're underestimating the potential."

"Well, if it reaches that point, before the deluge I'll buy you and the companion of your choice dinner at the Jockey Club."

"And if I'm wrong?" Rosecroft asked gravely.

"Then you can have me and the companion of my choice to dinner at the White House."

"You're on," he said, breaking into a smile.

We were now on the outskirts of Ann Arbor, coming down Washtenaw Avenue past big houses set back from the road, some of them standing majestically on top of hills that sloped gracefully down across emerald green grass to the road.

In about five minutes' time, we were in the heart of the campus, moving toward the Michigan Union, where we were scheduled to stay for the night. The press was not invited to the dinner with the Students for Rosecroft, which was fine with me. I had an opportunity to sit down for a minute, have a drink, and think things over.

I called the *Journal* to let them know I was alive and well. When I got the desk, Melinda told me that Jim Hoskins wanted to speak to me. I told her to let me speak to Elliott first. We talked for about thirty seconds, just long enough for me to make sure that they weren't expecting a story out of me and to tell him that I didn't have anything for the next day's paper. Then I was switched to Hoskins on the foreign desk.

"Jim," I said, "it's Tony. Melinda said you wanted to talk to me. Did you hear from Fournier again?"

"Not directly. I cabled him this morning about something else. I got a reply from his office this afternoon."

"So?" I said.

"Gerard was struck by a hit-and-run driver near his apartment yesterday. He's dead."

I just sat there. I didn't say anything for a moment. I felt a little numb.

"What do we—what else did they tell you? Do they know who did it? Or why?"

"I asked for details, whatever they could give me. He was hit by a dark blue Peugeot, according to a woman in his building who was looking out the window. It was raining a little. It was dusk, apparently. The car didn't have lights on. They don't use them over there the way we do here. She couldn't see the license number. The car hit him, swerved a little, and just kept on going."

"Did it look deliberate?" I asked.

"Tony, the witness is a woman eighty-one years old. Apparently she didn't see all that much. Her judgments on what she did see are even more limited."

"I guess so," I said. Hoskins knew what I was thinking and why I wanted to know. I wasn't just concerned to know if Fournier had found out anything before he died. And my curiosity wasn't simply a professional reflex. Had Fournier been killed because I had put him on to something without giving him adequate warning? The worst of it was the uncertainty. Not knowing if it was a grisly accident or another murder. And if it was murder, why?

Hoskins, at any rate, had made up his mind. He didn't come right out and say so, but the cool tone in his voice made it clear. "I haven't said anything to anyone here about what Fournier was doing for you," he said. "I'm not going to unless I'm asked."

"Right," I said. I could have said a whole lot more, because I was getting mad, but blowing up wouldn't have served any purpose. I wasn't even sure who I was mad at. I supposed a whole lot of people—myself, Hoskins, the driver of that car, Fournier for not being more careful, the goddamn police, the world. Hoskins should have known better anyway. That's one of the chances you take when you go after a story. We don't give up covering wars for fear that a reporter will get killed, and sometimes they do. Still, I felt guilty and confused. "Thanks for telling me, Jim. Find out whatever else you can, if you would. I'd like to know whatever we can find out."

He said he would and I hung up.

I turned off the light and lay back on my bed, trying to make sense out of it. Three things had happened. Les Painter had been murdered. I had been beaten up. And Gerard Fournier had been killed, maybe murdered. I didn't know if they were connected, and if so, how. I didn't know what nerve I was touching, if I was touching anything at all. Seld? That might explain why I was beaten up, but what did Painter have? Swiss bank accounts? Possibly. What about the Arab Consortium? What the hell was that all about? I was going around in circles. I needed to know more. Ideally, I'd have liked to go to Geneva, to try to retrace Fournier's footsteps.

But that was out of the question and maybe unnecessary. Painter had been killed in Washington. I still had that angle to work, assuming his death and Fournier's were connected. If they weren't, it was possible that Fournier had been killed by accident or had found out something entirely unrelated to Painter's murder. Or maybe not.

Fournier's death was a ghastly thing, and it jarred me. I had stepped into something serious, threatening, and I was finding out that I'd been walking through a minefield. Only I was still in the middle of it. I could quit, but I knew I wouldn't. What I had to do was to take stock, figure out where I was and what I should do next. I would do that as soon as I got back to D.C., I told myself. But for the moment, I wanted to forget the whole damn thing.

15

The mood I was in, I would have preferred to take a pass on Rosecroft's speech that night. But that wouldn't have been professional, I reminded myself. I tucked away my questions in the back of my mind, got up, showered, and ate a quick dinner.

The auditorium where Rosecroft was speaking was comfortable and plush, seats spaced widely apart and covered in a blue velvet material. The lieutenant governor of Michigan, a Democract, was there to introduce him, and Rosecroft stayed off the stage until it was time for him to speak.

I thought it was kind of risky, from a political point of view, to use an auditorium so large. If Rosecroft couldn't fill the five hundred or so seats—and it was close to final examinations—it would make him look bad. But with twenty minutes to go before the speech, every seat was occupied. Then the students started standing in the side aisles and in the back, so that the hall was packed by the time he went on

The speech Rosecroft gave will not find its way into history books. Some of the remarks he had made at lunch were served up again to the students. He talked about the need for sacrifice, without ever telling them what they would have to give up. "I believe government can be a great force for good in this country of ours," Rosecroft told them. "We can fight poverty, ignorance, disease, discrimination, apathy, and decay. We can begin to restore a sense of national purpose in the land and begin again to seek out the destiny that the Founding Fathers foresaw when they gathered in Philadelphia two centuries ago to write one of the greatest documents in the history of man, the Constitution of the United States."

Rosecroft was sporadically interrupted by cheers from the fresh-faced boys and girls, who all looked well-fed, well-dressed, and well-housed, if you get my point. There wasn't a whole lot of alienation in this audience—no discontent, no gnawing anxiety that they were no longer part of what was happening in the country, no worry that the nation that was once the last best hope of the world was losing faith in itself. Rosecroft's campaign was based on the premise that the kind of comfort and self-assurance he found here was widespread. If it weren't, he couldn't do much to win. He simply was not the man to call the multitudes to battle.

When it was over, I made my way backstage and found Rosecroft talking to a group of students, for the most good-looking young men. One of them—tall, blond, and slim—was familiar. I had a hard time placing the face. Then I recognized him as the boy on the beach with Rosecroft in the picture I had seen on Rosecroft's desk in his Senate office.

Peter Goldsboro was standing off to the side. I went over and stood next to him. "What did you think?" he asked me.

"I've heard parts of it before," I said. "I'm relieved to hear that he's resolved one problem."

"What's that?" Goldsboro asked.

"Whether or not to come out in favor of the Constitution."

Goldsboro just frowned at me and started to turn away. "Is that Rosecroft's nephew over there?" I asked Goldsboro.

"What?" Goldsboro said, not quite hearing me at first. "Where?" I pointed, attempting not to appear too conspicuous about it. Rosecroft saw me out of the corner of his eye, gave me a quick nod and went on talking. "Yes," Goldsboro said. "It is. Let's go find someplace where we can get a drink."

"Peter, there's hope for you yet. Let's do that."

I was not nearly so optimistic as I might have sounded. The news of Fournier's death was still hanging over me. I had a feeling that I was wasting time, that I should be back in Washington trying to unravel the tangled strings I had gotten caught in.

Goldsboro and I caught a cab on the street. When we told the driver we wanted to go to a bar, he took us to a place called The Falcon, which turned out to be nice enough—a long bar that went the length of a narrow room, with tables in the middle and booths along the wall. Behind the bar, near the cash register, was an enormous stuffed bird, the falcon that I suppose gave the place its name.

Goldsboro and I found an empty booth and squeezed in. He ordered scotch and I asked for bourbon. "You don't seem to be your old arrogant self tonight, Peter," I said, by way of opening an evening of friendly drinking.

"What?" he said, as though I had distracted him from thinking about something else. "Oh. No, I'm not I guess. I have less reason to be arrogant than I did when you were in the office."

"Such as?"

"You'll find out soon enough anyway. The Gallup Poll next Sunday will show us trailing Higgins."

"How the hell did you find that out?" I asked him.

"Never mind. I don't think that it's deadly, you know, the end of the campaign for us or anything like that. But it sure as hell isn't going to make it any easier to go out and raise money. Private money will be harder to get, which means that Rosecroft will have to rely more on labor unions and other big organizations. That's just what Higgins wants. That way he can talk about that goddamn bill of his and start painting us black at the same time."

"So what do you do about it?" I asked.

"We have strategy meetings when we get back. Meetings until we're blue in the face. I used to think that politicians really knew what the hell they were doing—the successful ones anyway. You know, that they had an instinct for picking the right position. I thought I was pretty sophisticated because I understood that they didn't always *believe* in what they're doing. But the truth is worse. Most of the time they don't even *know* what they're doing. Rosecroft and the people he listens to are convinced that the *only* way he can win is with a low-key campaign. That's just a guess on their part, based on some polls they had done and their analysis of the mood of the country. If they're right, someone will say after the campaign that they're a bunch of geniuses. If they're wrong, they'll be idiots. But the only way anyone will be able to make a judgment is after the fact, and then it doesn't take much to figure what we should have done. This whole thing is a hell of a lot chancier than I ever thought it was."

"Cheer up. Maybe you'll find the formula to turn political lead into gold."

"Very funny," Goldsboro said.

"How was the dinner?" I asked.

"It was all right. There were about twelve students. They sat there playing 'Meet the Press' with Rosecroft. They were impressed with him, anyway."

"Was his nephew there?" I asked.

"Yes. Why? Why the hell are you so interested in his nephew? This is the third time you've asked about him."

"Is there some reason why I shouldn't be interested in him?"

"Not that I know of," Goldsboro said, "but what the hell's the difference?"

With that, we began to concentrate on drinking and the conversation degenerated into shop talk about personalities. That way, at least, we could work off our aggressions by expressing strong feelings without doing violence to each other. We must have stayed at it for about two or three hours, because it was about one o'clock by the time we started making our way back. Peter went off to look for a cigarette machine and I took the elevator up to my floor.

I was fishing for my key when I heard loud voices in the room across the hall. From the sound of it, they were right next to the door.

"You're ashamed of me," one voice was saying. "You're ashamed of me. You don't love me at all. You don't care about me at all."

"Alan," this voice was an older man's. "You're not being reasonable. You're twisting what I'm saying. You understand very well what the situation is, why I can't see you for a while. You've got to understand. We'll have plenty of time together—later."

"No, not later," the younger man said. "Never." The door opened and the young, blond man came out and turned down the hall. Right behind him was William Rosecroft, dressed in a bathrobe, his face flushed. "Alan," Rosecroft said in a loud whisper. "Alan, come back here."

"Go to hell," Alan shouted. Rosecroft started after him and then for the first time saw me standing there. He stopped and stood looking at me for a minute. Then he just backed into his room and closed the door without saying another word.

I stood there for a minute trying to clear my head. I wasn't sure what it was that I had just witnessed, but my doubts about Rosecroft and his "nephew" were increasing. I didn't like to pry into family affairs, but I was beginning to wonder if that was what it was.

In fact, it sounded to me more like a lovers' quarrel. I wasn't ready to accept the full implications of that yet, but it was beginning to look more and more as though I was going to have to deal with it.

16

If I slept that night, it wasn't for long. The phone woke me at six-thirty and we were out at Willow Run Airport by seven-thirty.

Rosecroft was all business on the way out. Thompson was briefing him on who he would be seeing, what the local problems were, where the tender spots were and how to avoid them.

When we got to the airport, Thompson went off to make a call and Goldsboro to do an errand. Rosecroft and I found ourselves alone for a moment. "I'm sorry you had to witness that nasty little family scene last night," he said to me. "My nephew gets a little overwrought sometimes. He's a strange boy. The family tries to be understanding with him. Sometimes I think we're a little too indulgent, but now we have to live with it, for better or worse."

I didn't know what to say. "It's a difficult time in a person's life," was about the best I could manage.

"In his case it's even worse," Rosecroft said. "His father died when he was an infant, so in a certain sense I've been like a father to him, making sure that his education was taken care of, that sort of thing. I've tried to keep that part of my private life private, if you understand my meaning," he said, looking at me for assurance.

"I think you're entitled to a private life, Senator."

"That's nice to hear," Rosecroft said with a smile. "Sometimes I think you fellows think that public life requires us to make every aspect of our lives public.

"Only when it's relevant," I said.

Thompson came back to give some information to Rosecroft and then we all got on the plane. The rest of the day consisted of repeating the same basic drill in six or seven cities and towns in western Michigan. We would land at an airport, drive to Rosecroft headquarters, where he would start shaking hands enthusiastically with the volunteers working for him. The operation was identical in each place, since the Washington campaign office had issued a manual of instructions. But, ever the politician, Rosecroft acted each time as though he had never heard it before.

Lunch—tuna fish sandwiches on white bread with the crust trimmed off—was served in the Kalamazoo headquarters. We hit Battle Creek, Grand Rapids, Benton Harbor, Muskegon, Ludington, Manistee, and Traverse City before the day was over. By that time, I was dragging. Goldsboro didn't make it off the plane in Traverse City. On the plane, Rosecroft looked beat, although he had shaved and changed his clothes twice during the day.

Then flying back to Washington we ran into a front over the mountains—rain, wind, lightning. It didn't bother me particularly, except to make me even more tired. We finally landed around one-thirty a.m. Since it was now Saturday, I looked forward to sleeping late in the morning and a day of rest. Then I could begin examining the pieces that had turned up.

My hopes were cut short at nine, when the phone rang.

"Mr. Jordan?" she said. "Mr. Jordan, this is Harriet Olmstead."

"Oh, yes," I said, trying not to sound too weary.

"I hope I'm not calling too early."

"Not at all," I said. "I'm a follower of the teachings of Benjamin Franklin."

"So am I," she said emphatically. "I hope you can help me."

"I'll certainly try, Mrs. Olmstead." If the truth were known, I didn't want to help her at all. Harriet Olmstead was a snob and a hypocrite, a woman who used her money to collect interesting people around her as a way of covering her essential emptiness.

"I am having a hostess's nightmare," she said in that bored-with-life way she had. "The Argentine ambassador was called back to B.A. last night. I'm left with an unescorted woman and thirteen at my table. I'm hoping you'll get me out of a frightful jam by giving us the pleasure of your company."

"Well, I'd like to say yes..." thinking about what I had to do.

She cut me off. "Senator Daniels suggested that I call you. She said she had a feeling that you were free tonight and that you'd enjoy it."

"I'd like to come very much," I said, surprising myself at the way I was leaping at an opportunity to procrastinate.

"Oh, wonderful," she said, showing signs of life. "Come about eight-thirty. We dress for dinner."

"I wouldn't have it any other way," I said.

We hung up and then I dialed Charlotte. From the sound of her voice, she was still in bed. "One good turn deserves another," I said.

"What?"

"You put Harriet Olmstead up to calling me about dinner tonight. I had plans of sleeping till noon and maybe staying in bed all weekend."

"If it's any consolation to you," she said, "I think you're much more attractive than the Argentine ambassador. Are you coming?"

"Yes."

"Why don't I pick you up?"

"Why don't you."

"Eight forty-five," she said.

"We were invited for eight-thirty," I protested.

"Make it nine, then. That's even better. See you." She hung up.

I spent the rest of the day absorbed in trivia. In fact I sought out trivia as a way of avoiding everything that had happened in the last three days. I was going to have to come to grips with it sooner or later, but I couldn't get myself to focus. Yet the questions dogged me all day, so that I couldn't relax either.

My bell rang at eight-thirty. I had just climbed out of the shower, and my hair was wet, my face covered with shaving soap and my body with a formerly elegant terrycloth bathrobe I had lifted from a hotel in Paris. I opened the door to find Charlotte, impatiently tapping her foot.

"Don't you look nice," she said.

"I have a vague recollection that you said you wanted to be as late as possible," I said.

"I got bored," she said. "Finish getting ready and I'll make us a drink." She took off the spring coat she was wearing and dropped it on a chair. Her red hair was pulled into a pretty bun at the back of her head, she had a single strand of pearls around her neck, and she was wearing an emerald green long dress with a scoop neck. The combination of the dress, her hair, her pale white skin, and the perfume was staggering.

"We could forget about dinner," I said.

"The way you look right now," she said, "you're in no shape to make propositions. Just get dressed."

I shaved, put on my tuxedo and came out to let her do the bow tie.

"Who ties it when there's no one around?" she asked.

"I do it myself."

"So why am I doing it?"

"It gives me a chance to see if your hair is natural or dyed," I said.

I had to do a quick shuffle to keep her from stepping on my foot. "How was your trip with Rosecroft?" she asked.

"Exhausting, boring, and fascinating," I said.

"All at once?"

"No, at different times. Maybe we can talk about it later. I'll tell you what happened. One thing was very interesting."

"Why not now?" she asked. "The later we are the better. Harriet Olmstead will think we were someplace else first. Otherwise, she'll think you and I would have been left without a thing to do if she hadn't called."

"This is all much too complicated for me," I said. "We can talk about it later. Being late makes me nervous."

I picked up her coat and helped her on with it. She turned around, put her hands on my face, and smiled at me. "You *are* cute, even if you're compulsive." She kissed me, turned, and opened the door. I followed her out.

We were not the last guests to arrive at Harriet Olmstead's. The others included the Secretary of Interior, Harold W. Grosvenor and his wife, Martha; Edward X. Dunphy, the oil lobbyist, and— I don't know where Mrs. Dunphy was, if there was a Mrs. Dunphy;

Senator Horace Bullman, Republican of Oklahoma, and his wife, Clarissa; Thomas W. Adams, who was rich and known for being well-known, and his wife; Samuel Reid, a prominent architect, also equipped with a wife; Leonard Terry, a hard-nosed, successful Washington lawyer who was very political, with his wife, Irene. And Charlotte and me. The Grosvenors and the Bullmans were the last to arrive, as befitted their place in the pecking order. Bullman had been elected by the voters of Oklahoma, but it was lucky for his constituents that their interests coincided with the oil companies', because Bullman represented oil, not his constituents.

We all sat, or stood, around drinking for about an hour. Harriet Olmstead was everywhere, nosing in and out of conversations, speaking with that wonderful facility that upper-crust Easterners have, through clenched teeth. With her things were always "marvelous," "fabulous," and "just grand." She had a seemingly bottomless curiosity, listening with rapt attention and total concentration to a discussion on any topic, regardless of complexity, for ninety seconds. At that point, reacting as though she suddenly remembered she had a train to catch, she would extricate herself from the conversation, always promising to return to finish it later.

Not to say that she was stupid, because she wasn't. She had a reasonably good mind. She read. She knew what was going on, after a fashion. Her way of demonstrating commitment was to take out her checkbook. Generations of civil rights leaders, civil libertarians, and antiwar leaders had flocked to her house in Georgetown to shake the money tree. She cultivated that image of caring about deeper issues. But when the time came for a little fun, she found her company not among the dissidents or even the mavericks of Washington's political society, but right in the middle of the conservative power structure.

All in all, this evening did not promise to be my idea of a rollicking good time. Senator Bullman and Dunphy, the lobbyist, were over in a corner talking in code. Whatever it was that they were discussing, it probably involved the violation of at least a dozen federal statutes. Dunphy, with his face flushed not from merriment but from the explosion of tiny little blood vessels caused by excessive drinking, was one of the most accomplished practitioners of the art of lobbying in Washington. Some of the biggest corporations in America were his clients, including three major oil companies. He generally took on clients to help them with legislation, rather than dealing with problems they might have with the executive branch. Dunphy saw to it that senators and congressmen who could help his clients were remembered during election campaigns with healthy contributions; sometimes they were even remembered when election campaigns were still over the horizon.

So there we all were, a gathering of rich and powerful people—excluding me—getting together for dinner in Georgetown, just like it says in all the magazine stories.

When we finally went in for dinner, I was put down at Mrs. Olmstead's end of the table, with Eleanor Reid sitting on one side of me and Janice Adams on the other. Mrs. Adams and I established fairly quickly that we wouldn't enjoy being marooned alone together on a desert island. Eleanor Reid, whom I already knew, was another story. The only problem we had in talking in this setting was keeping the conversation sedate enough to suit the surroundings. She liked to plumb me for gossip and I liked to oblige when I could. Eventually, we got on to the subject of Les Painter and whether I thought Moose Petowski was guilty or not. Before I could even begin to discuss it, Bullman, who was sitting across the table, stuck in his two cents' worth.

"Well, if he's guilty, the police ought to let him go and public-spirited citizens ought to give him a reward. Whoever killed Painter performed a public service. I don't believe a more irresponsible SOB ever sat down in front of a typewriter. If he didn't have a scandal, he invented one."

Others at the table started to speak, but Bullman was just warming up. "He even called me—after all those stories he'd written about me—to ask if I knew anything about some Thursday Night Club!"

"Did you?" I asked.

"I suppose you want to write about it now?" Bullman challenged me, belligerently.

"No, not particularly. I was just curious," I said.

"Well, it's nothing at all," Bullman said. "I don't know anything about it. Painter told me that Steve Snyder, Bill Rosecroft, and some other members of Congress were in it."

"Who is Snyder?" Mrs. Adams asked.

"He's a congressman from Ohio," Bullman said. "One of those liberals who's going to make Congress into an effective instrument of government. I don't know what we'd do without all these young know-it-alls here to tell us how to run things right."

"Get a lot more done, Horace," Dunphy chirped in from the other end of the table.

"I think so," Bullman said. "When I came to Washington twenty years ago, being in the Senate was a good job. If Congress worked hard—and we always did—we were done with our work in nine or ten months, including a few recesses now and then. We didn't set out to legislate away every problem facing mankind. We didn't have all these regulations and restrictions that we've since imposed on ourselves. And the press respected us for public service. When Painter came along, things began to change. He did stories about individual men, making controversy where there was none and blowing little things all out of proportion. He was successful, so other reporters started picking it up and it became the vogue, so to speak. We were fair game for everyone. No private life at all, no respect for the sacrifices we were making."

I couldn't keep my mouth shut any longer. "What sacrifices are those, Senator?" I asked.

"Financial, for one. I could be earning two or three times what I'm earning now. Privacy for another—someone's always poking into my affairs or nosing around the family. I don't like it at all. I mean, for example, it's none of your business what my income is," Bullman said, his face flushing. "That's the point I'm trying to make, Jordan."

"Maybe," I said. "But maybe you recieve income from holdings that would raise questions about the way you do your job, so that someone might wonder if you had anything on your mind besides the well-being of the republic."

"Young man, are you accusing me of having a conflict of interest?" he shouted, becoming choleric.

"I'm not accusing you of anything," I answered. "I'm just pointing out why someone might be interested in your income—how much it is and where it comes from. If you want to keep something like that private, I think you probably have to stay in private life."

"That's the kind of attitude that bastard Painter had," Bullman said.

"I think," Harriet Olmstead said, ever so calmly but firmly, "that we'll have coffee in the living room." We started to get up. Mrs. Olmstead came over to me. "It's so marvelous to have a spirited discussion at a party," she gushed, "as long as it doesn't become personal or get out of hand. I'm so glad you could come this evening and I hope you'll be able to come again. You mustn't take

Horace too seriously. I certainly don't. If I did, I couldn't stand to have him around. But I don't think he means all those outrageous things he says, do you?"

"He's been saying them for twenty years," I said. "If his real feelings are any different, he's managed to keep them a closely held secret."

She gave me an indulgent little laugh and patted the arm she had been holding as we walked from the dining room. "Just don't take him so seriously," she said maternally.

The rest of the evening was spent with the guests in small clumps of conversation. Bullman and I stayed away from each other and when he and his wife left, he managed to say goodbye to everyone but me. Manners don't count for much in Washington. It's nice if you have them, but not critical if you don't. Some politicians owe their careers to organized crime. Others learn to survive by ignoring everything that's rotten in the country they're supposed to be governing. The man at the top periodically has to make life-and-death decisions. In that kind of a situation, things can get pretty raw. Even in Georgetown it's recognized that civilization is a thin veneer, that everyone is in the same rat race and you do what you have to in order to stay ahead. You meet a lot of rough people here who you might expect would be counted out of polite society. You might expect that, but you'd be wrong. What counts isn't money, which is nice to have, or breeding, which also helps. What really counts is power, and as long as you have that, Washington is a very forgiving place.

Charlotte and I left shortly after the Bullmans. When we got to the street, I was engulfed by the smell of honeysuckle that hung over Georgetown. It was a warm evening. Charlotte took my arm and walked close to me as we made our way slowly toward her car. I held the door open for her and then got in behind the wheel. She leaned across the seat, put her arm around me and kissed me. "Let's go for a swim at my place," she whispered in my ear.

When we got back to her house, she dug out a swim suit and a terrycloth beach robe for me. I changed and wandered out to the back of the house, where the pool was. The lights were on, but she had turned them down so that they cast a soft glow over the pool. The apron of the pool was black slate and the pool itself, which was about forty feet long, was black tile, making the water murky and sensual. I slipped into the water and took a dive. Because of the blackness, I had the illusion of being in a bottomless pond. I swam that way as long as I could and then surfaced, gasping for breath.

The lights around the pool had been turned off. I stayed where I was, treading water. I smelled the honeysuckle again, so sweet and seductive. I could hear Charlotte slipping through the water toward me. She swam past to the end of the pool, turned back to me and put her arms around me. "It's nice out here," she said softly.

"It beats arguing with Horace Bullman, anyway."

"Could you do something for me?" she asked.

"As long as it's legal," I said.

"Pour us some brandy and make a fire while I dry off." She pulled herself against me and I realized that she hadn't bothered to put on a bathing suit. She kissed me again. "I'll be out in a minute."

I went inside, took off my wet suit, and put on the robe she had given me. I got the fire going and poured Courvoisier into two snifters from the bar. Then I lay down on my back on the thick rug in front of the fire. She came in wearing a black robe and put her head down on my chest. "Are you tired?" she asked softly.

"Tired," I said, "but still breathing."

"That's a relief. I was worried I might have to spend the night alone." She raised herself up on her elbows and looked dreamily into the fire, which accentuated the redness of her hair against her pale skin. She slipped a hand inside my robe and started caressing my neck and chest. I closed my eyes. Slowly she opened my robe, and then lowered herself on top of me, her ripe, full breasts on my chest, her hands moving over my body, her lips caressing me.

"Tony," she whispered, "I want you."

We made love by the fire, with her taking the lead and then gently yielding to me as I felt an overpowering desire for her.

Later, we slipped into her bed and lay there talking. She had one leg thrown over mine and I was slowly gliding my fingers over her back. "It would be nice if we could just stay like this," she said.

"When I suggested it you wouldn't even give the idea a fair hearing," I told her.

"That was in a rational moment. I'm in a romantic mood right now."

"Should we talk business for a while?" she asked, later.

"If it makes you happy," I said.

"What happened with Rosecroft?"

I gave her a detailed account of the trip, including the report on

Seld, Fournier's death, everything that I had seen and heard of the incident with Rosecroft and the boy. "It was all so strange," I said. "Here was this pretty boy sounding like a twenty-year-old girl whose lover had just told her off. I might pass that off as effeminate immaturity, except that Rosecroft didn't say anything when he saw me standing there. Even if he was upset, he might have said something to acknowledge my presence. Instead he ducked back into his room as though he had been caught at something."

"Do you remember what I told you about Rosecroft?" she asked. "That he never touched me?"

"So?"

"So maybe he likes boys."

"I have trouble believing it, but I'm beginning to think so. Anyway, I'm going to have to let Rosecroft drop for the time being. The stuff with Seld and the Swiss bank account is a lot more immediate. I feel responsible for Fournier. I ought to at least try to find out why that happened, assuming it was deliberate."

"And you do assume?" she said.

"Maybe I'm paranoid," I said. "But I do. Anyway, as long as we're talking business and sharing secrets, you can share one with me."

"Which is?"

"How you ever got the President to sign that mining bill for Nevada," I said.

"You *would* have to ask," she said. "Promise me on your solemn oath that you'll go to jail and remain silent even if they use the rack on you to find out?"

"I promise on the First Amendment."

"After Theodore died and I was appointed to fill out his term, I decided that I wanted to stay here and that I could be as successful as any man in handling the job. The way I could prove it was to get that bill through, since my husband had been trying to for six or seven years without success. I was a little slow to come to some pretty basic understandings about a lot of things, but when I did it made it much easier."

"Could you elaborate on that?" I asked.

"Well, it took me a while to remember it, if I had forgotten. The President is commander-in-chief, head of our government, sovereign, chief of state, and head of his party. But the President of the United States is also a man. I'm an attractive woman," she said, smiling, "and when I found the President attracted, I took advantage of it.

"I was at one of those state dinners, for the premier of Italy I think it was. The President danced with me a couple of times, paid a lot of attention to me, kept holding me very close. So I decided at one point to raise the mining bill. He didn't miss a beat. 'Come over one day next week and we'll talk about it,' he said. I thought he was being polite, but I got a call from the White House asking me to come the next Friday afternoon.

"When I got there, I expected he would have some of his aides, but he sent Jackson out when I came in, and told him to make sure we weren't disturbed. We sat on the couch over by the fireplace for a while and talked about the bill. The President told me why he had found it so difficult to support it, and I told him why it was important that it go through. I was frank. I told him my career in the Senate was hanging in the balance.

"He didn't give me an answer yes or no. Instead, he asked me if he could show me around the Oval Office. I didn't think there was much to see, but I said why not. He fiddled around with this and that and then said, 'Let me show you the secret of my success.' He led me into a little anteroom off the Oval Office where there was a double bed made up. 'I take a nap in here every day for at least half an hour,' he told me. Well," she said, "one thing led to another. The idea of making love to the President right in the Oval Office appealed to me in a kinky sort of way. And he was not bad, not bad at all for a man of his age and with all the things he has to think about."

"Apparently he doesn't think about them as much as you imagine he does," I said.

"You may be right. I got another call about a week later telling me that the President wanted me to come up to Camp David that weekend as his guest to go over details about the bill."

"And you went?"

"I went. I had a delightful time! His wife was off planting trees and receiving the Mother of the Year Award in California. He's a fascinating man up close," she said.

"You ought to know," I said, wincing as she poked me in the ribs.

"You're interesting, too," she said, "though maybe not quite so powerful as the President of the United States."

"It all depends on how you mean it," I said, pulling her close.

17

Monday morning, after spending the weekend with Charlotte, I finally pulled myself together and began checking back with sources to see if I could open up anything new. I called my friend in the U.S. Attorney's office to see of they had anything on Seld and Swiss bank accounts. First he was coy, but finally he was direct. "We don't have anything like that at all," he told me. "We haven't determined finally and completely that we're dealing with funny money here. Internal Revenue is still doing a net worth on Seld to see if there's income there that we can't account for. The Swiss bank route would certainly make it more difficult for us, but we just haven't reached that stage yet. I'll tell you what, though, Tony. . . ."

"Yes?"

"If you find anything, you let me know, O.K.?"

"One way or another, you'll know," I said.

"I'm not sure what that means."

"I'm not either. Don't press it."

"See you, buddy," he said.

I talked to Hoskins on the foreign desk to see what he had found out about Fournier's death. But there wasn't much. Fournier had taken a week off from his regular job as a correspondent for *Le Temps de Paris* to work on something. He had not told his desk what it was, but he did say that it could be a very important story (*"une histoire très importante"*) that they would be interested in. That, I decided after thinking about it, could mean almost anything. That kind of bait is what every reporter gives his editor in order to get time without being specific about what it's for. If it doesn't work out, you just tell your editor it didn't work out. But if you tell him too much, then his juices are set to digest a meal you can't serve, and no matter what you put down in front of him, he wants to know where that steak is that you promised him. So Fournier may have had something big, or maybe he just was looking to screw around for a week. I told Hoskins to keep checking.

I went to see a friend of mine in the Senate—not a senator but an aide to one. This friend, who shall remain nameless at his request, was in a position to watch a lot of traffic. He knew the gossip on the Hill, knew who was getting what from whom, who was doing what to whom, and generally where the bodies were buried. One of the reasons he knew so much was that he made no judgments about his information. He was part of the Southern power structure, and if the devil had a vote, my friend would deal with him, if the cost weren't too high.

He sat in his little office, tucked away from the commotion of the Senate, and smoked his pipe, smiling at me with his big moon face. "Sump'in to drink?" he asked me.

"Coffee?" I said.

"How about a little of this?" he asked, pulling a Mason jar of clear liquid from his drawer.

"What?"

"This here is one hundred per cent, two hundred proof white lightnin', boy," he said. "It'll fix you up real good."

"All right," I said.

He pushed a button on his phone. "Marylou, honey, bring us in some clean glasses please."

A girl about twenty came in with two tumblers. She had lacquered hair in a bouffant, a miniskirt left over from the late sixties, and nice legs. "Thank you, honey," he said. She smiled and left. "Can't type or take dictation worth shit," he said after she closed the door. "But she's one fine piece of ass."

"I hate to keep you from your work this way," I said.

"For you, sir, it's no trouble. Drink up."

I took a sip and felt it burn its way down to my stomach. "Is there an antidote for this?"

"This is fine moonshine, boy. I was raised on this stuff. I am living proof that it is wonderful for you."

All this fooling around was not time wasted. Dealing with Southerners is special. One has to take the time to socialize, to talk about nothing in particular, to appear to be in no hurry, as though one has come upon a Bedouin in the desert. To rush to take up the business at hand would be bad form.

"Whatcha been workin' on?" he asked me.

"A couple of things," I said. "I'm watching Higgins's bill and the Quilling bill and doing some other stuff. Want to give me a prognostication?"

"Well," he said, sucking on his pipe, "the Quilling bill will make it, though it's going to be close. I guess folks thought it was all right when we were buying Arab oil and paying them peanuts, but now they don't like it when the shoe's on the other foot. So I guess Quilling can get the votes.

"Now the Higgins thing is a different story. It might not make it this time, but if he gets himself elected President, then he'll probably get his way after he's inaugurated. Personally I don't give a damn one way or the other, but I don't have to tell you that bill will make some fundamental changes in the way things are done around here.

"You didn't say anything about the other matter you were working on," he said, drawing on his pipe while holding a match over the bowl.

"Which is?" I said.

"Which is Layton Seld and the missing money."

"Jesus Christ!" I said. "How did you find out about that?"

"Just cuz I look dumb, talk dumb, and act dumb doesn't mean that I *am* dumb," he said. "Your business is to know what's going on. And my business is to know what's going on."

"Maybe you can help me then," I said.

"I can try."

"If Seld took money from his last campaign," I said, "and I emphasize the 'if,' then where did it go?"

139

"It would be nice to know, wouldn't it?"

"You're a big help," I said.

"No, I'm serious. It would be. I really don't know, though."

"How about money leaving the country?" I said.

"Keep going," he said.

"Into a Swiss bank account."

He smiled. "That's slick. Too slick for a slob like Seld. He would have had to find some way to transfer the money, someone to transfer it to who would do the arrangements. He couldn't do it himself."

"Do you know something about it?" I asked.

"I don't know anything. I'm just thinking about how it might have happened. I'll tell you what, though."

"What?"

"I hope you or somebody else gets that sleazy som-bitch. He owed us a vote a couple of months ago and welshed on it. We ain't gonna get mad, but we're sure as hell gonna get even."

"You got any suggestions about how to find out more?"

"Well," he said, "Seld has got a lot of unhappy people on his staff. He doesn't pay them worth shit and then expects them to work twenty hours a day. Why don't you talk to some of his secretaries?"

"Maybe I should do that," I said. "Tell me something else while we're on the subject of dirty linen. Do you know anything about the Thursday Night Club?"

"You mean that stag dinner thing Steve Snyder organized?"

"I guess that's what it is," I said.

"It's some group of high-type senators and congressmen that gets together once a month or so with young interns—you know, college students who work on the Hill. They spend a lot of time drinking and talking about good government and that civics bull-shit."

"Any women in it?" I asked.

"No. No. It's stag. Men only. Why?"

"I'm not sure. Someone was saying something about it at dinner the other night and when I asked about it, he wouldn't tell me what it was."

"Les Painter was in here asking me about it a couple of weeks before he was killed," my friend said.

"What did you tell him?" I asked.

"What I told you," he said. "That's all I know. Anyway. The other thing I know is there's a vote in five minutes and I've got to get over to the floor. If you need anything more on Seld, I'll try to help. I'll be talkin' atcha real soon," he said in an exaggerated drawl.

I left feeling not much closer to solving anything, but glad that he had given me an idea about how to proceed. I got hold of a *Congressional Staff Directory*, went through it to see who was on Seld's staff and then looked at some directories from six years ago to figure out who had been on the staff at least that long. I finally picked out one woman, and that night I drove over to her house.

She lived on Calvert Street, just west of Wisconsin Avenue, in one of those brick row houses that so well express the mind and temperament of the federal bureaucracy. Each house neat, trim, and exactly like the one next to it, sturdy, functional, and without a spark of imagination to give it distinction—the sort of place one buys in middle age to grow old in, picking the crab grass and the creeping vines away in summer, raking the leaves in autumn, shoveling snow in winter, and digging up the flower beds in spring.

My secretary had a coarse mat in front of the door where people could wipe their shoes before entering. In winter, she probably had a box on the porch where she left her boots, to keep dirt and disorder from invading her home.

I rang. It took a minute or so for her to come to the French door. She took a look at me through the glass. I told her my name and showed her my press card, and she opened the door by unlocking two security locks on it.

"I'm Tony Jordan from the *Journal*."

"I know who you are. What do you want?" she said. It was not the warmest welcome I've ever received.

"I wanted to talk to you if I could, for a minute."

"About what?"

"Your job."

She stood blocking the door. She gave me an indulgent smile. "I really don't see what could possibly interest you about my job."

"Maybe you underestimate yourself," I said. "Give me a chance. I may open horizons for you, expose vistas that you never imagined. Give me fifteen minutes. If you aren't satisfied by then, return the unused portion and you'll get double your money back."

She didn't smile. It wasn't all that funny, but she could have given way a bit. Well, she did finally unlock the door and let me in. Her living room was a living room, nothing to get excited about. It

141

had a couch, some chairs, a wooden table, a landscape on the wall. A window air conditioner groaned noisily in one corner of the room. There was a floor lamp in another corner and one table lamp. All in all, it looked like the waiting room in a doctor's office.

"This is very nice," I said with all the sincerity I could muster.

"Oh, no," she said, blushing, "it really isn't. I mean, it's nothing at all."

"Did you get the couch in Georgetown?" I asked.

"No, from Sears," she said.

"That print is really very nice," I said, gesturing toward the landscape. "It has a pleasant effect. It's a nice touch."

"Would you like some coffee?"

"I'd love some," I said. Coffee was a foot in the door. Once someone offers food or drink, they assume the role of host or hostess and you are a guest, even if you're a reporter. Then they have to be polite.

She excused herself, went out to the kitchen, and came back with two cups of coffee on a tray with skim milk and sugar. The coffee was the instant kind. Awful.

I made a stab at sounding as if I were apologizing for bothering her at home. "I would have spoken to you at the office about this, but I've been busy and I know how someone as conscientious as you are gets worried if she gets behind in her work. So I thought it would be better if I talked to you when you were more relaxed. I would have called this afternoon, but I didn't know until an hour ago that I could make it this evening."

"I'll try to help you if I can," she said. "But I really don't think you're going to be interested in anything I have to say."

"Well, let me judge that. How long have you been with Senator Seld?"

"Eight years."

"You're his confidential secretary, right?"

"Wait a minute," she said. "I'd like to know what all of this is for."

"Oh, I'm sorry," I said. "I thought I told you. I'm trying to do a piece on Senate staffs, you know the people who makes the offices work, who handle the non-glamorous but essential details."

"It's about time," she laughed. "Yes, I am his confidential secretary."

"What does that entail for you? What do you actually do?"

"I take dictation from the Senator, but not run-of-the mill things. Usually he gives me letters that are more..." She paused groping for a word.

"Sensitive?" I asked.

"Sensitive," she agreed. "Then I handle his social calendar, arrange his trips for him, make sure that he has hotel reservations, plane tickets, cash to spend, those kinds of things."

"Does Senator Seld travel a lot?" I asked.

"Oh, sure," she said. "He's away at least once a week, sometimes more."

"Who handles arrangements when he goes abroad?" I asked.

"Well, it depends what the trip is for. If it has something to do with Senate business, the State Department may make the arrangements or I may, depending. If it's not Senate business, then I probably would. Foreign trips are a real pain in the you-know-what to arrange." She smiled. I gave her an understanding smile back. The conversation was starting to get risqué.

"Does he go abroad a lot?" I asked.

"It depends what you call a lot. He goes two or three times a year."

"Where does he go?" I asked.

"All over," she said. "Look, excuse me, but I don't see what that has to do with what I do."

"Bear with me," I said. "Has he gone to Geneva recently?"

She just sat there for a minute, and I knew that I had blown it. When she answered, it was with that strained sort of politeness that reporters often get, as though I had asked her out of the blue to show me the contents of her lingerie drawer, or how often she had sex. She didn't want to answer. She couldn't quite bring herself to tell me to buzz off and she couldn't quite conceal her feeling that only some kind of moral misfit would be asking these kinds of questions. If you stay in the business long enough, either you begin to feel like a moral misfit, or you become one.

"I was just curious whether he had been to Geneva recently," I said. "It isn't a big deal."

"Well, I don't think I ought to be talking to you like this," she said. "I think if you want to speak to me, you should call the Senator's press secretary, Marion Wilson, and arrange an interview through him."

"That seems like a lot of trouble to go through," I said. "Why don't you just let me run through my questions with you since we've already started."

"No," she said, "I think you should call Mr. Wilson to do this. I shouldn't have agreed to speak with you in the first place."

"I don't understand," I said. "We were doing nicely until I mentioned Geneva. Is there something about Geneva that's sinister?"

"I just think you should call Mr. Wilson," she said. "That's the proper way to do it. And now I don't want to seem rude, but if you've finished your coffee, I'd like you to leave."

I know when I'm not welcome. I'm very sensitive to subtle signals people send out. I decided that she probably didn't want to talk to me any more. So I gave her my card and told her that if she had a change of heart, she should call me. I stood on the porch for a minute and listened to her lock both the security locks on her front door and then turn off the living-room light. If she had had shutters to close, she would have done that, too.

That visit was only the first of many I made to members of Seld's staff that week. Some people think that reporters in Washington sit around waiting for someone to drop stolen government documents into their hands so that they can expose a scandal. I was beginning to wish that someone would drop a document into my hands. All that happened was that I met two kinds of reactions—those like the one I just described, and a really warm, sincere, friendly, eager-to-help kind of reaction. The trouble was that when they were willing, it turned out that they didn't know anything. I was beginning to think I would go back for a second try at the confidential secretary when I got a call from Elliott asking me to come in to see him.

"Our campaign coverage is flat," he told me. "Our stories don't give any drama, don't get beneath the surface at all, don't capture the idea that a power struggle is going on. We're not getting a good picture of the candidates. That piece you did for us after your trip with Rosecroft in the Midwest was good. We need more of that."

"I've always said I was a fine reporter," I told him. "And underrated. I'm glad you're finally turning to me for advice on how to handle the news. You need intelligent advice, and you'll get it from me."

"I don't want your goddamn advice," Elliott said. "I want you to let go of the Senate for a while and cover the campaign."

"Are you kidding?" I said. "I don't mind an occasional trip, but a steady diet? I hate politics."

"Tough shit," he said. "I didn't ask what you want. *I* want you to."

"It's nice to be consulted once in a while about one's preferences."

"That may work for preparing the family meals, but I'm not going to run my staff like that. I want you to pick up the Higgins campaign. I want you to work at it day and night. Work with those people, eat with them, sleep with them. I want to get a feel for that campaign. Don't worry about daily stories unless something strong happens. Concentrate on several longer pieces. I want a piece about the volunteer effort—how it was that Higgins had an organization ready to get off to a running start when he declared. I want a profile of Higgins. I want a piece about the way he campaigns. I want another one on what his candidacy means, whether it's more politics as usual or if it's a departure from tradition. I want you to use your head and come up with some stories of your own."

"I don't want to do it," I said quietly. "I'm working on something important and I don't want to take the time for political bullshit."

Elliott slammed his fist down on his desk. "Listen to me," he roared, then realized he could be heard by half the newsroom. He got up and closed the door. "Listen to me, goddamn it. I don't give a shit what you want. You work for me. You forget that once in a while. I'm grateful for the opportunity to remind you. You've got it too soft up in that clubby atmosphere in the press gallery. You guys sit around scratching each other's backs. When someone asks you to do a little work, or to do something for the good of the paper, you start hollering."

"You've got plenty of other people you can assign to cover Higgins. I don't see the point in yanking me out of the Senate to do it," I told him angrily.

"Look, whether or not you see the point doesn't make a goddamn bit of difference to me. I don't care if it makes sense to you or not. It isn't necessary for me to justify it to you."

"I don't like it, Frank. I'm not the least bit happy about this."

"What you don't seem to understand is that it doesn't matter what you like. Either we run this paper so that the reporters are happy—which means we indulge your whims, let you work at your leisurely pace, and turn out an inferior product—or we run it the way it should be run and make you unhappy but productive. I'm not interested in your happiness. I'm interested in covering the news.

When the two are incompatible, your happiness will have to suffer."

He was mad and so was I. On the one hand, I didn't trust him. His silence at that lunch with Walters had not encouraged me to put my faith in him. Now he was distracting me from working on the Seld story. It all seemed to be part of a pattern. Perhaps he had heard I was talking to Seld's staff. On the other hand, maybe I was being paranoid. Elliott had never killed a decent story before. He didn't roll over and play dead when a reporter came in with something hot. He always insisted on careful reporting, but that was just good editing. I had no evidence that he was purposely trying to block me.

I sat there without saying anything, looking out into the newsroom. Elliott was glaring at me. What the hell, I told myself, the Seld story isn't going anywhere fast anyway. It will keep. Maybe in a month something would develop to open it up. It wouldn't be the first time.

"Well?" he said finally.

"O.K., Frank," I said. "You're the boss."

"You're goddamn right I am."

"I'd like to have an understanding about one thing, though."

"Which is?"

"Which is that I can take time periodically to touch base in the Senate so that when I go back there I haven't completely lost track."

"When there's time to do that and it doesn't hurt your coverage of Higgins," he said, "you can do that."

"Some concession," I said.

"Don't get me going again, Tony," he said edgily.

"Do you have a knife or something in your drawer?" I asked.

"For what?"

"I'd like to cut off a finger as a sign of fealty to you." I said.

"A nice thought, but it would slow your typing down. Get the hell out of here."

18

The next several weeks were busy and chaotic for me. I traveled with Higgins through the primary states for a while, watching him in action and getting a feel for his campaign. I also spent time at his headquarters in Washington, meeting the people who were doing the nuts-and-bolts work that kept him on track.

I must say, his operation was impressive. He had transformed much of the organization from the non-partisan Americans Together into an effective, smooth-functioning campaign staff, operating in almost every state down to the ward and precinct level. And as a result, he was doing exceptionally well. He split Michigan and Illinois with Rosecroft, and looked strong in Oregon, California, and New York. He might not take the nomination on the first ballot, but the tide was running very strong in his direction. He was beginning to get good crowds. A large part of the Washington press corps was traveling with him now. And, one of the most important considerations, they served decent food on his plane.

Sometime in late May, I drove up to Baltimore with him for a speech he gave in Dundalk to a group of steelworkers. Dundalk is over in the eastern part of the city, with block after block of identical row houses on treeless streets in the shadow of one of the world's largest steel mills. Even at night, the sky is bright orange from the reflected glow of the big blast furnace at the Bethlehem plant nearby. The area is overwhelmingly Democratic, ethnic, and strongly union—the kind of place where Higgins might not be expected to get an especially warm reception. If he could do well there, his chances for winning both the nomination and the election were excellent.

The speech was not a major event in Higgins's campaign, and Baltimore's proximity to Washington gave the rest of the press corps a chance to get home for some clean laundry and a decent night's sleep. Dedicated reporter that I am, I decided to take the one-hour trip up to Baltimore with Higgins. We drove up in the evening, and I sat in the front seat with Higgins's driver, Richie Vallone. Higgins was in the back, going over his speech and taking care of some other business with his secretary, Virginia Wilson.

That Virginia Wilson worked for Higgins at all symbolized the incestuousness of politics in Washington. She was the wife of Marion Wilson, Layton Seld's press secretary. It seemed to bother no one— not her, or her husband, or Seld, or Higgins—that she should be working so closely with Higgins, while her husband worked for Seld. For the Wilsons, the only thing that ultimately mattered was the money they brought home. They were working for a living, not for an ideal. I suppose they liked the men they worked for, but it wouldn't have mattered if they didn't. As long as the pay was decent, they could suppress their feelings.

Richie Vallone was a different story. We started talking on the trip up to Baltimore that evening and had conversations often during slow minutes in the campaign in the following weeks.

Richie seemed like a nice kid—earnest, concerned about national affairs, reasonably well-informed if not terribly bright, and totally dedicated to the campaign of Philip Higgins. Richie told me about being a Marine in Vietnam. "I went over there really gung ho, you know what I mean? I got out of high school and I joined the Marine Corps. I wanted to fight for my country and I hated all those peace demonstrators who were tearing the country down. I went over to Nam as a grunt, a rifleman. When I got there I just wanted to kill as many gooks as I could. We were up in Eye Corps, near Da Nang."

Richie's experience in Vietnam, as he told the story, wasn't unique. That was part of the tragedy. He had friends in his platoon, young kids like himself who were fresh out of high school, full of themselves and unable to accept their own mortality. Richie got a lesson in how things were the second week he was in Vietnam. His squad was on a patrol. It got hit. Fifteen Marines were killed.

Then he was in another operation, a big offensive dreamed up in Saigon called "Operation Texas." The idea was supposed to be to catch the Viet Cong by surprise in a valley between two mountain ridges. B-52s were supposed to soften them up first with saturation bombing, and then the Marines were supposed to sweep through and mop up whatever was left. It sounded perfect on paper. But the B-52s had to fly with a heavy cloud cover and the air strike wasn't as surgical as the military wizards had planned. Instead of bombing the valley, the B-52s unloaded on the mountain ridge, wiping out a series of friendly Montagnard villages. The Marines were diverted to help the Montagnards. And the irony was that the V.C. had known the operation was coming and had cleared out. So the whole thing had been for nothing.

Then Richie was sent into Hué during the Tet offensive. He lost more of his buddies. Whatever enthusiasm he had had for the Marines, for the war, for the Vietnamese, had turned into hatred for all of them. I wasn't exactly clear on what happened to him after that. His story jumped to the junior college he had gone to for a while. He had dropped out, tried a couple of jobs, and then heard about Americans Together. He got a job as an office boy and started driving Higgins around Washington when he needed to get somewhere in a hurry. When Higgins announced his candidacy, he took Richie with him.

Richie stuck with Higgins because he thought Higgins "would make a difference." I didn't agree that Higgins or anyone else would make much of a difference, but I found Richie's naive faith in Higgins touching. It gave me an insight into the kind of appeal that Higgins had. Richie was not well-educated, not from a comfortable background, not part of the self-styled intellectual liberal elite that determined so much of the Democratic party's agenda. But he shared a feeling that something was terribly wrong in the country. The elite believed in the reforms Higgins was pushing. Richie didn't fully understand Higgins's program, he simply believed in Higgins. I suspected that millions of Americans responded the same way Richie did. They believed in Higgins the way their fathers and mothers had believed in Roosevelt.

The speech Higgins gave that night demonstrated why he was such a strong candidate. The audience was composed of union men who had scrubbed the dirt out from under their fingernails after a day of hard work, eaten a meal of meat and potatoes, put on open-necked sport shirts, and then come down to the union hall to hear a man who their union leaders told them was dangerous to their interests but who nonetheless might be the Democratic candidate for President.

Higgins didn't evade the issue. He could sense the unfriendly if not hostile atmosphere and he confronted it. "One of the reasons why I wanted to come speak here to you tonight," Higgins told them, "was to give you an opportunity to see that I don't have horns and a tail." There were a few chuckles. "I know what you've been hearing about me. So I thought it would be only fair if you heard from me. I thought I should have a chance to give you my own version of what I hope to do when I become President.

"In the first place, you've heard that I'm anti-union, that I want to break the power of the AFL-CIO. It's true that the AFL-CIO and I don't see eye-to-eye on every issue—especially on the need for reforming our campaign spending laws. But take a look at my record when I was in the Senate. Year after year," he said, repeating it for emphasis, "year after year, I voted down the line for bills that labor wanted. Did I do that because I was under pressure from the AFL-CIO? No! I did it because I believed in the same things that union people believed in—strong foundations for collective bargaining, a decent minimum wage, barriers to importation of cheap foreign labor, an opportunity to get a fair return for increased productivity, protection for you against the hazards of industrial accidents.

"I still believe in those things and if I were in the Senate today, my vote would be recorded in support of them. This is a difficult time for us all. It is a time of transition for our country. We face a changed world. Our former enemies are now among our closest allies. We're adjusting to that reality abroad. But we have to adjust to realities at home as well. In the last twenty years our elections have become commodities to be sold as if they were auctions, with the winner more often than not being the highest bidder. Each of you contributes, voluntarily," he stopped while ironic laughter swept the hall, "voluntarily, to a political fund controlled by your union. The cost of elections is going up. The stakes are enormous. Big business is prepared to spend millions, hundreds of millions and billions to protect its interests.

"If you're giving fifty dollars now, are you prepared to give a hundred and fifty or two fifty or five hundred? Inflation isn't hitting you just at the supermarket or at the shoe store when you take your kids to get a new pair or when you take your wife out to dinner at a restaurant. Inflation has hit our elections, too. And the only way to deal with it is to impose strict limits on how much a candidate can spend and how much an individual can give.

"But if we leave the process open to groups, you are going to be priced out as individuals. Individuals built this country, made it great. Are we now going to say that the individual is obsolete? That's what they say in other countries. They don't have faith in the individual, only in the collective. But I don't accept that and I don't think you do either. I say that left to your own devices, you will make an intelligent choice. You don't need to be coerced into contributing—voluntarily—to some election fund. You will give, many of you up to the one hundred dollar limit I propose, to the candidate of your choice. My way is the democratic way. Since the limit is low, you'll be on an equal footing with businessmen, doctors, lawyers, oil tycoons, millionaires, and all the rest of the moneyed interests. That's the whole point, to give everybody an equal voice and realize the dream that Thomas Jefferson expressed in the Declaration of Independence."

Higgins was being interrupted by applause now. Occasionally they were on their feet for him. A change had come over him. The suave, cool exterior had been relaxed and the fervent side of his personality, the evangelist in him, was coming out. The men were being swayed by it. In spite of themselves, they were being drawn to him. And I was seeing first hand why Philip Higgins more than likely would be the next President of the United States.

When Higgins finished, they gave him a standing ovation. He came down off the speaker's stand, handed his coat to Richie Vallone and, sleeves rolled up to reveal two muscular arms, he began circulating among the men, vigorously shaking hands and taking gulps from a beer someone had given him.

We stayed in the hall for another hour while Higgins meticulously worked his way through it, talking to the men. I won't say that he made everyone there a Higgins supporter, but he did something just as important—he convinced them that he was not the dire threat to their livelihood that they had been told. For Higgins that was important. After he had the nomination, it would be important for him to keep voters like these from deserting the Democratic party. If he could transform their hostility to indifference and then to mild or strong support, a major problem would be solved. The evidence of that evening was that he could do it.

When we left, Higgins invited me to ride in the back seat with him so that we could chat. Virginia Wilson had long since gone back to Washington, and a Secret Service agent rode up in the front seat with Richie Vallone.

Higgins was tired but ebullient. I was beat. It had been a long day for me, and even longer for him, but he was still going. "How did you think it went?" he asked me.

"I thought you got a good reception at the end, especially after the beginning," I said.

"The staff thought I was wasting my time coming up here—not enough people. But that wasn't the point. We've got to start thinking ahead to the campaign. We've got to come to grips with the animosity of traditional Democratic voters who've been told that I'm poison. I've got to find a way to talk to them directly, over the heads of their leaders, and convince them I'm not a threat. That's why I wanted to come up here tonight. I think I know how to do it, but you never know for sure until you try it out. I think it worked just fine. I think they understood perfectly when I explained it. Better than understanding it, they responded. That's important, Tony. The response. It does something for me as a candidate, that kind of feedback."

"Let me pose a practical question," I said. "Suppose big labor withholds the usual contributions, doesn't throw its workers in to help you, and other big money stays away, too. How are you going to run a successful campaign?"

"Tony," he said earnestly, a little as though I had hurt his feelings, "I meant every word I said about not taking contributions from organized labor or any other group. I am going to accept contributions only from individuals and no more than a hundred dollars per person. This campaign is going to be financed with the spare change of America."

"And you think you can get enough to conduct a credible campaign?" I asked skeptically.

"I already am," he said with emphasis. "You don't understand that my position has a lot of appeal out there. When people realize that their contributions and their votes count for something, it turns them on. It makes them feel important. They understand in a way that you reporters still don't grasp what my candidacy represents. When I'm elected, there's going to be a fundamental change in the politics of this country. We're going to take on the big interests and make the people sovereign again. You probably think that's corny or naive, but look at the returns, boy, look at the returns. Look at the polls. When you take away the ability of big business to pour all kinds of money into campaigns—or big labor—you'll find a lot of politicians taking their noses out of those troughs. Otherwise, they're going to find their asses booted out of Washington. They'll be replaced by men and women who will do what the public wants them to do.

"Every liberal Democratic President since Franklin Roosevelt has wanted to do what I'm going to do—build a popular majority in Congress and transform this government. Roosevelt wanted to do it but wasn't quite sure how, and then the war intervened. The rest of them never really had a chance. I'm going to do it. By the time I leave office, you are going to see some profound changes in this country. We'll finally be able to deal with poverty in an effective way. We'll be able to bring black and white voters together. I'm just going to be continuing the work of Americans Together from a more effective platform.

"But it can't be done, none of that can be accomplished until we break the grip special interests hold over the electoral process. That's why big business and big labor are united in their opposition to me, because I understand and tell the people that those interests are united in their opposition to the public.

"How do you feel about that, Richie?" Higgins called up to the front seat.

"Yes, sir," Richie said, keeping his eyes on the road. "Let him have it."

Higgins lowered his voice. "There's a good kid, Tony," he told me. "I've offered to get him jobs that would pay more or to help him go back to school so he can get a college degree, but he just wants to stay with me. He came back from Vietnam fed up with the whole goddamn country. Now he's fired up. His mother wrote me once how he's changed—how dispirited he was when he came back. They had him out at Walter Reed for a while for treatment. Now

153

look at him—back on his feet, a useful, productive member of society. That's the spirit of America at work. You can snicker at it if you want to, but that's what this campaign is all about. Anyway," he said in a kind of sigh, "I don't know whether you've gotten what I've told you or not. But I can tell you, we're getting our message across."

By now, we were off the Baltimore-Washington Parkway and coming up New York Avenue. Out the window of the car, across the warehouses and tenements in that part of town, we could see the Capitol shining bright white in the darkness, standing out against the summer sky. Higgins sat there for a while, looking out at the Capitol in the distance, not saying anything, lost in thought.

Finally he turned back to me. "Are you coming with us to California in the morning?" he asked.

"No. I'm going to stay back here. Felshin is going to make the trip. I want to do a story on your campaign organization."

"Well, it's an open campaign," he said. "The staff has been instructed to give you guys carte blanche. You can go anywhere you want in the office, see anything you want to. We don't have any secrets."

"That certainly makes life easier," I said.

"Richie," Higgins said, turning toward the front seat, "Drop me off at home and then take Mr. Jordan wherever he wants to go."

"O.K., Mr. Higgins," Richie said.

We drove out the Whitehurst Freeway, along the Potomac, with a full moon hanging over the city, reflected in the water. Washington in May is one of the most beautiful cities in the world—perhaps *the* most beautiful. Shimmering in the moonlight, the Potomac was a silvery invitation to romance and adventure, gently curving as it rolled gracefully past the capital. From this perspective its waters looked cool and inviting, the perfect antidote to a hot summer's day. But the truth was something else. The truth was that the Potomac was hopelessly polluted, an open sewer running through the city to the Chesapeake Bay.

We dropped Higgins at his home and then turned back toward town. Richie started talking as we drove. "We're going to go all the way, Mr. Jordan. You could see it tonight, the way he turned those guys on. He's got a God-given gift."

I couldn't argue the point. I was impressed with what I had seen, whatever my own doubts about Higgins. I thought about doing a story on what Richie was talking about, Higgins's ability to ignite people, to inspire them in his cause, and to renew their faith and interest in government. I played back in my mind what I had seen and heard that evening. Then I recalled that weeks before I had had an idea to do a similar story about Richie Vallone and about politics as a way for people to escape the meaninglessness of their own lives.

I saw Richie as a good vehicle for getting into the story, humanizing all those faceless volunteers who were being drawn to Higgins.

"Richie," I said, "I'd like to do a story about how Mr. Higgins has done it—I mean gotten where he is in the campaign. I'd like to talk to someone who was completely turned off to politics and then turned on again by Higgins. I wonder if you'd be interested?"

He thought about it for a minute. "Sure," he said. "I guess it'd be O.K. I'm not sure when we'd talk, though. I'm going to be out of town with him for the next ten days or so. This next couple of weeks is going to be really tight."

"No problem," I said. "I can talk to other people and work on some other stories, too." Something Higgins said to me came back at that moment. "I don't know how sensitive you are on the point," I said, "but if it's all right with you, I'd like to talk to your folks, too, so I can get another view on how Higgins has changed your attitude."

"Well, you can talk to my mom," he said, "but my father's dead."

"Your mother then."

"I'll call her for you in the morning and tell her you'll give her a call. She lives up in Harrisburg. She's working for the campaign up there. She's crazy about Higgins, too."

We pulled up in front of my apartment. Richie gave me his mother's phone number and we said good night.

19

Mrs. Vallone lived in a tidy little frame house in a working-class section of Harrisburg. I got there around ten o'clock in the morning three days after my conversation with Richie. I took a cab to her house. She had over-dressed for the occasion, as though my visit to interview her were a big event in her life. I suppose it was, although it depressed me a little to realize that my presence could be a source of excitement for someone.

She was wearing a cotton skirt and a blouse. She had on some inexpensive costume jewelry. Her house was neat as a pin. On a table next to a couch was a picture of a young man in an Army uniform. The picture had evidently been taken years ago, judging by the looks of it. Next to it was a picture of Richie in his Marine Corps dress blues, peering intently into the camera. Although he looked as though he were trying to smile, what came through was the hard, hostile stare of a warrior preparing himself for battle.

Mrs. Vallone—she introduced herself to me as Anita—had a nice grip when we shook hands. I guessed that she was somewhere around forty-five, and it looked as though the last twenty or so years had been tough ones for her. There were flecks of gray in her brown hair. Her clothes, though neat, were a little worn. Her hands had the appearance of having worked. The polish on her nails was chipped in some places. She was a handsome woman who, from the looks of her, had endured hardship without triumphing over it.

She gave me some coffee and we started talking. In addition to working as a secretary in a small electronics firm in Harrisburg, she worked nights and weekends in the Higgins campaign. She had gotten involved in Americans Together after Richie had started with Higgins, after Higgins had worked his evangelical magic.

I asked her to tell me about that. She took a deep breath. "I don't know how much I should tell you," she said. "It isn't a simple story."

"I'm not sure I know what you're talking about," I said.

"Well, Richie had a very bad time of it for a while when he came back from Vietnam. He's all right now. I just don't want to call attention to a problem that already has been taken care of. I mean he's better now and I don't want to create doubts in peoples' minds about him."

"That's up to you, Mrs. Vallone. I don't want to embarrass Richie or hurt him. I just want to do a story about Higgins and this uncanny ability he seems to have to inspire people. It would help for me to know what Richie's been through, but I don't think I have to put every detail of it in the story. I hope you would trust my discretion."

"You seem to be very nice," she said. "Why don't I tell you what I feel I can, with the understanding that you'll try to leave out the parts that might not be so good for him."

I agreed that that would be an acceptable way to proceed.

She started in telling me about herself. Her father had been a coal miner in West Virginia. She had grown up poor and had known the violence in the hills when the United Mine Workers had come to organize the miners. In 1948, not long after she finished school, she married her high-school sweetheart. He was a mechanic and made a living, but they weren't looking for tax shelters for any surplus income. Richie was born the same year. She didn't say so, but I got the feeling that they married sooner rather than later because she was pregnant. When the Korean War broke out, her husband managed to avoid being called for a while. He was drafted in 1952, when Richie was four, and sent over to Korea after he finished basic training. Since he was a trained mechanic, Army logic dictated that he be put in the infantry. He was killed somewhere up near the Thirty-eighth Parallel. Richie was then five.

Anita Vallone raised Richie herself, scratching to make ends meet. She had never remarried, for reasons she didn't go into and I didn't ask about. "That was probably a mistake," she said. "Richie needed a father. He desperately wanted to have a father. He loved his father. He remembered things about him. I thought I was doing the right thing, but now I don't know." She paused for a minute. "When Richie finished high school in nineteen sixty-six, that was when the war in Vietnam was really starting to get very big. Richie was exempt from the draft because he was the sole surviving son and because his father had been killed in Korea. But he wanted to. You know how patriotic kids can get, how wildeyed they can be when they really believe in something. It seems funny now to think that kids could get so excited about the war in Vietnam, but those times were different.

"I didn't want Richie to go. I was afraid he'd be killed the way his father was and I couldn't stand that, to lose both of them. I didn't care about the war at all. I just wanted my son to be alive. But he insisted. He didn't say so, but I think he wanted to be like his dad. I couldn't stop him, not legally anyway. And he wouldn't listen to me. He joined the Marines and went over in the summer of nineteen sixty-seven."

As she told it, Richie had been a good Marine. He went through Parris Island as the top recruit in his platoon. He was sent to Vietnam within a matter of months. At first, he wrote regularly, describing his friends, his officers, the patrols he went on. He accepted his job there without thinking about it much. As the year wore on, he started writing about how one friend had been wounded, another killed.

"I noticed that his enthusiasm wore off," she told me. "He started questioning what he was doing there. Then I started hearing from him less. Finally there was a period of a few months when I didn't hear from him at all. I was going crazy I was so worried. That was right around the battle for Hué in early nineteen sixty-eight during that Tet offensive. I was falling apart. I didn't know what to do. My boss, Mr. Simpson—a wonderful man—saw what was happening to me. He got our congressman to find out from the Marine Corps where Richie was and what was wrong with him. They had him in a hospital in Da Nang. He hadn't been wounded or anything. He was suffering from battle fatigue, they said. They brought him back here to Walter Reed Hospital in Washington. I went to see him there. I hardly knew him. He was so quiet—sullen. He barely would speak to me. He told me that he wished he had been killed in Vietnam. He was just—terribly disillusioned. He said he felt empty, lost."

The psychiatrist treating him, a young doctor named Hoffman, told her Richie had become unable to function in Vietnam. He had become anxious and preoccupied. He lost weight because he wouldn't eat. Richie may have been fooling around with drugs, too, but the main problem apparently was mental, Hoffman told her. Richie had been moved to Saigon, where a Navy psychiatrist examined him and ordered him to be sent home early.

"Richie was in Walter Reed for five months. They put him on some drug and Dr. Hoffman asked me if I could come down several times a week to participate in family therapy. I didn't think I could do it, but Mr. Simpson was terrific about it. He gave me the time off with pay, and even paid some of my expenses." She sat looking at her hands for a minute, clasping them together.

"I read some books about mental illness—you know, to try to understand what Richie was going through. I asked Dr. Hoffman if Richie was schizophrenic, because sometimes he seemed perfectly fine and then other times he was so withdrawn. Dr. Hoffman told me that Richie had some of the symptoms of schizophrenia, but that he could be treated. I wrote down what he told me," she said, getting up from the couch where she was sitting and taking out a piece of paper from a desk drawer.

"He told me Richie 'suffered from a profound sense of loss—loss of identity and purpose.' There was a 'profound psychological assault on his self-esteem and concomitant depression.'" She stumbled over these last words a little, laughing at herself for her difficulty in pronouncing "concomitant." Then she continued on her own. "He said Richie had gone to Vietnam in an attempt to join his father, but Richie lost his father when he saw how bad the war was. So really Richie lost his father twice, in a way—first when he was killed in Korea and then again in Vietnam. I guess, the second time was even worse than the first."

Mrs. Vallone looked at me bravely, and kept going with her

story. Richie was sent home after Walter Reed, but he continued as a psychiatric out-patient. Gradually, he was taken off the drugs they'd been giving him. He got better, but not the way he had been. When the doctors told him to get a job without much mental stress, Mrs. Vallone's boss found him a job at a playground. Later they said he should try moving out of the house into his own place. Then they said he could get a job with more responsibilities, so Mr. Simpson helped find him something better. Finally, they said Richie could stop seeing the psychiatrist, that he was all right.

"He still didn't seem to me the way he had been before, but I guess war changes people and he *was* getting older," said Mrs. Vallone. "Richie worked in a bank for a while, until he decided to go back to school. He wanted to go to college. He tried that and didn't particularly like it, although he did all right." She looked out the window for a moment, trying to collect her thoughts.

"He was still so negative about things. Then all of a sudden, he said he wanted to move to Washington, wanted to be with friends he had made while he was in Walter Reed. I was against it, but Richie wrote me or I called him a couple of times a week, to make sure he was all right. A friend got him his job with Americans Together. He began talking about Mr. Higgins, dropping him into his conversations, and then talking about him more and more—very enthusiastically. He was crazy about Mr. Higgins. Mr. Higgins was taking him to all kinds of fancy places and bringing Richie inside instead of making him stay outside in the car the way other people in Washington do. I could see right away that Richie acted like Mr. Higgins was a kind of a father. I mean, he was like a kid— listening to what Mr. Higgins said, doing what he was asked to do, and really enthusiastic. And when the doctors saw Richie again after a year, they agreed he'd really done just marvelously well.

"So I'm personally grateful to Mr. Higgins. I'm hoping Richie'll go back to college after a while, but I know he wants to be in the White House." Mrs. Vallone smiled her pretty, faded smile.

It was quite a tale. We talked some more about Richie, about the campaign, about Higgins and things in general. The longer we talked, the heavier the conversation got. When it got toward lunch time, Anita Vallone offered me a drink. I really didn't want one, but she kept insisting, so I had a Bloody Mary. She poured herself a bourbon, which she took care of pretty quickly, and then had another one. She was into her third drink when I decided to pull her out before she fell into the bottle. We went to a restaurant not terribly far from her house where they overcooked the steak and wilted the lettuce before serving it. I did not enjoy lunch. I dropped Mrs. Vallone off back at her house, feeling sorry for her—for what she had been through and for the life she hadn't had—and took a cab to the airport to catch a flight back to Washington.

What she had told me about Richie was interesting, in some places fascinating. As usual, though, most of what she had said couldn't find its way into a story. Even if I hadn't promised to be discreet, I would have wound up with too much material. Whenever you're reporting—if you do it right—you wind up with much more material than you can use, and that was the case here.

I played around with the stuff, interviewing others who supported or worked for Higgins to get their views. Then I had what I thought was a masterstroke—I would call some of his contributors, some of the people who sent in five or ten dollars in crumpled bills, to find out what they did and why they were supporting him. It wasn't an original approach, but journalism isn't a profession where a premium is put on breaking new ground. I figured that if the contributors didn't fit in with my idea for the story focusing on Richie, then I could split the stories and do them separately.

So a couple of days after talking to Anita Vallone, I went over to the Higgins headquarters to get the names of some contributors. I talked to Herb Edelman, one of Higgins's financial wizards, to get some help on how to get the names. He invited me to watch some of the staff open the mail. "It's fantastic," he told me in his enthusiastic way. "You're not going to believe what you see. Just make sure you keep your sticky fingers off the table."

He took me into a back room with an armed guard posted outside the door. Inside were five or six heavy bags of mail. Sitting around the table were ten campaign workers, who carefully opened envelopes, extracted money from them, recorded the amount and the name of the donor if it was included with the money, and then put the money into stacks of singles, fives, tens, twenties, checks, and other drafts.

Herb wanted to introduce me to everyone. "Stop, everybody. Stop. Stop," he said. "I want to introduce Tony Jordan and warn you. He's an underpaid reporter—so as long as he's in the room, keep your eyes on him. He can look, but no touching."

Herb turned back to me as the workers went back to gathering in the money. "I will now turn you loose. If you need anything, let me know. We've got a staff meeting two minutes ago, so I've gotta run."

I stood watching as they all quietly went about their business. Whenever one of the workers found a check for more than a hundred dollars, it was put into a return envelope with a form letter thanking the donor and explaining that Higgins had imposed a limit of one hundred dollars for contributors. Even so, he seemed to be getting a lot of money.

I stopped behind one woman, who had, like the others, a large pile of maize and gold slips in front of her. She must have had fifty or sixty of them, and the others also had that many or more. I asked her what they were.

"Postal money orders," she said. "We get a lot of them. The people who don't have checking accounts like to send them because they're cheaper to buy than a commercial money order. They're convenient for us, too, because the people usually put all the information we need—name, address, and zip code—right on it. Right here, see?" she said, indicating a place in the center of the money order that held all the information. "They're really safe, in some ways safer than checks. So we don't mind getting them, even though they cause us some other administrative problems."

I asked her if I could have a couple to copy down the names of the donors. "It's all public record," she said. "I don't see why not." She gave me five postal money orders.

I copied down the names and the numbers off the money orders. There were two contributors in Manhattan, another in Chicago, one in Cleveland, and a fifth in Los Angeles. I gave them back to her and then addressed myself to the group. "I wonder if I could interrupt you for a minute," I said. "I'm trying to do a story. I wonder if you all would mind totalling up the money you each have and let me know how much is on the table right now." They let out a collective groan, but started counting and then gave me their totals, not counting the checks that were being sent back. In all, they had about three thousand dollars in checks of one hundred dollars or less, two thousand dollars in bills, and six thousand dollars in postal money orders. They told me that that amount was the result of about an hour's work opening letters. "Is that what you usually get?" I asked. "I mean is this normal?"

"We usually don't total it up this way," the woman I had been talking to said. "But this looks to be about average."

"How many hours a day do you work at it?" I asked.

"There are people doing this twelve or fourteen hours a day," she said. "We don't like to leave unopened letters in here overnight. What isn't deposited in the bank during the day is put in our safe overnight and deposited the next day. But envelopes and all would be too bulky. And anyway, every day there's another load like this."

I did some quick figuring in my head. "So you get about a hundred and thirty thousand to a hundred and seventy thousand dollars a day like this?" I asked, not quite believing it.

"If that's what it comes out to," she said.

I understood now what Edelman meant. I made a note to check the figures with him to make sure they were right. If I had estimated accurately, the Higgins campaign was pulling in somewhere between three quarters of a million and a million dollars a week. That was a hell of a lot of money. I was more than impressed with the way Higgins was making good on his determination to finance his campaign with the spare change of America. He seemed to be succeeding beyond the wildest expectations of anyone, except perhaps himself.

If I had planned it, things could not have worked out better. By pure coincidence, I was having lunch that day with a friend of mine, Carla Huntington, who was in the business of helping people raise money. Most of her efforts had been toward assisting research projects, civil rights groups, reform organizations, citizens' associations, and that kind of activity get money from private foundations. She had helped a few political candidates, but she was very selective about whom she worked for. She also had a reputation, although she was no older than thirty, for being one of the best in the business.

Carla is beautiful—olive skin, long black hair, a memorable figure. She also has extraordinary intelligence, wit, charm, and good horse sense. We've never been romantically involved. We are, as they say, just good friends.

We were eating at a Chinese restaurant on Fifteenth Street. We ordered lunch and then I started telling her about my morning's activities. I told her in detail what I had just seen, because I was knocked over by it. When I finished, she looked puzzled. "That's really strange, you know?" she said after reflecting on it.

"What's that?"

"Well, I was just trying to think. I don't remember hearing anything about Higgins's putting on a mail-solicitation campaign."

"And?" I said, waiting to hear the rest.

"Well, mail-solicitation campaigns are a big deal to organize. You have to buy lists of potential contributors, you have to get a solicitation letter written and printed. The stuff has to be mailed. It may not sound complicated, but it really is. Just knowing which list to buy, for example, is an enormously important decision. And if you don't know what you're doing, you can pay a lot of money for a list that's not even going to bring you back the purchase price, much less substantial contributions. There are a couple of companies here and in New York that do nothing but mail solicitations—that's their business. What you're telling me about sounds like a big undertaking, and I haven't heard of anyone doing that kind of work for Higgins."

"Maybe one of them is doing it and you didn't hear about it," I said.

"No," she said thoughtfully but firmly, "I would know about it. I would have heard. That would be a really plum contract to get."

"That's interesting," I said. "I'll ask Herb Edelman about it."

We talked about it some more until the waiter brought over our dishes—first hot and sour soup, then moo-shu pork and diced chicken with peanuts.

As it turned out, Carla couldn't linger over lunch, since she had a two-fifteen meeting. So we went our separate ways after agreeing to get together again in a month or so.

I went back to the office and got on the phone, first to Herb Edelman, who confirmed my estimate of about seven hundred and fifty thousand to a million dollars in contributions a week. "I told you you wouldn't believe it," he said. "I don't believe it, but there it is. It's a campaign treasurer's dream."

"One other thing, Herb," I said. "Who's doing your mail solicitations for you? Where did you get your lists and all?"

"We're not using anyone. We didn't have a mail campaign," he said. "Phil asks people to mail in money when he speaks, but that's it. We couldn't afford a mail campaign. Do you know what they cost?"

"I know they're expensive," I said.

"Expensive isn't the word," he said. "You pay in blood. No, we just took our chances and we're doing it on our own. It just proves that the people want Higgins," he said.

"I think I'll get off before I start crying," I told him.

I called Carla and told her what Edelman had said. "Well, that's worth a story in itself," she said. "I don't know if you appreciate that or not, but that's an accomplishment unheard-of in the business. It's just incredible."

We talked a little more and then I hung up. Since I had time on my hands, I called New York information and asked for the phone numbers for the two Manhattan contributors whose names I had copied off the money orders. One was Golda Weiss, with an address on West 73rd Street, and the other was a Berenice Golden on East 65th.

I called Golda Weiss first. An old woman answered the phone. She spoke with a thick Yiddish accent. I told her who I was and why I was calling.

"What?" she said.

I thought maybe her hearing was bad. "My name is Tony Jordan. I'm a reporter for *The Washington Journal*. I'm doing a story about Philip Higgins's presidential campaign. I noticed that you contributed money to his campaign. I wanted to talk to you for a minute."

"What?" she asked again. I contemplated recording the statement and playing it for her on a machine to save my voice.

"Did you hear what I said?" I asked her.

"I heard," she said.

"Did you understand?"

"Look, Mr. Jordan. I'm here thirty-six years. I understand English. I don't know what you're talking about. My husband is dead ten years. I live on a small pension and Social Security. Money for politics I don't have."

"You didn't give money to Philip Higgins?" I asked.

"Sometimes I don't even vote," she said. "For Roosevelt I would have, but I wasn't a citizen then. For Truman, yes. For Stevenson and for Kennedy. But lately, no. Do you want to know why I don't vote?" she asked belligerently.

"Why?" I asked, beginning to regret the entire conversation.

The answer that followed was a five-minute speech, supplemented with Yiddish when her English was inadequate to the task. When she paused for a breath, I broke in. "Mrs. Weiss," I said quickly. "I'm terribly sorry that I bothered you for nothing and I hope that you find a candidate of your choice someday and that you'll be happy with him or her or it. Goodbye."

Next, I tried Berenice Golden. Berenice was a New York sophisticate. After conveying her disappointment that I was with the

Journal and not the *Times,* she went further. "I don't do politics, Mr. Gordan," she said.

"Jordan," I corrected her. "Like the river."

"Yes," she said. "Anyway, I don't do politics. I didn't send any money to the Higgins campaign. I don't know who told you that I did, but I didn't. Politics is so—tacky," she said. "It used to be fun, but it's really passé now. Nobody does politics any more."

I had to agree with her that politics didn't seem to have the same grace and charm it once had had. I apologized to her and got off, now zero for two. I double-checked with New York information to make sure I had everything right, which I did.

I was a little puzzled, but not overly so. Campaigns always have those little quirks. I decided to check out the contributors from Chicago, Cleveland, and L.A. When I got through doing that, I still hadn't talked to a contributor. Worse than that, there was no listing for anyone bearing the names of the contributors at the addresses given on the money orders.

That was more than coincidence, it seemed to me. I was damned annoyed. First of all, these discrepancies were screwing up what I had thought would be a good, easy story. Now I would have to go back and get more names in order to do the piece. But more important, I now would have to put in time finding out why the names hadn't checked out. From a professional standpoint, I was obligated to do that. From a practical perspective, I wanted to overlook it. I already had too much work to do.

20

On top of all the other things I had to do, John Forman called me about this time asking me for more money. I didn't argue with him—I trusted him completely—but I reminded myself again that I should have gone to law school when I had the chance. I had to get hold of Mary Painter to arrange a transfer of funds and then get the bank to issue a check to Forman. I had to go to the bank personally, since our arrangement was such that I couldn't do it by phone.

I had fully intended to get back to Higgins's headquarters right away, but the Quilling bill was scheduled to come up for debate and a vote on the Senate floor. I wanted to cover it since I considered the bill, if passed, a landmark in American history.

Fortunately, without my saying a word, Frank Elliott came to the same conclusion. He told me to drop what I was doing "for the time being, and go back up to the Hill for this and this alone. Then it's back to the campaign."

At the time I didn't think that any of this was getting me any closer to finding Painter's killer, but I was wrong. Things were beginning to move.

I didn't notice any bunting or signs up when I came back to the press gallery after being gone for three weeks. Crowds did not rush forward to grab my hand or tear my clothing. There were no bands. But I was glad to be back there. I liked my senators. And I was coming back just in time to watch them roll over a lot of oil-rich Arabs. Think of all the banks, factories, software computer firms, trucking companies, airlines, refineries, shipping companies, and a lot of other heavy businesses that they were going to protect for true-blue Americans.

Actually the debate on the Senate floor focused on two issues: first, whether American manufacturers and other companies could safely be allowed to pass into foreign ownership without jeopardizing national security, or at least fundamentally altering the structure of the economy; second, whether the United States could block foreigners from investing their money in the United States without risking some form of retaliation. For four days, the debate went on. Visitors might not have sensed that anything important was happening if they showed up at the wrong time, because usually not more than ten or twenty senators were on the floor. During those four days, though, the bells were ringing in the Senate office buildings, as one amendment after another was offered in a vain attempt to cripple or water down the Quilling bill.

But Quilling was ready. He had drafted the bill tightly. It had no loopholes. He had done his homework. He knew the Senate rules, and he avoided the parliamentary traps his opponents tried to set for him. He was quick to see the damage that an amendment might have on the whole bill. He had his votes and could deliver them when he needed them.

Administration lobbyists were trying quietly to get votes to defeat the bill. The President would have to sign it if it came to his desk, and so he was trying to stop that from happening. So far, he wasn't succeeding. Finally the opponents ran out of amendments, and the agreed-upon time for the vote came. It was a dramatic moment in the Senate. The galleries were packed with spectators. The press crowded in. But for all the drama, the vote wasn't terribly close—fifty-five to thirty-nine. Quilling had passed his bill and now it would go to the House, where passage was a virtual certainty. For better or worse, Congress was making an historic law.

I wrote the stories that Elliott had asked me to do, and when they were in, I avoided speaking to him. I didn't ask if I could stay on the Hill. I simply decided I would, to find out what was happening with Higgins's bill, and Elliott would get ahold of me if he wanted me.

As it happened, Elliott was too preoccupied with the primaries and the preliminaries to the Democratic convention to worry about me. Higgins picked up most of the delegates in California, New York, and Oregon to give him a strong lead for the nomination. He might not be able to get the nomination on the first ballot, but unless Rosecroft or someone else pulled a rabbit out of a hat, it looked like he would be the Democratic nominee. The various convention committees were holding hearings in Washington, so that the Congressional Democrats could participate and still go through the motions of representing their constituents. The platform committee had three or four difficult issues, including busing, price supports for farmers, Higgins's campaign reform bill, and oil pricing. The credentials committee was hearing challenges, brought by Rosecroft and Higgins mainly, trying to knock out each other's delegates to the convention. All in all, it was a typical preconvention performance, but that didn't make it any easier to cover. So Elliott was preoccupied and I was left alone for a while.

Summer had come to Washington with a vengeance. By midday, it was ninety outside. By late afternoon, the downtown streets were an alfresco sauna. No one ventured outside, away from air conditioning, unless there was no choice. At night, even after the sun had set, the mass of concrete and stone in downtown Washington gave back the heat it had absorbed through the long, torpid day. The air hung like Spanish moss over the city.

But the Senate continued to grind away, trying to clear up as much of its calendar as possible before recessing for the conventions. In the Senate reception room, next to the senators' cloakroom, I ran into Mike O'Connell one afternoon. I asked him if he was going to Chicago.

"Yeah, I'm going," he said. "It isn't really my show but the old man is getting desperate. He wants to block Higgins. He's got all our local unions sending bodies to Chicago to be ready to do whatever needs to be done. He wants me to go, too. I've gone to every convention—Republican and Democratic—for the last twenty-four years. It's the same every time. I wind up with a week-long hangover. I suppose it helps me here to buy drinks and get around there. But

I'm getting too old for all that playing. I'd rather just go fishing and do my drinking alone.

"Anyway," he continued, "I'm glad I ran into you. I've been looking for you for the last couple of weeks and haven't seen you." He stopped and glanced around. We were standing in the middle of a clump of people—Senate aides, tourists, and assorted lobbyists. "Come sit over here where we can talk," he said, pulling me over to a bench under the window.

"I'm going to die of curiosity," I said.

"Take it easy," he said, pausing to light the stub of a cigar. "There's something strange going on with this Higgins bill."

"Like what?"

"Support is showing up in places where it shouldn't be," he said.

"I told you when we had lunch a couple of months ago that there was a lot going on in the country you weren't taking into account," I said. "I guess you're just seeing the results of what I told you."

"Don't kid yourself," he said. "That isn't it. I mean there's money floating around in support of the bill that's coming from unexpected places and going to unexpected people."

"Am I supposed to play Twenty Questions with you? Who's paying and who's getting?"

"I was talking to a senator the other day, a conservative—not someone who votes labor, but we get along. I think he's a very decent guy, although he has a kind of shady reputation among you fellows. I think you're wrong about him, and what he told me confirms it as far as I'm concerned."

"Who are we talking about?" I asked.

"I'm not going to tell you," O'Connell said.

"East or west of the Mississippi?" I asked.

"Save it. I'm not going to tell you. And that isn't the important thing anyway. He told me . . ."

"You're talking about this much-maligned conservative senator friend now?"

"Yeah. He told me he had been approached by a lobbyist with a promise of a big campaign contribution."

"How big?" I asked.

"A hundred thousand. The lobbyist talked about the dough, then he brought up the Higgins bill and urged my conservative pal to vote for it."

"What's so strange about that?" I asked. "It's probably illegal, but you shouldn't be shocked. You knew that money would change hands over Higgins's bill."

"Yeah," he said, "but I didn't expect a lobbyist for big oil to come up here in favor of a campaign reform bill."

Now I was getting interested. "For what?" I demanded.

"Edward X. Dunphy," he said, giving emphasis to each part of the name. "What the hell is he doing going around lobbying for a bill that would reduce his clients' effectiveness? This senator told me Dunphy had told him not to worry about money for his campaign, that money would always be available for the right people."

"What did the senator say?"

"He got pissed off, told Dunphy to get screwed."

"So why doesn't the senator go public with it?"

"You really are a naive son of a bitch, Jordan. The senator already has a shady reputation. If he went public, he's afraid you guys would miss the point and start after him rather than after Dunphy. He doesn't want any trouble. He figures he's discharged his obligation by staying honest. The way you survive in politics is to develop tolerance for human failings. Besides, he hates reporters."

"That could be anybody," I said.

"Why don't you make some calls?" he said. "Do something constructive for a change."

"You're beginning to sound like an editor," I said. "I'll look into it."

It would be nice if all the information the government has were on a computer accessible to reporters. It would be nice if all the information the government has that's supposed to be available actually were available. I spent two hours on the phone trying to reach the office on the Hill where lobbyists registered. When I finally reached the office, they said I had to come over, they couldn't help me over the phone. When I went over, I found that their records were spotty, incomplete, and in a lot of cases years behind. That included Dunphy's file.

So then I had to get on the phone again. After about three hours of calls spread over that afternoon and the next morning, I finally got hold of a lawyer I knew in the counsel's office at United Oil, one of Dunphy's clients. We talked small talk for a little while and then I eased into the main question.

"Listen," I said, "I'm working on something that involves your legislative representative here. Dunphy is still your man, isn't he?"

"No," he said. "Jerry Murphy is."

"What about Dunphy?" I asked.

"He doesn't represent us any more. Not for the past six months or so. We insisted. Amalgamated and Southern dropped him, too."

"What happened?"

"The whole thing was kind of quiet and sensitive," he said. "I don't think I can go into it."

"What's so sensitive?" I said. "He has to register his clients with the Clerk of the House of Representatives and the Secretary of the Senate. It's public record."

"Maybe so," he said. "Only it didn't come from me if anybody asks, all right?"

"Guaranteed," I said.

"He started representing the Arab Consortium in addition to us. We deal with the Consortium closely, but our interests and theirs aren't always compatible. We told Dunphy he'd have to give up them or us. So it was us. I guess they must be paying him a lot because he was getting about a hundred fifty a year from us, and I imagine Amalgamated and Southern were paying a similar amount."

"So he's representing the Arab Consortium now, and not you?" I said.

"That's about the size of it."

We talked a little longer and then I hung up and sat there trying to figure things out. I had so many different leads I should be working on that I didn't know what to do first. Why was Dunphy spreading money around? I was still wondering about Seld and the Swiss bank account. I wanted to go back to Higgins's headquarters to find out why none of the names on the postal money orders had been correct. Then there was Fournier's death, my mugging, Rosecroft, and the central question—Painter's murder. I felt paralyzed by the prospects. And none of them was even close to being finished.

I was saved from further self-criticism by Elliott, who called me into his office. "Do you know Steven Snyder at all?" he asked me. "He's—or I should say he was—a congressman."

"What happened to him?" I asked.

"He was found dead a couple of hours ago in one of those fleabag hotels on New York Avenue," Elliott said.

"What was he doing there?" I said.

"He had gone to meet someone in a room," Elliott said.

172

"A woman?"

"No, a man."

"And the guy killed him?" I asked.

"It doesn't look that way," Elliott said. "Police founa Snyder in bed naked. There was sperm on the sheets and everything. The guy told police that Snyder picked him up in a bar a little bit before. They went up to the hotel room, undressed, and climbed into bed. The guy told police that Snyder had a heart attack. The medical examiner looked at the body there. He's going to have to do an autopsy, but it looks as though it was a heart attack. I've got to get someone to do the obituary. It isn't very pleasant. I want to report the circumstances of his death, but I don't want to be salacious. Anyway, do you know him?"

"I just know who he is," I said. "I didn't know him except to say hello."

Elliott frowned. "Shit, I've got all this stuff with the Democratic convention and I have to be sidetracked by queer congressmen with weak hearts. All right. Thanks. I'll have to find someone else."

I went back to my desk. That whole business about the Thursday Night Club was coming back again. One more item to add to my list of things to do. I saw myself drowning in a sea of unfinished stories. Nothing was getting done. I had been drifting along, letting events take me from one point to the next. At the rate I was going, my suspects would die of old age before I ever made a dent in Painter's murder.

Then I got mad. I was going to have to cut some corners.

I picked up the phone and called Rosecroft's office and asked to speak to Goldsboro.

"I want to see Rosecroft today," I said.

"You're out of your mind," he said. "I might be able to get you something in about four months."

"Look, Peter, I'm not going to kid around. I want to see Rosecroft. Just tell him I want to speak to him about his nephew and the Thursday Night Club."

"Is this some kind of code or something, Jordan? Come on. Let me in on it."

"Just tell him that, Peter."

I hung up and waited. About half an hour later the phone rang. It was Goldsboro. "He says you can have ten minutes if you come up right now. I'd like to know what the hell this is all about."

"I'll be right up," I said.

It took me about half an hour to get up to the Senate because it was rush hour. Washington cab drivers like to go home before rush hour so their cabs don't get scratched in the heavy traffic.

I had to wait about five minutes, but then the receptionist told me that I could go in. Goldsboro walked in with me. "Hello, Tony," Rosecroft said. We shook hands. "Uh, Peter. I think Tony and I can talk alone. You ought to get back to that stuff you were working on." Goldsboro looked disappointed, but he left. "Now what is this?" Rosecroft asked, his tone suddenly changing.

"Steven Snyder died of a heart attack this afternoon in a hotel over on New York Avenue," I told him.

"I heard about it. I'm quite upset. Steven was a friend of mine."

"Did you hear all the circumstances?"

"What do you mean?"

"He was found in bed, nude. He had been with another man. Did you know that Steven Snyder was a homosexual?"

"Are you going to ask me if I'm a homosexual, too?" Rosecroft asked.

"I guess I am," I said. "Before he died, Les Painter was checking around about you, asking people about you and the Thursday Night Club. Snyder was a member of that, too. Now he turns up dead in a hotel room. Painter's already dead. I heard, without intending to, an argument you had with a boy you tell me is your nephew. It sounded more like a lovers' quarrel. I told you then that it didn't make any difference to me what you did in your private life as long as it wasn't relevant to your public life. Now it's become relevant."

"Why is it relevant?" Rosecroft demanded. "What goddamn business is it of yours?"

"Because," I said calmly, "you are a leading candidate for the Democratic Presidential nomination. A friend of yours is a homosexual. That would be politically embarrassing, if it turned out that you were homosexual, too. It could knock you out of the race and out of politics. Another man, Painter, has been killed. Why shouldn't I believe that you had him killed after he discovered that you were a homosexual?"

"Sit down, Tony," Rosecroft said quietly. "I'm going to tell you something. I'd like it to be off the record, but I'm not going to insist. I'm going to tell you what I told Les Painter about a month before he was killed. He knew about Snyder, and about the Thursday

Night Club. He was right about Snyder, but the club is just a club. That's all. And I am not a homosexual."

"What about your nephew?" I asked.

"Well," he said, taking a deep breath, "my nephew is not my nephew. He's my son. I don't like to use the word 'illegitimate,' but that's what people call it.

"Twenty years ago, before I got into politics, I had a brief affair with a girl from a small town in Pennsylvania. A beautiful girl. But she and I were worlds apart. The only thing we really shared was our lust. She got pregnant. I wanted her to have an abortion. She was Catholic. She refused. She wanted me to marry her. I refused. We would have both been miserable and then we would have been stuck with each other forever.

"She had the baby. Alan. That's him, in that picture with me at the Vineyard last summer. I've stayed in touch with them, given her more than enough money to take care of herself and him. I've made sure that he's had the things I would have wanted him to have if we were living together as a family. I've tried to be a father to him." He paused for a breath. "And that's what I told Painter."

"What did he say?"

"Painter said that if what I told him was true, it probably wasn't worth a story."

"Probably?" I asked.

"Look, the whole thing would hurt me if it came out. I would prefer that it didn't. I was hoping Painter wouldn't do anything with it. It isn't exactly the kind of thing a candidate likes to see on the front page. But it isn't worth killing someone over, either," he said. "I'd like you to believe that, because it's true."

"And because you'd like to leave the past buried," I said.

"That, too."

"I don't know," I said. "I'm not sure what to do. I'm going to have to wrestle with this myself."

"Will you let me know if you're going to do a story?" he asked.

"Certainly," I said. "That would be only fair." I got up and left. Goldsboro was waiting for me.

"Well?" he said.

"Ask him," I said. "I'm going to get a drink."

I wandered back to the paper, hoping to find someone to save me from drinking alone. Elliott was still huddling with people on the desk, going over the day's news and worrying about tomorrow. He called over to me. "Don't go anywhere until you see me, Jordan. I want to talk to you."

From the sound of his voice, he wasn't going to be giving me a raise. At the moment, I didn't care one way or the other. I just wanted to dive into a bottle of bourbon. I called Charlotte while I waited for Elliott. "I solved the Rosecroft mystery," I told her, "but it doesn't get me any closer to home plate."

"You want to come tell Mama all about it?" she asked, her voice suggesting a slight hint of sympathy.

"I feel like getting shit-faced drunk. How would you like to do that?"

"I've got something better than that," she said. "Come on over. I'll give you something to eat and then see what we can do to make you feel better."

"I'll see," I said. "I've gotta go."

Elliott was motioning me to come into his office. When I walked in, he shut the door. It was going to be another one of those sessions. "You know," he said, "you used to be a pretty good reporter—dependable, fast, steady, accurate. Something's happened to you. You haven't done anything worthwhile in weeks. I send you up to Senate to cover one story and you disappear. I'd think you were in love or something, but you're too old for that. You're not a big drinker, so that can't be the problem. You're not married any more, so I know there's no trouble at home. What the hell is your problem?"

"I don't know, coach. I've been watching movies of myself at the plate, trying to figure out what I'm doing wrong. I feel like I'm still swinging the same way, but I can't seem to hit the ball good. I know I'm in a slump, but I'll break out of it soon. Give me a break, O.K.?"

"I'm going to give you a kick in the ass if you don't start following up your assignments," he said. "I told you I wanted stories about Higgins's campaign. The convention starts in two weeks. We're going to be wanting stories in advance. You're going to Chicago to stick with Higgins when he goes. In the meantime, I want at least—at least—two big stories from you about his campaign. Get it?"

"Anything you say, Frank."

"Goddamn right. Now get on it."

I went back to my desk and sat there feeling sorry for myself for about fifteen minutes. I clocked it. When the fifteen minutes were up, I figured that was enough self-pity for the week. I picked up the phone and called Herb Edelman at Higgins headquarters.

176

"Herb, I'd like to come over tomorrow morning to do some more work on your campaign financing, if it's all right."

"Sure," he said. "We're busy, but I think it can be arranged. What do you want to do?"

"I want to watch them open the envelopes again and get the names of some more contributors."

"What was wrong with the names you got the last time?" he asked.

"Nothing," I said, leaning back in my chair. "I had trouble reaching them. I thought I should get some more."

Edelman laughed at the other end of the line. "You know," he said, "you guys are all alike. Big-time reporters. Les Painter did the same thing about six weeks before he was killed."

"What?" I said.

"Painter did the same thing. He came over here, watched them opening envelopes. He took down the names of some contributors and then came back and said he needed more names, that the first batch didn't work out. What the hell is wrong with you guys?"

"Wait a minute, Herb. Painter was working on the same kind of story and said he had trouble with the names?" I was sitting up straight now, taking notes on the first piece of paper I could grab.

"Yeah, why?"

"What kind of names did he get?" I asked.

"Contributors. I told you that."

"No. I mean what kind of donors were they—big donors, small donors, people who sent in cash, checks, or what?"

"I don't know," Edelman said. "I'm not sure. He asked me a lot of questions about the postal money orders. Why are you so interested?"

I didn't want him to know just how intriguing this was. "I'm not, in fact, I said. "I'm just always fascinated to hear about the way Les worked a story, that's all."

"He was a hell of a reporter," Edelman said.

"Yes, he was," I agreed. "I'll see you in the morning."

I sat there thinking, thinking about money orders. I called Sid Jacobson, our police reporter, at home. "I'd like a favor," I said.

"I'll try to help," he told me, chewing whatever it was he was having for dinner at the same time.

"I'd like to look at whatever the police found in Painter's pockets the night his body was found."

177

"The police don't like to let you do that, Tony."

"I know they don't, Sid, but I'd like to anyway. It's important."

"I'll do my best. Call me down at the cop shop tomorrow around eleven."

"Ten-thirty," I said.

"O.K., ten-thirty."

"One more thing, Sid. I'd like to keep this between you, me, and the cops. Don't say anything to anyone around the paper about it, all right?"

"I understand," he said.

After that I went to Charlotte's. She was wearing a peasant blouse and cotton skirt. She put her arms around me and kissed me warmly. I guess I didn't respond. "Maybe it's my breath," she said. "I thought I looked pretty good."

"You look great," I said. "I was just thinking about something."

"Important?"

"I don't know yet. I may not know for a while. It may be important."

"Rosecroft and Painter?" she said.

"No, not Rosecroft."

"Who?"

"Didn't you say something about fixing me dinner and then helping me get my mind off my work?" I asked her.

"Only if you promise to tell me," she said.

"Then I'll starve to death. I'm not ready to tell anybody anything."

"Come on," she said, "I'll give you dinner."

Dinner was perfect. First she served some cold cucumber soup, then avocado stuffed with shrimp, a salad, and fresh strawberries. She opened champagne with the strawberries. I helped her clear the table and then we went upstairs. She put on some music, and then proceeded to take my clothes off, slowly. "Can I ask what's happening?" I said.

"You're going to get a nice relaxing massage," she said. She brought a towel from the bathroom and told me to lie down on the bed. Then she went into the bathroom. She came out wearing a negligee and Arpege. She started rubbing my back, and after two or three minutes, she stripped down to the Arpege. I closed my eyes while her hands worked the muscles in my shoulders, then down my back and my legs. Then she told me to turn over and she started the same thing on the other side. After about five minutes of that, I took her hands and drew her down near me. I kissed her, pulling her next to me, feeling her against me, straining to get closer. Then she found me and guided me into her.

When we finished, we lay there for several minutes without talking. "You don't want to tell me what you're doing, do you?" she said.

"I don't want to think about it," I said. "If I tell you, I'll have to think about it. It's been a miserable day, and I'm afraid tomorrow's going to be worse."

"Is it that bad?"

"Maybe. I'm not sure. I'll let you know when I know."

She finally closed her eyes and went to sleep. I lay there thinking about Washington, how it had been when I had come there in 1959, in the last dull days of the Eisenhower administration. I thought about how the town seemed to come alive overnight with anticipation when Kennedy had been elected. We were all a lot younger then, thinking we knew the answers and had the energy to make them work.

That was before a lot of things—before Kennedy's assassination, before King's, before Robert Kennedy was killed. That was before Vietnam, before a lot of my friends were killed trying to cover themselves with glory reporting a miserable war. And it was before a lot of people, American and Vietnamese, were killed for nothing. We had started out to cure what we thought was a disease over there, and we had come down with something ourselves that looked to be incurable. All that killing and we were still suffering. And it wasn't over yet.

Lying there, next to the warmth and fragrance of Charlotte, I was tempted to chuck the whole business. Maybe I wasn't cut out to be a reporter after all, dredging up dirty little details about people in public life, stripping away the masks they so carefully constructed. What, after all, was so harmful about illusions?

Then I remembered something that Painter had said to me once after I had criticized him for a story I thought had been a little too personal. "All these guys in public life try to reconstruct themselves in God's image. That's understandable enough. The problem is that if they're successful, they'll have God's power over our lives. And that's dangerous."

So what he had done and what I was doing was honorable, despite the abuse we took. I was probably going to be in for a lot more abuse, maybe enough to knock me out of reporting for good. That was the least of my concerns—the professional risk. There was a personal danger—I could wind up like Fournier and Painter. I'd have to chance it. If I didn't take my best shot now, I might as well quit.

21

I got up around five-thirty in the morning, dressed, wrote a short note to Charlotte, and went home to change. If I was right, I was going to have a lot to do, and all of a sudden I wasn't sure how much time I had to do it. I wanted to do everything at once, now that things were beginning to click. I was so nervous and hyper I couldn't sit still. I made a list of things to do, beginning with a call to Hollis Crandall. I sat looking at the clock, waiting for it to be seven-thirty. I felt schizophrenic about time, wanting it to move faster so I could get things done more quickly and wanting it to slow down so I could get more done.

At seven twenty-nine I called Crandall, apologizing for calling so early. I told him I wanted to be sure he would be in his office later. He said he would be and would tell his secretary to make sure to put my call through.

Crandall worked for the Post Office Department. If my hunch

was right, I was going to need his help to unravel the whole mess.

The next item on the list was Geneva. I would have liked to go to Geneva, but again I didn't have time and Elliott wouldn't let me go in any case. I toyed with the idea of going anyway, but I knew I would waste a lot of time spinning wheels there, so I did the next best thing, which was to call a friend of mine in Paris who makes his living doing mysterious errands. He and I had found each other years before, drinking in a bistro in the south of France. We had a deal, my friend and I. He would help me when he could to get information or whatever else I wanted, and I wouldn't ask him about how he made his living or how he found out what I wanted to know.

You might find that arrangement something to raise your eyebrows about, but I've managed to come to terms with it. I know all about moral contradictions and dilemmas. If you want to tell me you've heard too much of my kind of rationalizing, save it. I'll be the one who loses sleep worrying about how I make my way.

So I called my friend in Paris, which is something I should have thought to do before. I made it clear that there wasn't much time, but that I would like to know as much about Fournier's death as he could find out. I didn't know if he could handle it or not, but the effort had to be made. He was my only chance.

At nine o'clock, I was at Higgins headquarters. Edelman and I bantered for about sixty seconds—we were both in a hurry—while he took me back to where they were opening envelopes. There were only four people working, three women and a high-school kid. After about forty-five minutes, I had what I wanted—the names and addresses of thirty more donors who had sent in postal money orders, along with the ten-digit numbers on the drafts.

Next I went to police headquarters. I found Sid Jacobson reading the paper and drinking a cup of coffee in the press room. "Did you take care of that for me?" I asked him.

He pushed his hat back on his head. "I said I would and I did. We won't get an answer for a while."

"How long?" I asked.

"A couple of days."

"A couple of days?" I said, not believing it. "I can't wait that long. What's the big deal? They should be able to do it in a matter of minutes. This sounds like the State Department."

"Just a minute," he said, "wait here. Let me go talk to someone."

"I'll come with you," I said, getting up.

"Just wait here, sonny. If you come with me, you'll wait a week for the stuff."

I sat there for almost an hour, drumming my fingers on the table, reading the paper, drinking coffee, and getting nervous. Finally, Jacobson came back and handed me a sealed envelope. "What's this?" I asked.

"Open it up," he said.

Inside the envelope, I found three pages of photocopied materials, including a matchbook cover, a folded press release, a newspaper clipping, and a piece of paper with five rows of numbers on it.

"Is that what you wanted?" Jacobson asked me.

"Is this all there was?" I asked.

"That's all of it, they said. They wanted to know why I wanted it."

"What did you tell them?"

"I said I'd tell them later. Will I tell them later?"

"I hope so," I said. "It's going to take some time."

I went to a pay phone in the building and called Crandall at the Post Office. I read him a bunch of numbers, including the ones I had gotten on my first visit to Higgins headquarters and my second visit that morning, and the numbers from the piece of paper that Sid Jacobson had gotten from the police.

"This is going to take a while, Tony," Crandall told me. "I'll have to get a postal detective freed to do it. They're understaffed as it is. Tell me again just what you want done."

"I want to know where these money orders were bought. When they were bought. And if it's possible who bought them."

"Well," he said, "where they were bought and when is no problem. The numbers will indicate that. But who bought them is an entirely different story. Anybody can buy an order. We don't require their names when they buy them. You put your name on it yourself before you send it out, if you want to."

"So you could put any name on the money order that you wanted to, right?" I asked.

"I guess you could, but what would be the point of that?" he said.

"I'm not sure. You just said that you could tell from the numbers when they were purchased and where."

"That's right."

"Can you tell me where and when those money orders were bought?"

"I think I can. I'm a little rusty at this. Give me a minute or so to get something." He put me on hold, then he came back on the line. "O.K. Now. Where should I start?"

"Anywhere you like," I said.

"O.K. I'll start with one nine one three eight nine six five two zero eight. The first ten numbers there are the serial number. The eleventh is a computer code number so that we can verify whether the money order is legitimate or not. Now look at the next six numbers. They show the date of purchase—so this money order was bought on May fifteenth this year. Then you have six more numbers, which indicate the zip code where the money order was bought. So this one was bought at the..." He paused for a minute, as though he were double checking against a list. "...the main post office in Manhattan."

"What about the other ones in that same group?" I asked.

"Wait a minute," he said. "O.K. Of the others, two were bought in Chicago and two in L.A. on two different dates."

"What about the first five?" I asked.

"O.K. This earlier group," by which he meant the numbers I had gotten from Painter's body, "these were bought on February seventh at the big post office in Brooklyn."

"Fine. I wonder if I can ask you to do one more thing in addition to everything else?"

"You can ask," he said.

"After these things are cashed, what happens to them?"

"We put them on microfilm to keep a record and destroy the originals. We don't need them any more and we don't have space to store them. But we keep a record."

"So you could tell from looking at the microfilm who these were made out to? See, this group from February I've never seen. I just have the numbers. I'd like to know the names of the purchasers and recipients."

"Tony," he asked pointedly, "would you tell me what this is all about?"

"I'd like to, but I can't. I know it's a lot of trouble for you, but I think it's important."

"O.K. It will take about three, maybe four days, to get these numbers traced, assuming the money orders have been cashed."

"It can't be done more quickly?" I asked.

"More quickly?" he shouted. "Jesus Christ, man, this is the Post

Office Department, not NASA or the Air Force. We're lucky to be able to deliver a postcard within a week in the same city where it's mailed. Don't press your luck."

"Sorry," I said. "What about finding out who bought them?"

"Well, the names will be on them."

"Right," I said. "Let me put it to you a little differently. Would you ask someone to check around at the post offices where these were bought to find out if there are one or two people who have been buying lots of money orders on a regular basis for the past several months?"

"What is this all about?" he repeated.

"Just, please, trust me. It's important. I'll tell you more as soon as I can and be responsible, O.K.?"

He wasn't happy about it, but I had done him a large favor a few years ago and had never collected on it. I had never intended to, until this happened, but now I was glad I had the credit with him.

In the next few days, I had a million things to do. I wanted to finish the stories that Elliott had assigned to keep him off my back, and at the same time I had other leads to follow out. One thing I did was to call the people whose names were on the new postal money orders I had gotten from the Higgins campaign. My experience with the first five names was repeated: I couldn't find a single one who had actually sent money to Higgins. Either the people I reached denied that they had sent the money orders, or I couldn't locate the people whose names were on them.

Then I tried to check people who had sent cash or checks. I took twenty names. In some instances, I had trouble with the cash, but I was able to find all but one of the types who had sent checks. That one, I learned with the help of the local newspaper, was away on vacation, but a neighbor said the family was outspoken in their support for Higgins.

Finally, I tried checking with Rosecroft headquarters to see how many postal orders *they* were getting. They had virtually none at all. So it appeared that the Higgins campaign was unique in receiving so many postal money orders.

I had hoped that Crandall would be back in touch with me within two or three days, but when I hadn't heard from him by the fifth day, I got concerned. I started brooding about how it took two or three weeks for an airmail letter to go from Los Angeles to Washington. I gave him a call.

"I know you said it would take some time, but I'm getting a little anxious," I told him.

"Maybe if you explained to me what the need for speed is, I could get it done more quickly," Crandall said.

"I'd like to, but I don't think I should. Look, I'm really sorry to be so circumspect, especially when I'm asking you for a fairly large favor."

"O.K. I'll put in a call and try to find out where the thing stands. Then I'll get back to you, as soon as I hear from my people."

That was about the best I could hope for, but it wasn't much. I tried to be patient, resisting the temptation to call him again when he didn't call me back that day, or the next morning. Late the next afternoon, he gave me a call.

"They're preparing a report in New York now. It should be ready tomorrow. I can call you when I have it and tell you what's in it."

"Have they told you what they found out?" I asked.

"No. That isn't the procedure. All information about their activities is supposed to be transmitted in a formal way. I didn't see any point to going outside of our established procedures."

"Can I have a copy of the report when it comes in?"

"Not supposed to do that," he said.

"You're not supposed to do a lot of things," I said.

"Including doing investigations for reporters," he said.

I dropped it. He was giving me a hard time for a good reason. I decided I'd pursue the point after he had read the report and briefed me. "Should I call you or will you call me?" I asked.

"I'll call you."

I am not a person who endures waiting gracefully. I suppose it's a fault left over from standing in too many lines in the military. Until a thing is in my hand, I worry about its getting there. The report was critical. It could blow my whole theory out of the water or be so incomplete as to be useless. Or it could confirm my suspicions, in which case I still wasn't sure what the hell to do next.

So the next twenty-four hours were miserable ones for me. I fooled around with my meals, fidgeted, yelled at operators, and generally wasted a day of my life.

When he hadn't called me back at noon the next day, I called him. His secretary told me he was at a meeting with the Postmaster General and could not be disturbed. I asked her if he had received a teletype report from New York. She responded as though I were an idiot. "He receives thirty to forty teletype reports a day, from New York, Chicago, Los Angeles, Keokuk, Glens Falls, St. Louis . . . do you want me to go on?"

"No," I said. "I get the picture. Just tell him please that I am hanging by a slender thread waiting for his call."

I managed to get Melinda to watch my phone at one point so I could go to the bathroom. She bought my lunch and brought it in so that I wouldn't have to leave in case he called while I was out. I sat typing nonsense to give the illusion that useful work was being performed. Elliott came over at one point to congratulate me for being so industrious. When he asked to see what I had written, I got evasive and told him it wasn't ready to be looked at.

Finally, at about five-thirty, when I had all but given up hope, Crandall called me back.

"Come over tomorrow morning at nine and I'll let you look at it," he said.

"What's wrong with telling me over the phone?" I said, trying not to yell.

"Because I don't want to discuss it over the phone."

"Why can't I see it now? Why not just leave it in an envelope for me with your secretary?"

"My secretary went home half an hour ago."

"A guard then."

"Jordan, if you want the goddamn thing, be at my office at nine. You don't want to tell me what this is about for your reasons, and I don't want to tell you what's in the thing or leave it with a guard for my reasons."

"O.K.," I said. "Nine o'clock." I had the feeling I was being jerked around for no good reason, but he was now in a position to make me dance to his tune. I couldn't tell him what the whole thing was about yet because I was afraid of leaks. The body doesn't exist in Washington that doesn't blab a secret to the first person it runs into. That wasn't going to happen this time.

So at nine o'clock the next morning, after Sleepless Night Number Two, I was sitting in his outer office waiting to be shown in. He called me in at nine-fifteen. I could see the report sitting in front of him, since it was the only thing on his desk. It never ceases to impress me—the more important the bureaucrat in Washington, the less work it looks like he does.

Before he would show it to me, he had to go through a little lecture about rules and regulations, and then he tried prying out of me again what I was up to. I had a little speech of my own ready, designed to placate him and promising to give him the full story as soon as I could.

It seemed to work because he finally flipped the report across the desk.

"I think you'll find quite a lot of information in there," he said with a smile.

I read it quickly once and then more slowly a second time. He said nothing while I was reading.

"Can I have this?" I asked.

"The original?"

"A copy will do."

"It's against our regulations. Make notes on anything you want in it."

I started writing things down.

"One of the reasons it took so long was that they got intrigued up in New York and really busted their asses on the thing. It turns out that this guy has been showing up every week or so for the past seven or eight months at a dozen post offices in the New York area as well as Chicago, Cleveland and Los Angles. He's been buying what totaled up to be fifty or sixty thousand dollars' worth of money orders in each city every week, all in little penny-ante amounts. The clerks started looking forward to his visits. 'Mr. Moneybags' they call him in New York. So then the postal detectives decided to tail him. Our New York guys managed to follow him on the whole route from Manhattan to Brooklyn, to Queens and the Bronx. And they followed him to that office on Park Avenue, right up to the door. After that they circulated a picture of him to the other offices around the country just to make sure they had gotten them all. One thing that took them so long was that they mailed the picture to all the post offices. That alone took three days. We got positive identifications from Chicago, Cleveland, and L.A. and tentative identifications in Detroit, St. Louis, Kansas City, and Boston. He started out buying a couple of hundred or a thousand dollars' worth of them a week and then gradually increased the total amount. Nobody thought much about it until the postal detectives came around asking questions.

"As for the rest of it, who those money orders were made out to, that's in the report, too."

"I know. I saw it," I said.

"Can J ask you a question about that?" he said.

"I'd rather you didn't," I said.

"If you've got knowledge of a crime being committed involving the Post Office, you have a moral, if not a legal, obligation to tell me about it."

"I'm not aware that this guy is committing any crime," I said.

"So what's this all about?"

"I'm not entirely sure."

"What difference does it make if you tell me?" he asked.

"Not much," I said, lying diplomatically. "I know I can trust you to sit on this for a while."

"I don't even know yet what I'm sitting on," he laughed. "For instance . . ."

I cut him off. "Do you have your office swept regularly?" I asked.

"The cleaning people come in every night," he said.

"No, no. I mean for bugs—electronic devices."

"I've never thought it was necessary," he said, puzzled.

"Maybe it isn't," I said, "but I'd just as soon not discuss this in any more detail. I just don't want to take the chance." I managed to wring a promise from him that he would not mention the whole business to anyone until he heard from me. He gave me his word after I had made my best, but futile, effort to get a copy of the report. I badly needed a document for support. In that respect, we played to a standoff. I suppose I could have gotten the thing if I had told him why it was so important. As it turned out, I could have saved everybody—myself included—a lot of grief if I had told him and gotten the goddamn piece of paper.

22

With the information I had in hand, I figured it wouldn't take me more than three or four months at a minimum to nail the story down. By that time, assuming I had everything I wanted, the election would be over. That wouldn't work, I decided. In the first place, the story had to go before the election—before the Democratic convention if possible. Once the election was over, the story would get harder to do. Records would disappear, sources would scatter, interest would wane, resistance would harden.

But I was still on square one as far as having something to put in the paper. I decided to get as close to the horse's mouth as possible. I called Mary Painter.

We had spoken often in the weeks since she had called me to get a lawyer for Moose Petowski, but our conversations had been about money. This one was different, and I didn't waste any time getting to the point with her.

"Mary, I think I may know what Les was working on when he was killed."

"What is it?"

"It has something to do, I think, with funny money coming in to the Higgins campaign. Did he ever say anything to you about that?"

"No," she said, pausing for a minute before completing the sentence, "I can't think of anything he said about it. Have you asked Phil Higgins? Maybe Les talked to him."

"No, I haven't yet. Did Les ask you to do anything unusual for him in the weeks before he was killed?"

"Such as?" she asked.

"I don't know. I don't know what his habits were, so I wouldn't know what unusual would be. Anything out of the ordinary as far as you were concerned."

"I can't think of anything. He asked me to do some errands, I think, but nothing beyond that."

"What kind of errands?" I asked.

"Really important things," she said with a trace of sarcasm. "I had to take a suit of his to the cleaners. I took a pair of shoes to have new heels put on. Do you want me to go on?"

"Anything you can remember," I said.

"I had to buy a saw at the hardware store. And he asked me one time when I was going to the post office to get something for him."

"What?" I said.

"I hadn't seen one in years," she said. "One of those money orders they sell at the post office."

"Did he say why he wanted it?" I asked.

"No. He just said he wanted to see what one looked like when you bought it at the post office, before it was filled out. Is that important?" she asked.

"I think it is. And he didn't tell you anything more about it? He never said anything to you about what it was for, why he wanted it, what it meant?"

"No," she said, "he just asked me to get it. He told me to get one for a quarter or whatever the lowest amount is that you can get one for. I got him one for a penny. I never asked him about it and he never brought it up."

"I wish you hadn't destroyed his notes and files," I said. "It's for sure that he must have had something about this in there. I need help, and I don't know where I can get it."

191

"Well, I'm sorry I can't help you any more than I have," she said. "I can't undo the past."

"I know," I said. "If you think of anything else, please give me a call, day or night, here or at home. Anything at all, Mary."

I made a few other calls, one of which would have been moderately productive if I could have made a breakthrough somewhere else. Otherwise, the information was useless.

And Elliott gave me my assignment for the Democratic convention. I listened distractedly, trying to pay attention but preoccupied with thinking what I could do to move the story along.

"You'll be with Higgins writing color. Don't worry about doing substantive stories, but if you see something let us know. If Felshin can use it, he will. Otherwise we might ask you to do a separate. Then the night they ballot—or however long it takes—you stay around Higgins's hotel suite. If they have reporters in, you'll be there for us. Naturally, if he gets the nomination, then you'll do a piece on how it was in his room and that kind of thing. If he doesn't get the nomination, then maybe we'll do something else. I want you to be in Chicago on Saturday, all set up when he gets there, which I think is either Sunday or Monday."

I thought about saying something, and then thought better about it and kept my mouth shut. I usually wind up saying too much and prematurely at that. For once I was able to discipline myself. Elliott was not his usual self with me, I noticed, but I didn't bring the subject up. He had a lot on his mind for one thing. And he was down on me for reasons I understood.

The next couple of days, I kept busy getting ready for Chicago and making phone calls to people I thought might be able to help me get another leg up on what I had found out. I didn't get anywhere at all.

That last Friday was a big day for phone calls. My day began at five a.m. (ten a.m. in Paris) when my French friend called me collect to tell me what he had found out about Fournier. That turned out to be essentially two things. One, word was out in less than polite circles that Gerard Fournier's death had been about as accidental as an Apollo moon shot. Two, he had not been killed by the usual run-of-the-mill hit men who work the Continent. For this job, apparently, outside talent had been brought in. They came, did their work quietly, and left.

I pressed for more details, but I got a lot of verbal shrugging of the shoulders and protestations about not giving enough time, not giving enough information, not understanding the difficulties, not putting out enough money, et cetera, et cetera. I couldn't complain. I knew more than I had known before he called.

But it wasn't enough. Not by half. I needed to know a lot more. I needed a file full of documents mysteriously turning up on my desk. Or a little old lady showing up with a shoe box full of incriminating evidence. The mood I was in, I would have settled for a simple manila envelope.

What I got instead was a phone call late that afternoon from Mary Painter.

"Did you remember something?" I asked her.

"No," she said. "Nothing like that. I don't know what to do. I'm in a quandary. I want to do the right thing. I just don't know what that is."

"Why don't you tell what the problem is?" I asked.

"I don't think I should talk about it over the phone. Could you come over this evening?"

"Name the time."

"Seven-thirty."

"I'll see you then."

I took a chance on a hamburger in the snack bar at the *Journal* before driving out to Mary Painter's. It was a hot night, hot enough so that I wished I had air conditioning in my car. I found myself driving too fast and slowed down just in time to miss getting a ticket from a Montgomery County cop who had a radar trap set up on Wisconsin Avenue going towards Bethesda.

"Let's sit outside," Mary said when I got there. It was pleasant in her yard and about ten degrees cooler than in downtown Washington.

She offered me some iced tea, which I took. I didn't want to rush her into talking about whatever was bothering her. Eventually, though, she got to the point. "I told you when I called that I was confused. I want to be honest, but sometimes that conflicts with other considerations that are just as important. I haven't slept well since you asked me about Les the other day. What I told you then was the truth. He never talked to me about those money orders or 'funny money' or anything like that.

"But," she said, taking a deep breath, "I'm afraid I misled you about one other thing. I didn't destroy Les's notes and records. I have them."

I was dumbstruck. "Where are they?" I said.

193

"I have them. They're safe. I still don't want the police to have them, but I don't want to see Moose convicted because I refused to turn them over. I don't want your story to be stopped, if it's so important, simply because I wouldn't let you see the notes. You said your story was important, didn't you?"

"It's very important," I said quietly.

"Then I'm going to let you see the files," she said. "I don't know how you'll use them or what will happen if the police find out. I'll have to worry about that later. For now, I've decided that this is the right thing to do."

"Are they here?" I asked.

"No, they're up at Deep Creek Lake. We can drive up there in the morning."

"How about now?" I said.

"I can't leave the kids that way," she said. "It will have to wait until morning. It's about a four-hour drive."

"But I'm supposed to go to Chicago tomorrow," I said. "What am I going to do about that?"

"I'm sorry I didn't call you sooner, Tony." She sounded genuinely apologetic.

"It's O.K.," I said. "I'll figure something out. What time do you want to get started?"

"I could leave by eight in the morning," she said.

"I'll be here at seven forty-five," I said.

We left by about eight-thirty the next morning. I was on time, but Mary still had things to do for her kids before we could go. Deep Creek Lake is all the way at the western end of Maryland in the mountains of Garrett County. The only way to get there, unless you own a private plane, is by car. Under different circumstances, it might have been a beautiful drive—through a rolling countryside of thick forests and lush pastures gradually giving way to undulating hills and finally to junior-size mountains.

But I didn't have time to enjoy the view. For one thing, I already had missed my plane to Chicago. Getting another flight from Washington or even New York was going to be next to impossible because everyone else was going out to Chicago for the convention, too.

Mary couldn't tell me much about Les's files, except that they were not well organized. She told me that she had driven them up to their cottage at Deep Creek Lake the day after Les's body had been found, when the police started pressing her. "I didn't want to let them see the files, but I didn't want to destroy them, either. And then I thought to bring them up here, where they would be out of the way. Not many people know we have a place up here, so it was unlikely that the police would think to look for them here if they got around to searching."

When we got to the cottage—I told Mary I didn't want to stop for lunch first—she took me in and showed me where she had put his papers. Then she went into town to buy some food.

Painter's notes were a total mess. He kept everything, and also took notes on everything—paper, envelopes, matchbook covers, pieces of napkins, corners of menus, etc. Besides that, he had virtually undecipherable handwriting. The notes were in file folders. Painter may have had a coding system that he understood, but I couldn't begin to penetrate it. That meant that I had to start going slowly through several hundred files, dating back over a period of years, in the hope that I would find what I wanted. I didn't tell Mary everything, but I gave her enough so that she knew what we were looking for. She helped me, but it was painfully slow going.

We worked all of Saturday afternoon and evening, and started in again Sunday morning. We kept at it Sunday all day and all night, until one or two in the morning, when neither of us could see straight any more. In the middle of all this I called Elliott to tell him that I had gotten desperately ill and would be late getting to Chicago but that I would be there as soon as I could. Elliott's response employed language not found in a family newspaper. He heaped abuse on me for five minutes or more, tracing the history of our entire professional association, illuminating each of my character defects, and comparing me unfavorably with incompetent colleagues. To the extent that I thought he was merely venting his spleen, making it up just to get me angry, I got angry. But he meant a lot of what he said, too, and that depressed me. By the time the conversation ended, our working relationship was at an all-time low. It was clear that he thought I had gone completely to pot. But I couldn't do much about it; he and I had drifted too far apart for me to trust him now. I needed to have the story locked up first.

Monday was another long day going through one file after another. I was afraid to skip anything, so I combed all the folders. I could understand why the FBI, the CIA, the police, and half the rest of the world wanted to get their hands on them—they were fascinating.

In Chicago, the convention got under way. Higgins and Rosecroft were far ahead of the rest of the field, and though Higgins was not expected to win the nomination on the first ballot, he would probably pick it up on the second. I kept one eye on the television and the other on Painter's files. I wasn't sorry about missing the muggy crush of a convention in Chicago, but I did have the feeling I was watching a party I badly wanted to go to—even though things weren't going to be fun, if they came out the way I wanted them to.

By Tuesday morning I was getting frantic, plowing through the papers as fast as I could, not bothering to put things back after looking at them. Paper was everywhere and I despaired of finding what I wanted. Just as I was beginning to think that the whole idea had been a hopeless waste of time, I found what I needed. It was all there—a clear, detailed explanation of the entire scheme, complete with an outline of the column that Painter had been planning to write. His information corroborated what I had. He had had a lot of good stories during his career, but this would have been the biggest of them all.

It took half a day to go through everything, to make sure we had it all. Then we went into town so that I could make photocopies of what I needed. Trying to get something photocopied in Oakland, Maryland, is a story in itself, but it will have to wait.

By the time we were finished, it was late Tuesday. Driving back to Washington would have taken four hours and I wouldn't have been able to get a plane to Chicago until three the next afternoon. That was too late. Luckily Mary had the wit to suggest Pittsburgh, which was actually closer to us than Washington. I was able to book an early flight to Chicago the next morning, so she drove me to Pittsburgh and we took rooms in a motel near the airport. At eight a.m., Wednesday, I was on my plane to Chicago with seventy-three pages of photocopied notes from Painter's files.

My first stop was to see Elliott, who was still sleeping at ten-thirty. Conventions are night-time affairs, with the first event not scheduled to begin until after lunch. I called him on the house phone at the Conrad Hilton, where he was staying along with almost everyone else who mattered—Higgins, Rosecroft, Seld, Charlotte, and about half of Congress.

Elliott was too sleepy to say much over the phone, except that he would be down to have breakfast in forty-five minutes and I should meet him in the lobby.

The way things were going, it now looked as though Higgins would be able to pull off a first-ballot nomination. He had been maneuvering quickly and skillfully to pick up stray delegates and was doing very well at it. Since the situation was changing constantly, it was hard to gauge with any precision. The only certain test would be the balloting.

Elliott made it down in an hour and ten minutes. We went in for breakfast.

"Miraculous recovery you made," he said icily. "You been shacked up with the Queen of England or something? I tried calling you at home yesterday but there was no answer."

"I wasn't there."

"No kidding."

"Frank," I said earnestly, "I'll tell you all about it when you finish eating and we can go for a walk."

"What's wrong with right here?"

"Too many people."

"Well, I don't have time for a walk. It's too goddamn hot. I also don't have the time or the inclination to deal with personnel problems. That will have to wait until we get back to Washington."

"We're not talking about a personnel problem," I said. "We're talking about the biggest news story you'll ever handle in your life."

"And that is?"

"Les Painter's murder."

"Have you told the police so that they can release that kid they arrested and go out and get the real killer?"

"I'm not sure yet who the real killer is."

"A mere detail," he said sarcastically. "Already this sounds like a hell of a story. Tell me more."

"When you finish eating," I said. "We can't talk about it here."

He took his time getting finished. I hadn't knocked him off his feet with my introduction, but I thought that when he had heard it all, he would agree with me.

We took a walk up Balbo Drive to the harbor that runs along the lakefront. We walked along slowly, Elliott watching the small sailboats bobbing up and down in the water while I filled him in. I went through the whole thing, everything I had done from the beginning, laying it all out for him as it had happened to me. I told him about the postal investigation, the report I had gotten on Fournier's death, about finding out that Painter's papers were intact. I

197

told him what I had found in Painter's notes. When I finished, he went right on walking. Then he stopped and looked me straight in the eye.

"So you weren't sick when you called me and said you were?" he asked.

I couldn't believe he was focusing on *that* after what I had told him. "No, I wasn't," I said as calmly as I could. "I'm sorry I lied to you. What do you think about the story?"

"What do you think we should do?" he asked.

"I think I should start writing," I said.

"And when would we run it?"

"Tomorrow if possible. Or the next day. It has to be done quickly." I was beginning to feel better. Then he answered me.

"No."

"I'm sorry?" I asked, thinking I had misunderstood him.

"I said no!" He said it loudly and distinctly. "We are not going to run that story tomorrow or the next day and probably not for some time to come, if ever."

"Why the hell not?" I asked.

"Because, pal, you don't have the story."

"I just told you the whole damn thing," I said, shouting. "What do you call that?"

"I call that a strong lead. You have weeks, maybe months of reporting ahead of you. I wouldn't even ask for a comment based on what you have. Let's run through it. You say that you've checked fifteen purported donors to the Higgins campaign and either they deny having given or they don't exist. Fine. That's a story, maybe even a good story. But that isn't murder. Some French mobster gives you the latest gossip on Fournier. Mere speculation and probably irrelevant. Then there's this Post Office report—a copy of which you've seen but don't have—establishing that a man whose name you don't know has been buying postal money orders totaling millions of dollars. And the report says that numbers found on Painter's body correspond with numbers for money orders that were mailed to Higgins. Finally," he said, pausing to work his sarcasm up to a peak, "you have the notes of a dead man which, you say, confirm everything you've found and add to it."

"And you don't think that's something?" I asked.

"Are you kidding? That's barely a start. I really don't know what's gotten into you, Tony. Your story has, conservatively speaking, a dozen holes in it."

"I can't believe it!" I said, almost shouting. "We're talking about Les Painter, not some goddamn rookie. Considering his reliability and everything I've found, I think we have no choice but to do a story now, to stop this thing."

"That isn't our obligation, goddammit. Our obligation is to print the news, not to try to influence it. We try to make it accurate, comprehensive, and fair. That's hard enough right there. Let someone else figure out what to do with it after we print it."

"Under ordinary circumstances, I'd agree with you," I said. "But that isn't the situation here. We're talking about the future of the country."

"Listen, pal," he said, patronizingly, "this country has been around quite a while and was doing fine without you. I'm sure it can take care of itself."

"It has nothing to do with me. You're misjudging the whole thing. You ask me what's happened to me. I'm beginning to wonder what's happened to you. I think Walters has gotten to you. I think you're worried about paying your mortgage and putting your kids through school. I think you're getting scared. You've lost your nerve."

He just stopped dead in his tracks and looked at me again. "Then we have nothing more to talk about. Tonight you will be in Higgins's hotel suite. You will be there to watch the Democratic nominee as he receives the nomination. You will write a color story on what you see. You will not discuss this matter with him or anyone else. When we get back to Washington, we will discuss the story and your future with the *Journal*." He stopped for a moment. I could see that he was restraining himself from really letting me have it. "Now get lost. I don't want to talk to you any more."

23

That night I went to Higgins's hotel suite as Elliott had instructed me to do. It wasn't what you would call an intimate gathering. At any given point in the evening, anywhere between ten and fifteen reporters were in the room, watching Higgins watching the balloting. In addition to the reporters, every campaign aide above the rank of corporal, family, friends, Secret Service, and the usual hangers-on were there. Higgins was shuttling back and forth between the sitting room, where the crowd was gathered, and the bedroom, where the real business was being conducted, to get reports and talk by telephone to his floor managers. Otherwise, he sat in the large outer room in the midst of a mob scene. Every thirty seconds or so, someone would approach him, either to shake his hand or to kiss him. Television film crews popped in to shoot footage, still photographers were brought in and out to get the same shots to put on front pages of morning papers all over America. By now, it was virtually certain that he would have the nomination on the first ballot. A bandwagon had started and it appeared that nothing could stop it.

That's what had me on the edge of my seat. I had hoped Elliott would agree that we could go ahead. His refusal had thrown me back to my own initiative. I had spent my professional lifetime being an observer of events. I had tried to keep my own views out of what I wrote, tried not to be a participant, either by making things happen or by preventing them from happening. That was the professional ethic. But this was no ordinary situation. I was not going to sit still and let a murderer become President of the United States.

We sat there watching the balloting, listening to the droning roll call of the states, starting with Alabama, then working up through Illinois, Minnesota, and Ohio. As the roll approached Washington state it was clear that that was where Higgins would go over the top. I took a piece of paper out of my pocket, walked across the room to the big chair where Higgins was sitting, and casually slipped him the note I had written earlier. He took it without looking at it or taking his eyes off the television screen. My note was simple. It said, "Painter, postal money orders, and the Arab Consortium. I'd like to talk to you. Tony Jordan."

I went back and sat with my eyes fixed on Higgins, waiting for him to open my note. He fingered it, folded it, unfolded it, chewed on it, and did everything but look at it as the roll call got closer and closer to Washington state.

Finally, the clerk got to Washington, and it cast thirty-five votes for Higgins and ten for Rosecroft. By prearrangement, balloons in the convention hall came falling from the ceiling, the band struck up "Happy Days Are Here Again," and the delegates in the convention hall went crazy.

In Higgins's hotel suite there was a lot of applause, cheering, black-slapping, etc. Champagne appeared out of nowhere. Flashblubs were exploding with a staccato rhythm. His wife came over to kiss him and to pose for pictures. Then everyone wanted to shake his hand, including Richie Vallone, who looked as though he were on the verge of ecstasy.

I waited for a moment when there was a lull and I could say a word to him. I waited, waited, and waited some more. Then Larry Samuels, Higgins's press secretary, stood on a chair to announce that Higgins would appear at a press conference in fifteen minutes to make some announcements. The whole thing was irregular, but then Higgins was an irregular candidate.

Finally, I just blundered forward. "Congratulations," I said, trying unsuccessfully to avoid shaking his hand. "You ought to read my note before you go downstairs."

"Note?" he said, giving me a quizzical look. "Oh! Right. Sure, Tony."

Samuels came up to him and turned him away to whisper something in his ear. Higgins listened closely, at the same time slowly unfolding my note. He stopped from time to time to concentrate on what Samuels was telling him. When he opened it, he took a look at it for a minute. I didn't notice any change in his expression. He went on listening to Samuels, raising his head to gaze slowly around the room trying to catch someone's eye. When his gaze finally came to rest on me, he gave me a reassuring glance and nodded ever so slightly.

After Samuels had finished, Higgins turned to me as he spoke to Samuels. "I'll be out in a second," he said. "Keep this mob out of the bedroom."

We went into the bedroom and Higgins closed the door. "What's this all about?" he said as though it were a complete mystery.

"I'll tell you what it's about," I said, sitting down. My knees were shaky and my voice quivering. I was scared as hell.

"I don't have much time, Jordan, so I'd appreciate your being as quick as possible."

"Right," I said. "I'll make it short. Several weeks ago, I told you I wanted to do a story about your organization. You told me you were running an open campaign and your staff confirmed it.

"I watched them opening letters from supporters who were sending in money. You were getting a hell of a lot in postal money orders —I hadn't seen one in years. I wrote down about five names from those orders, and I checked them out. I couldn't locate a single one. I went back a week or so later to get some more names. And then Herb Edelman told me something funny—that Les Painter had done the same thing a month before he was killed. That struck me as strange—maybe coincidental, maybe not.

"So then I checked to find out what was in Painter's pockets when his body was found. There was a piece of paper with numbers written on it, and those numbers turned out to be for five money orders. I had those traced. They all had been bought in New York at one post office on the same day, and they were all cashed by the Higgins for President Committee."

Higgins glanced at his watch. "Look, this is all fascinating, but I'm having a press conference . . ."

"I had a friend in the Post Office Department do more checking for me. There's a swarthy little man with a mustache who visits post offices in New York, Chicago, Cleveland, L.A., and a bunch of other cities every week. They can't be precise about it, but the postal people think this guy has bought somewhere in the neighborhood of between ten and fifteen million dollars' worth of money orders in the last seven months. They call him 'Mr. Moneybags.' They put a tail on him and followed him right back to the Park Avenue offices of the Arab Consortium. Odd, isn't it? You're getting these huge numbers of money orders at the same time that this Arab is buying huge numbers of them."

"I don't have any time for this," Higgins said. "Get to the point. What does this have to do with me? Naturally, I'd be concerned if there were irregularities in my campaign. I'd want to know everything about it, especially considering the stand I've taken." He started toward the door.

"This won't wait," I said. "It can be a story in tomorrow morning's paper, right alongside the one reporting that you got the nomination. You told me once that your campaign was being financed with the spare change of America, but that wasn't quite the truth. Your campaign is being financed with the spare change of the Arab oil sheiks. Would the Arabs be dropping millions into your campaign without a wink from you that the investment was worthwhile? They're very conservative about what they do with their money, you know. They don't like to speculate or gamble. They like sure things."

"Right now it sounds to me as thought you're the one who's speculating, Jordan." He spoke without emotion, almost as though he weren't even interested.

"Up until yesterday, that would have been the case. But I've been reading Les Painter's files. Mary didn't destroy them after all. She said it would have been like killing Les a second time."

I watched the color drain from Higgins's face. He turned back from the door, listening closely now, barely maintaining the calm exterior of the moment before. "I've spent the last four days looking at his files. It's all here," I said, holding up the copies I had made. "How he found out about the money orders the same way I did. How he put it together with some other things he had picked up.

How he went to Geneva to check it out. How he found out much more there. Along the way you must have found out he was on to it.

"Painter was a threat to you and to them, just as Fournier was later. It was a neat scheme. You'd get to be President and the Arabs would have their man in Washington—in the White House no less." Anger crept into my voice. "Painter also got on to Dunphy. Was it your idea or the Arabs' to buy up Congress?"

"You don't seriously expect me to answer this, do you?" he said angrily, walking toward me.

"It doesn't matter. I'll finish, so you can go to your press conference. The Arabs' first concern was the Quilling bill. But they couldn't lobby against it directly—everybody would notice something obvious like that—so they planned to get you elected President first. Dry up other sources of campaign financing. Then elect a Congress they could control through you. After that they could repeal the Quilling Act. And that'd be just for starters." I paused to catch my breath and looked him squarely in the eye. "And you went around convincing everyone that you were the last honest man in Washington."

"It's an interesting theory," Higgins said, pausing for emphasis, "but I don't see how you figure I had anything to do with Painter."

"That's easy," I said. "Painter picked up the story. He had sources all over. And you knew he was on to it before he came to you. But he was careful, so no one else except maybe the Arabs knew what he had. You put him off when he tried to see you. He thought that was strange. He had never had trouble talking to you before. Now all of a sudden you were too busy. It must have been hard for you, if Painter was really a real friend."

"He was," Higgins said quietly.

"You wanted to be President so badly. There was so much you wanted to do. Now your pal had picked up this little secret that would wreck your campaign and probably send you to jail. But finally you decided. I don't know, maybe the Arabs were pressing you or maybe you did it on your own. You were already dangerously indebted to them. You wanted to handle this one yourself.

"Obviously, you couldn't get rid of Painter yourself. That wouldn't work. You couldn't hire someone to do it. That was too risky, and you didn't know how to do it in any case. You needed someone who knew how to kill, who had done it before. Someone you could trust. Someone who would do what you instructed without question. Someone who believed in you, even when you asked him to kill."

"You got it all figured out, don't you, Jordan?" a voice said behind me. I turned to find Richie Vallone standing by the bathroom door. He must have heard the whole thing. Now he was facing me holding a gun with a silencer on it. "I don't know where you got all that stuff about the Arabs and everything. That wasn't what Painter was going to write, was it, Phil? Tell him what Painter was going to write about you."

"I'd like to hear what you told Richie," I said to Higgins. "You couldn't have told him the truth, could you? Richie is a patriot. He loves this country in his own way. You didn't tell him about the Arabs, so what did you tell him?"

"I'm going to kill the son of a bitch right now," Richie snarled. "He's just like that goddamn Painter. What's he talking about—Arabs, and you lying to me?"

Now Higgins was talking. "Just take it easy, Richie. There's nothing to worry about. He's the one who's crazy. We can deal with him later."

"By later the story will be in the *Journal*," I said emphatically. I had to play this thing on the edge and hope it would break my way. "I'm not going to sit on this. I'm going to print it. Your campaign hasn't even started and it's over. I'm going to blow you out of the water."

I could see that Richie was getting edgy. I had to count on Higgins's being rational. "Your only hope is to shut me up," I said, "but sooner or later you'll have to tell Richie the truth. Then what will he do to you for taking advantage of him? You're going to have to be careful, Higgins. A mind like his is dangerous—loving one minute, hating the next."

Richie erupted. "I'm going to kill him," he said, moving toward me with the gun raised. "I'll kill the son of a bitch."

I felt naked, groping for something to hide behind and finding nothing. Already I could imagine the searing pain of a bullet tearing into my stomach. He was about four feet away, just next to Higgins. Richie's finger started tightening on the trigger. Higgins turned quickly, slamming his fist into Richie's gut. Richie's mouth came open as he gagged and gasped for breath, and then he crumpled in a heap on the rug. I didn't stay around to take pictures. I jumped for the door and found a wall of human flesh in the outer room. The convention had moved into Higgins's suite. I struggled through the mob, pushing, being pushed, shoving and being shoved. While I was being jostled, someone slapped a campaign hat on my head and kept trying to put a drink in my hand. The drink wound up on the back of a woman's dress. I don't know what happened to the hat. I felt as though I were clawing my way through the hold of a sinking ship, climbing over bodies to get out before I drowned. I was frantic to get out of that room. When I finally reached the door, I knocked over a stand of television lights set up in the corridor. Some beautiful young man with a microphone started to protest, but I stiff-armed him and started down the hall at a lope. Turning at the corner about thirty yards away, I saw Richie Vallone stagger out of Higgins's suite, his hand inside his coat pocket.

I ran to the elevator and pushed the button, keeping my eye out for Richie. We were on the twenty-seventh floor and the nearest car was on twelve. Richie was now about ten yards away, wearing the feverish look of a man intent on doing harm. I made a mental note to complain to the management about the slow elevator service as I fought my way through another crowd and ducked into the stairwell, taking the stairs down two at a time.

Then I could hear Richie behind me, rumbling down the steps, and I could hear my own heavy rasping as I gulped for air. On the third landing down, the light was out. I had to watch where I put my feet since I wasn't used to crashing down stairs this way. The first step was fine, but as I put my right foot down, I missed the next step, catching it with my heel and turning my left ankle as I tried to get my balance back. My left leg crumpled and I went down in a heap, pitching forward, tumbling down the concrete stairs.

I landed with a smack at the bottom—stunned, but not unconscious. My head was foggy. My survival instinct told me that if I didn't move, I'd be gone. I tried getting up. My right leg seemed all right, but when I shifted weight to my left foot, it threatened to desert me. Richie was getting closer. I called out to him.

"Richie. Richie. Listen to me. I didn't make that up. I was telling the truth—about the Arabs and Higgins. He lied to you."

Richie was now standing at the top of the flight, ten or twelve feet above me. "Tell me again," he said.

I started to spcak, gasping for breath. The gun flashed, I felt a tugging at my sleeve, and a huge chunk of the wall behind me splattered. Richie didn't really want to listen.

Leaning heavily against the wall, I half ran, half slid down another flight of stairs. I grabbed the door for the corridor, yanked it open and started lurching down the long hallway, weaving from side to side, checking for open doors.

After two or three tries, a door opened. I barreled in, not sure if Richie had seen me go into the room or not. I locked the door and then just leaned against it, my eyes closed, gasping, feeling drops of sweat rolling down my flushed face. My sleeve was torn, but I hadn't been hit when Richie had fired at me. My pants were ripped at the knee, but I still was in one piece. All I had to do was stay put for a couple of minutes and pray he hadn't seen me.

"Is that you, Ted?" I opened my eyes to be confronted by a woman coming out of the bathroom in a slip.

I started to speak, to try to reassure her, but I didn't have a chance.

She screamed and then started shouting. "Get out! Get out!"

"Wait a minute," I said. "Just take it easy."

She screamed again. I panicked and opened the door again. Richie was standing about three feet to the right, looking a little stunned. I didn't have a lot of time to weigh options. I came out quickly, straight at him, hoping my left leg would hold. I ducked as I approached him, then came up hard, jamming my shoulder into his gut and knocking the wind out of him again. He smashed into the wall and I kept going. I figured that if I wasn't successful, I would never hear the shot that killed me.

My only chance was to return to the stairs, go down one floor, run to the other stairwell, and go down a flight or two there, working my way back and forth past the elevator, on the off chance that I might catch one before Richie caught me. It didn't seem like a terrific idea, but I didn't have a lot of time to come up with anything better.

We must have spent about three days doing that. Richie took another shot at me on one of the stairs, coming close but not doing any damage. I caught glimpses of him turning corners in the hallways, but I had given up trying to apply sweet reason. I was worried that he might figure out the pattern and just stay on one stairwell until I came back to it, but finally as I was lurching down the corridor on the seventeenth floor, I saw a passenger getting on an elevator. "Going down," I yelled.

"We're going up," the elevator operator said, as the door started to close. I squeezed myself in, just avoiding the snap of the doors.

207

Then, not caring what professional ethics or federal laws I was about to violate, I pulled out my wallet and quickly flashed my White House press card so that the operator could see it was something official with a government seal, but not be able to read it.

"Secret Service," I said. "Take this car down to the mezzanine." The operator started to speak. "Now!" I shouted at him. The other passengers looked frightened. He brought the car to a quick stop, and I felt my stomach go up another floor as we reversed and went hurtling down the shaft. He let me off at the mezzanine. "Sorry to have held you folks up," I said, stepping off.

The only safe place for me was at Higgins's press conference. I knew what I had to do now. I didn't have any more time. Let the crazy bastard try to kill me there, I told myself. I was so tired and panicked I was past the point of caring, but I figured if Richie was going to get me, I would get him, too. I could have played it the conventional way, the way Elliott had wanted me to, but it was too late for that now. I was going to have to put it all on one desperate roll of the dice. If this didn't work, I'd be through in journalism. Or dead.

I worked my way to the rear of the ballroom, but I found the door blocked by a Secret Service agent, a real one, with a button in his lapel, a walkie-talkie plug in his ear, a gun, and everything. When I came chugging up and showed him my convention press credentials, he just waved me around to the front. "You can't come in this way," he said.

I started to argue but gave up. Secret Service agents aren't programmed for logical discussion. I would only waste time, for one thing. For another, I saw Richie Vallone steaming toward me from the other direction. He was like the creature from the Black Lagoon. I couldn't get rid of him. I backtracked quickly, turning the corner, darting down the hallway and coming into the ballroom at the side. He was still padding along behind me. I fought my way to the front of the room, knocking a "reserved" sign off a seat next to Hal Karsten from the AP.

"You can't sit there," Karsten said. "It's reserved."

I started to answer, but then he took a good look at me—at my torn sleeve, my shirt tails hanging out, my trouser leg torn, my suit jacket sopping with sweat, my hair a matted mess. "Hey, what the hell happened to you?" he asked incredulously.

"Attacked by media groupies," I said, panting.

"Media groupies?" he repeated. "I don't get it."

"Thought I was Woodward and Bernstein."

"How could they think you were both?"

"Kids aren't very well informed these days," I said.

Just then Higgins came in and the room went wild with applause and cheering. Higgins stood there, his wife and kids by his side, waving to the crowd. I noticed Richie over on the far side of the podium, working his way to the center. Higgins's Secret Service agents, who knew him, let him through. He circled around and positioned himself behind Higgins, in direct line of sight with me. We weren't more than about twenty feet apart.

Higgins posed for pictures with his family before finally holding up his hands for quiet. He went through a statement thanking the delegates for nominating him and promising to run a successful campaign. Then he said that he wanted for his running mate some-one who could be considered Presidential material on his own. Higgins went to great length to describe the characteristics he was look-ing for, but wouldn't name the person he had in mind. It sounded pretty clearly like Rosecroft, who had already announced he wasn't interested. This was Higgins's way of putting pressure on him.

When the questions started, Higgins dodged attempts to get him to confirm that he wanted Rosecroft. I sat in my seat, turning the copies of Painter's notes into a tight roll. I was waiting for my chance. I thought I had it at one point, when Higgins appeared to be finished answering a question, but he found something more to say. I tried getting up a moment or so later, but he ignored me, taking a question from someone behind me. Richie just stood there, staring.

I was frantic. I had to pull this off regardless of the risk. I'd never have another chance. Higgins sounded as though he were about to wrap it up. This was it, I told myself. I had to get up and do it. I found myself on my feet, shouting my question to drown out a reporter from UPI who was also trying to ask a question. Higgins had turned to face him, trying to ignore me, but the UPI correspon-dent got flustered when I wouldn't stop. I started my question over again.

"Mr. Higgins," I said, "I wonder if you'd mind commenting on some apparent irregularities in the financing of your campaign to date?" He started to speak, but I cut him off and kept talking. "I'm referring to a number of persons who are listed as contributors who could not be found by this reporter and another reporter who checked your records."

"Well," Higgins said, smiling, "I'm not aware of any such

irregularities. Naturally, I would be concerned if what you say is verified, and I'll ask my staff to look into it, but that isn't the purpose of this press ..."

I cut him off again. "Could you tell us what you know about the murder of Les Painter?" I said. "He was the other reporter I was referring to."

My colleagues started murmuring. A few yelled to me to sit down.

Higgins smiled again. "As far as I know, the police have arrested someone for the murder of Les Painter, who, many of you know, was a close personal friend. I know nothing about that, Mr. Jordan, other than what has been publicly reported. Now I think I'll take a question from over there."

I was about to put everything on the line and I wasn't even sure what I would say. I did something unheard of in a press conference. "You're lying," I said—calmly, but loud enough to make my voice heard over the clamor. "Your answer is a lie, just as your whole campaign is a lie. I have documents proving a connection between millions of dollars in money that has been funneled into your campaign by Arab oil interests and Painter's murder."

The room went up for grabs at that point. People started hollering at me to sit down. Other people were hollering at them to give me a chance to speak. Someone tried to push me back into my seat, but I ducked around and stood in the aisle.

"Just give me one minute," I shouted. "I'm asking you all to give me one minute. The Arab Consortium has been pouring money into Higgins's campaign, laundering it through Geneva, bringing in dollars and converting them into postal money orders. Cash would be suspicious and checks mean bank accounts. But postal money orders are ideal. Anyone can buy them. You can make them out to anyone and put anyone's name on them as buyer. The Post Office does all the transferring of funds and there are no incriminating records. Twenty out of twenty money orders sent to Higgins that I checked had phony names on them."

I turned and faced Higgins. "The sloppy, lazy press being what it is, you counted on us to overlook all this—assuming any of us would bother to find the money orders in the first place.

"But you hadn't counted on Painter. He picked up the money chain from Geneva and followed it back here. He had the story cold."

"Get on with the press conference!" someone in the back of the room shouted. Higgins's press secretary moved toward the microphone. I was running out of time.

"So you had him killed," I shouted. "But you couldn't tell the killer the real reason for it. You had to fabricate some other threat."

Higgins wasn't smiling now. Someone behind me was bellowing, "Sit down. Oh my god. For god's sake. Sit down."

Karsten, who thought I had gone around the bend, was pulling on my sleeve. "Sit down," he said. "You're making a goddamn fool of yourself."

A television camera in the center aisle had swung off Higgins and was aimed on me. "I don't think we have to listen to any more of this, Mr. Jordan," Higgins was saying.

Time was up. "What did you say to convince the killer?" I asked. "How did you betray his trust in you? A boy looks upon you as a father and you trick him into doing your dirty work."

Out of the corner of my eye, I could see Secret Service agents coming at me. Someone shoved me from one side. I turned and was hit from the other side. People kept yelling for me to sit down, get out, sober up.

Then I heard a voice over all the din in the room. "Answer the question," the voice commanded. "Answer the man's question." It was Elliott. The room seemed to quiet down a bit. Elliott spoke one more time, more softly, but firmly. "The question deserves an answer."

Higgins looked at Elliott, then at me, and then cast a glance over at Richie. It was a funny kind of look that Higgins gave Richie Vallone—pathetic and pleading and apologetic at the same time. In that moment Higgins's years of discipline and training failed him. The public mask slipped. He was looking at Richie now, but I can't describe any better the look on Higgins's face because at that precise moment, Richie Vallone pulled the gun from under his coat and fired it three times, straight at Philip Higgins.

EPILOGUE

I didn't win any Pulitzer for the story I wrote. I suppose I might have if I hadn't blown it all at the press conference. They're still arguing about whether I should have done what I did. The issue is hotly debated in the *Columbia Journalism Review*, in the bar of the National Press Club, and in newsrooms all over the country, including that of *The Washington Journal*.

I'm not particularly glad about the way it turned out. I'd rather that Richie hadn't killed Higgins and that he hadn't been shot by the Secret Service. I would have liked to handle the whole thing the way they do it in the movies, printing the stories and watching the power of the press right the wrong and bring the villain down. I just didn't have faith that it would turn out that way in the end.

After the excitement died down, I went into a tailspin. I was depressed, drained, and generally aimless. I couldn't get interested in anything and found any sort of story too much to do and not enough to bother with, all at the same time.

I spent a lot of time thinking about everything that had happened. Most of it was pretty clear to me, but I'm still bothered by two points. First, I wonder who beat me up that night in front of my apartment. And second, I'm still wondering what Fournier found out about Senator Seld's Swiss bank account.

We know more or less that someone connected to the Arab Consortium killed Fournier, but I suppose we'll never nail the guys responsible. As time went on, I found myself spending more and more time thinking about Fournier and what he had been doing those last days of his life. Which brings me to the last point.

Elliott called me in to see him some time after things had quieted down. We had had a lot of conversations after Chicago, but always about stories. Neither of us had spoken about the blowup between us. And then one day he called me in to talk.

I had a little speech all ready, trying to apologize for the things I had said to him in Chicago, but he cut me off.

"You're just going through the motions," he said with a wave of his hand. "You wouldn't have done what you did if you hadn't believed what you said to me. And now that you think you've been vindicated, you figure you can be magnanimous about it. Save it for someone who needs it."

"Well," I said, "at least I'm sorry that I felt forced to do it that way. I would have rather done it your way."

"We could have done it my way," he said. "But you didn't trust me. You thought I'd take a dive, that I'd rather keep my job than print the news. You're all wet.

"In the first place, it wouldn't have been an issue. You underestimate Walters. In the second place, you underestimated me. If you ask me if I'm angry, I'm not. I'm more hurt than angry, and I don't mind saying so. You were on to a hell of a story, but it wasn't in shape to print. You wanted to go with it to stop something from happening. I thought that was wrong. And it would have been just as wrong not to print the story, when it was ready, out of fear that it would influence events."

I just sat there looking at him, not saying a word. I understood what he was telling me and I didn't disagree with a word of it. I was simply skeptical, and he knew it.

"I can see you don't believe it," he said.

"Let's just say I remain to be convinced," I said.

"Well, I don't know what I can do to prove it," he said.

"You'll have an opportunity. I'm picking up that story about Layton Seld again. This time I'll make it stick."

"Just do me one favor," Elliott said.

"Yes?"

"Don't call a press conference to announce your findings."